STEEL ANIMALS

We gratefully acknowledge the support of the Canada Council for the Arts and the Ontario Arts Council for our publishing program. We also acknowledge the financial support of the Government of Canada.

Cover design: Val Fullard

Steel Animals is a work of fiction. All the characters, situations, and locations portrayed in this book are fictitious and any resemblance to persons living or dead, or actual locations, is purely coincidental.

Library and Archives Canada Cataloguing in Publication

Dyment, SK, 1967–, author
        Steel animals / SK Dyment.

(Inanna poetry & fiction series)
Issued in print and electronic formats.
ISBN 978-1-77133-533-1 (softcover).-- ISBN 978-1-77133-534-8 (epub).--
ISBN 978-1-77133-535-5 (Kindle).-- ISBN 978-1-77133-536-2 (pdf)

        I. Title. II. Series: Inanna poetry and fiction series

PS8607.Y64S74 2018   C813'.6   C2018-904347-4
                                                                              C2018-904348-2

Printed and bound in Canada

Inanna Publications and Education Inc.
210 Founders College, York University
4700 Keele Street, Toronto, Ontario, Canada M3J 1P3
Telephone: (416) 736-5356 Fax: (416) 736-5765
Email: inanna.publications@inanna.ca Website: www.inanna.ca

MIX
Paper from
responsible sources
FSC® C004071

STEEL ANIMALS

a novel

SK DYMENT

inanna poetry & fiction series

INANNA PUBLICATIONS AND EDUCATION INC.
TORONTO, CANADA

For epicyclic thinkers

1.

JACKIE IS SLEEPING NAKED now. "To understand love," she murmurs, speaking to the empty room in her sleep, "I will need to fit all this heart machinery together." The treacherous fan with the sharp metal blades whirs sympathetically from her windowsill and Jackie dreams that hot fingers are undressing and seducing her on the floor of a desert. An African violet has kicked out a spray of dirt and small rocks in the night, allowing earth to rain from the sill. The mess has fallen onto Jackie's alarm clock, which is set for six a.m. In defense of the violet, it merely surrendered to a caress, a stroke of wind that entered through the window at three a.m., touching down on her turf as she slept. Her cactus had watched. The cactus knows the retro fan will be blamed for everything. The fan drones on through the pre-dawn heat, exposing her wires at the outlet source. It appears that it won't be long before she sparks and creates a fire- or sputters out altogether. A sort of revenge to surprise the violet.

Jackie knows about her fan. When she wakes, she is going to cannibalize her toaster and swap cords. The fire will never materialize. She is clever, mechanical, likes to tinker and comprehend. In relationships, she fights the desire to take people apart entirely, controlling her impulse to examine their interlocking psychological pieces. Typically, when her intimates plead with her to return to them, they beg her to reassemble their emotional health with the deft use of her muscular hands.

The ruby-headed cactus studies her face as she sleeps. She is a woman who waters her cactus in correspondence with her menstrual cycle. To the cactus, her love is a desert where it rains every twenty-eight days.

Jackie shifts, her black hair falling into her eyes, drifting through a mindscape of sunlight and sex and hot surfaces. It is delicious for her to be at home in her bed. She has just spent a brief stint in custody for a crime she did not commit. As she has explained to her lawyer by phone, the actual perpetrators were copycat criminals responsible for a sloppy rip-off of Jackie's talent in heisting unattended banking machines, and so it was a butchering of something fine. Technically innocent, she clattered home on her rollerblades a free woman.

The only positive note to the insult has been a chance encounter with Wanda, a charming dreamer who was not only physically affectionate, but knew a lot about motorcycles. After several modified performances of Macbeth's final moments staged atop a holding cell bench, Wanda had taken her hand and declared, "Never have I met such a lady as thou," causing Jackie to inquire as to whether Wanda was queer.

"Not!" she had answered. "I love only a lost rogue biker prince named Ben."

Applauding, Jackie decided to accept the offer of friendship and the invitation to stay connected to the social stability Wanda's heterosexuality represented. If she had known how unstable that world was, Jackie might not have felt so reverent.

Sociologically speaking, Jackie has never been granted the easy, light-hearted safety of boyfriends with motorcycles and guitars. She occasionally longs to be sheltered by things defined as normal: not deviant, not criminal, not psychologically twisted. She has always known she was different, and was, for those wishing to psychoanalyze her, a basic case of cleverness and gender ambivalence combined with being broke.

The violet and the cactus agree that Jackie should get a new honey. It would be nicer than living with this incessantly rattling forties-style fan, and in the right conditions, if the new romance was a waterer, the cactus could outlive Jackie. At the moment, they are in rhythm together, and the cactus feels peace rushing through her stem and along her strong green torso. She feels it roar in the red part of her head. Because it is in love with Jackie, it does not mind waiting for her to menstruate, watching her plan her next desperate life move devotedly from the sill.

2.

NOVEMBER. A skiff of snow has descended on Vancouver. The snow dusts the green peaks that embrace it. They look like torn paper unwrapped by a curious child, abruptly crumple-pressed against a backdrop of glowing blue blending to bone.

Wanda is walking far past her usual stroll. She is walking to move her body, to feel the blood coursing through the muscles in her limbs, to feel her long legs stretching. Defiance, when it visits her, does not want anything to slow it down. Glancing at her reflection in a parked car, she sees her strong features, her pouting lips, the way the cool air has coloured her face. "This is a mountain wind," she sighs, "a breeze descending from snow."

When she was a young girl, her mother had married a man who took them to Switzerland. They stayed at a resort on the Schilthorn, where she listened to the man and her mother argue as they drank. Wanda had slipped out, feeling the now familiar restlessness that sometimes overtook her, and she skied off-piste, far from the sounds of anybody, into the snow. A storm had risen, and she had felt a child's sense of satisfaction that she was lost.

She walks down to where the Lions Gate Bridge starts, thinking about that day in the storm, and then she heads out along its length. She does not know where she is heading, only that work is not a pleasure; her life is not a pleasure.

Because she feels angry, she doesn't care that she is far out on a lonely bridge in the middle of nowhere.

She considers how to tell her aggressive, high blood pressure employer that she's quitting.

"Well, we'll always have Paris, sweetheart..." says Wanda, imagining the expression. She laughs to herself.

"Blessed are the pacemakers," she adds.

Normally reserved and even shy, she is made shyer by an unfocused eye for which she refuses to wear glasses. Her nose, broken in her girlhood, would cost next to nothing for a Canadian middle-class person to straighten. Because of this, the broken nose represents to many people a quirky decision to look off-kilter. In fact, to some it represents a girl who has been in some fights. She adapts to the misconception by developing a talent for smartass remarks. Her right hand is a prosthetic. Not one of the more expensive kinds, but a functional, basic, fake one. Many times, she has put on velvet creations sewn by her artist-friend Vespa, the sister of her lover, Ben. She has stepped out in her velvet and attended parties with people living in comfortable homes. Afterwards, her head would ring with the banter of politically suggestive remarks and ignorant laughter made to sound informed. She knows that in many people's minds, the poor are embarrassing as windblown garbage, as if they represent excess instead of desperation. Her young face, while hopeful, is already pocked with the marks and scars of hard living, and her teeth are not covered with the kind of enamel that well-heeled people buy to appear more than natural when they smile.

"'Oh woman tempest-tossed!'" Wanda shouts in her best theatre-club growl. She giggles.

Pressing her toes against the guardrail of the Lions Gate Bridge, she stares at the cold water shimmering two hundred feet below her, a small blizzard beginning to obscure the waves. When she was a child, she skied into a storm of whirling snow until it overcame her. She had rested finally, on the side of an alpine forest, the wind chill cutting through her. Her right hand was the loser in the event, and in her memory is the sight of her girl-fingers turning white and then blue. Slipping into unconsciousness, her skis at crossed angles, she had started to freeze to death, beginning the descent from warm, runaway child to cold, hypothermic tragedy.

She walks to the centre line of the bridge. But the bridge has changed. An off-duty taxi is rushing at her. The men inside are chatting away like two teenage girls on a romantic date. She glances up. There is a warm light of human life inside the car. Too late they see the woman on the road. The driver pumps the brakes, but the speeding car slides into the oncoming lane, then turns around three hundred and sixty degrees. Spinning another one hundred and eighty, they come to rest inches from Wanda, facing backwards into town. Knocked off her feet, Wanda has been swatted by the fender on her backside and lands plumb on her bottom. Her leg does not feel anymore as if it is attached. *Who really knows?* thinks Wanda. Things detach, fall away, new ones are brought in to represent them. She looks up at the snow swirling down from the gathering darkness. Moments earlier, she thought she had grappled life by the horns. Now, she realizes any person can just as easily be killed by something random.

The driver, whose face appears as shocked as Wanda's, reaches to the dash and turns on the service light, wrongly indicating that he is accepting rides for fare. They lock eyes.

Uncertain, Wanda flashes him a quirky, perplexed-looking smirk through the mirrored surface of the window.

He shudders with relief. "You're still alive!" he shouts from window. He hops out, together with the passenger who had been sitting next to him.

She rolls down her window and looks at the car. "Heading back into town?"

"Yes. We are taking you to a hospital at once. My name is Swan."

"Swan, that's new."

The two men lift Wanda into the back seat. They notice she smells of alcohol, and the passenger gives her a mint. "My name is Gus," he tells her, and she notices he has muscular arms, interesting tattoos, friendly teeth. His friend Swan is slighter, with soft black curls and brown-gold eyes with wet lashes.

"Thank you. It was nice of you to stop."

"Well, you were struck."

"I thought your car was going to plunge over the edge of the rail, and then I thought you were going to hit me."

"We both did. How does your leg feel?" Gus asks. "Do you think it is broken?"

She looks down at it. "Broken or reluctant."

"Good Lord."

"Isn't this a romantic evening turned nightmare," says the driver.

Gus hands her another mint and leans over the seat.

"Why were you out in the middle of the road?"

"Only way you can hail a taxi in this town," she answers him, her old self starting to surface through the storm.

"She's in a state of shock," comforts Swan, unaware that Wanda is flexing her sense of humour.

By the time they arrive at the hospital, Wanda has eaten three mints and nine butterscotch Life Savers.

"I feel sick," she tells them.

Without waiting for ambulance attendants, the men carry her into the nursing station.

"I have seen my life flash before my eyes twice tonight, once in each eye." She gives Vespa's number to a nurse. Vespa tells the nurse she is talking on her emergency cellphone while modelling for an art class in the nude, which she is. She sends her brother Ben to go see Wanda in her stead.

Gus and Swan, having given their report to the police in the waiting room, stand around idly. No one will be charged. From the room where she is having some routine tests, including pupil tests for brain injury, Wanda can watch them easily. She can hear them, and they do not seem to be aware she is listening. Gus is staring at his own reflection in a pop machine. He looks distorted, like a carnival mirror, older, wider, his handsome form removed. He wonders aloud where he has seen the young woman before.

"An image of a young girl who has run away from her parents is drifting in and out of my mind," he tells Swan. "I was much younger, scarcely a teenager, my first real job. A ski patrol in the mountains. They were all looking for the girl lost in the wooded slopes. I reached down to pick her up, and she was sleeping in the snow."

"Sleeping?" says Swan.

"Well, her lips were blue, but she was still alive. Her hands were frozen, but I pressed them in my own. They were white, bloodless, like the hands of a statue in the local town square."

He raises his brows. "But then one of them moved, just so slightly, and it curled tightly around my fingers. She was still sleeping, but she was alive."

Wanda worries that while they are waiting, a tired, over-protective Ben will turn up and start some sort of man-to-man fight. Swan sighs and expresses the wish to go to a steam bath to unwind, perhaps to pick up a charming man called Gus.

"But this has already happened," he laughs.

"Then we are ahead of schedule," responds Gus.

The door to the hospital slams open and Ben indeed enters with the attitude of a gunfighter coming to settle a score. His dark frame is tense but tired. Ben is likely booking off from work. He will call his kid sister later and Vespa will leave the studio and she will wait. Later, the phone book will be covered with Vespa's dramatic pen-and-ink designs portraying the day's events.

"You hit her with a car?"

The men begin to argue.

"Are you sure your name is Swan?"

"Yes, S-W-A-N."

"What kind of name is that? That's a girl's name! That's a bird's name! Are you certain that's your name? You don't want to take the heat for this. It could be 'Sven' instead."

"It could be 'Swine,'" says Gus, "but it isn't."

"Oh, for pity's sake. I hit the girl, but it wasn't my fault. I'm not afraid to take the heat. She was walking on the road, in the middle, and my car spun around like a vitamin on a plate."

"We'll see what Wanda says to that," says Ben, sweeping into the room where Wanda is being treated.

Gus waits, immobilized. His eyes slip shut. Behind them he is again engulfed in snow, mountains, his eyes blurring from the bright white, and then there is the girl. He picks her up, carries her back to the emergency station on the mountain. His skis sing *hush hush hush* beneath his feet.

"It's not their fault," says Wanda softly.

Ben tells her it appears to have been an accident, and everyone has waited and spoken to the police. But he has no idea why they are still sitting there. She sees he is still shaking with adrenaline. He tells her his day has been long, the hurried pace dangerous. Ben has been working for B.F. Turner, a notorious mass-producer of condos. At first, it had been drywalling, but then he had come within inches of his head being chopped off from thrown rubbish slicing through the air at dumpsters from ten floors above. A death trap. Later, welding. The supervisors turning the other way.

"Darling," she answers, and he tenderly strokes her brow. She observes that twice in her life, a disaster of her own folly has brought her affection and concern.

"All day, do you know what I have been doing? Welding together supports for upper floors. And thinking if there was even a small tremor, the whole place would drop like a house of cards. Water everywhere, electrodes destroyed, workers fired. I think of you more than I can admit. And then this, an accident! Look, my hands are shaking!"

She looks, and a self-indulgent feeling that the hands belong to her seeps warmly into her senses.

Beyond it, the battered blue Chevy pickup Ben has just bought sits in a badly parked position in the hospital lot collecting snow. A ticket flutters underneath his wiper blade.

The tests completed, her leg wrapped, Wanda rolls back out in to the room where Ben has shouted at the men.

"You know," says Swan, "I am thinking about a young boy running by the Pacific Ocean. He does it every day, although he is too shy to try out for the track team at his school. He does it to avoid the other boys. They tease him because he is beautiful. Because he is homosexual. And because he has the name of a bird. Once again, everyone is asking me how a good person such as I can be so fucked-up. And now he has hit a girl!" A tear slides from his eye and a sob shakes him. "I love girls. I would never hit a girl, even out of anger. I wonder if you have the same principles as I do. I wonder if Ben would ever hit a girl."

"Hush," says Gus. "It's a woman and you didn't hit."

Wanda, a cane lying across hers knee, is overwhelmed by the emotion in the three male faces. "Ben, these men are the kindest people in the world. Don't be angry with them. It was my fault. They risked their lives to stop."

Gus nods. He looks at both her hands, but they are hidden in her lap. Turning to Swan, he sees he is crying. Gus gives him a mint.

"I was drinking, Ben," Wanda says, "and I walked right out into the middle. This man, this expert driver, spun around three times attempting to stop. Everyone thought the taxi was going to fly off the bridge."

"Fly?" says Ben. Wanda, who sleeps at his side, knows that Ben toils on the fifteenth floor of a skeletal building and dreams every night of dropping his tools and flying.

"They almost drove over the rail and into the water just to save my life. It was almost their lives."

Swan seems to be crashing emotionally, his face drawn. Inspired to help, she reaches out her hand to thank him. Their eyes meet, and she allows the hand to come off in his grip.

"Good God!" he cries out, then, gaining control, he says wonderingly, "it's a prosthetic!" He turns to Gus, who once saved the child Wanda, a young skier in the snow.

"Sorry," Wanda says, "I can be disarming. Yes, the hand is a prosthetic." She puts the prosthetic back in its place. Then, she extends her hands and Gus embraces them, feeling clearly that one is not real. The two men rise to go.

"Ben," says Wanda, "do you ever feel like you know something before it happens, like the colour of a truck coming down your street, or the face of a person running into your arms?"

She rises from the chair, still smiling at Gus, who now stares back at her in boyish curiosity.

"Call us if you ever need your life saved again," he says, and he hands her his card. The sliding doors hiss, and the pair are gone.

Testing, Wanda hobbles from the drink machine and back again with her cane. "Let's walk backwards," says Wanda.

"But you can barely walk frontwards," Ben says.

"Let's walk backwards and talk backwards all the way to Vespa's house ... and sit in cafés with words painted on the windows backwards, so we can read them from behind as if nothing is strange at all. And, baby, let's quit work."

Ben nods consent, and as the two lovers leave the hospital, they place their feet backwards in the footsteps of the men who carried her in.

3.

JACKIE HAD OTHER NAMES: "Sparky," "High Volt," "Hammer Hips," "Chipper." She had a lot of other names when she was working her regular job as a welder with a Vancouver outfit that contracted her out—when she was out. Some of the other names she was called by the part-time workers who encountered her were not nearly as endearing because Jackie was not an easy woman to get to know. She was not as interested in people as some people felt a woman was supposed to be. This opinion was most often voiced by men. And she was not certain they were a scientific necessity in the first place, only that they were responsible for ninety percent of society's violent crimes. Jackie had rubbed a few women's fur the wrong way as well. When she was a girl, not many people were around to look after her, which made her a loner. She needs someone to care about her, and she does not even know it. Her ambivalence about gender rules is healthy, her ambivalence about which side of the law she is on is hurting her. Kindness is something wavering in the distance like a heat mirage, and to her credit, she moves towards it, but she cannot grasp what it is or be certain it is real.

Walking alone as a child, she had gone to the shipyards in Vancouver and watched the warm fire of acetylene and the electric blue of arc welding in the enormous hangars by the docks. It was the arc machines that filled her with her first sense of meaning, and a further feeling of love; they were warm, responsive creatures that made her feel safe. Jackie was in love with arc welding, and the machines were in love with her.

To Jackie, the instant banking computer was not only a machine with money and no life, it was an entity without a soul. When she stole one, her final, crashing, forklift-operating argument was difficult for an automated banking machine to reject, cancel, or contradict with a preprogrammed series of greetings and replies. To those ATMs that were removed by Jackie's forklift and transferred into the back of her truck, a visit from her was a dream come true. To exchange their predestined animation with a brush of her restless, indestructible soul actually meant more to their solitary spirits than any amount of money she could dream of tearing from their vandal-proof magnetic stripe-reading bellies. After a spell of hard drinks, it became obvious to Jackie that they pined for her, they dreamed of a woman like her, and they were nothing but flattered when she tore cash-issuing dispensers and paper currency free from their submissive frames. Sensitive to machines, Jackie ripped out their cables and wiring with all the fury in her small body, loading their overstuffed selves onto the forklift in a rough manner that contradicted their sedentary experiences up to that moment. It was just this longed-for destiny that sent their circuitry into surrender.

Rough handling soon became a signature of Jackie's moonlight work, and at night, money and broken pieces of cash-dispensing coils lay scattered around her in an anonymous Vancouver storage locker on the edge of town. She extended her naked body across them, threw back her head, and laughed soundlessly. Bedding down on a cardboard box for the night, she sipped a beer, stroked her calloused hands across her muscular torso, and dreamed that computer cables enamoured with love were winding around and around her legs.

4.

IT'S HAPPENED AGAIN. She has just done another six-week stretch for possession of a stolen vehicle that was not ever in her possession, a stolen vehicle that, finally, no one could even prove she had stolen. Because of her unrepentant involvement in past robberies, the Vancouver police are beginning to perceive her as a recidivist with a limited social conscience. If she is ever to develop a mature sense of her own morality, someone needs to save her.

She is only twenty-one, but she feels a thousand years older than everyone else. The only good thing that has happened is that just before this stint, she had met Wanda, a woman with a perceived understanding of the truth in the world, and someone who phoned her every day she was inside.

Wanda has told her she is going to prove it is better to live in Toronto than out West. Wanda had run East with Ben to Toronto after her bridge accident, determined to make a new start. But now her boyfriend has returned to Vancouver to visit his sister, Vespa, to convince her to join them in Toronto. Wanda tells Jackie that Ben has plans to open a motorcycle shop, might even be someone Jackie could meet.

"Come join us as well," says Wanda.

Jackie considers the promise of a warm, humming arc-welding unit waiting to heal vintage motorcycles in Ben's shop. "I'm not certain if I can travel yet," she tells her. Wanda's promises are hard to gauge.

Wanda and Ben have roots in Toronto, Jackie has not. Ben's sister, somewhere in Vancouver, is someone Wanda has assured her she would completely love to meet, telling Jackie that they would all make a fabulous team. Jackie doesn't know anything about love, yet the words flow from Wanda over the long-distance line in a way that is enticing. It makes Jackie want to trust them, realizing that trust is also something she knows nothing about.

At the moment, to cover her ATM tracks, Jackie has decided to break her biggest rule. She has taken a job with a fast-paced, dangerous Vancouver construction company. Ben had worked there and been fired. There is no picket line, no protest, but she knows that she is taking over the job of one of twenty workers who had walked off the job together.

The story behind their employment does not endear her to the other welders at her site or them to her. But with a mask to protect her from the arc weld, a monkey suit, a gritty face, and an anti-social attitude, each worker remains unrecognizable.

The pay is next to nothing, but it is an immediate position. "My name is Patricia," Jackie tells the men at her workplace, and before she takes the job, she dyes her hair an amber-brown colour that while not quite convincing, is at least her most memorable feature. She brings her own gear and uses company-supplied machines.

"Second-rate, danger…" she whispers her first day, having arrived on-site earlier than anyone else. Around her, half the machines have exposed cables, peeling electrical tape from previous repairs, and other broken or improvised parts.

"I choose this one."

The machine she chooses has a strong, reliable electrode holder, but the ground-lead clamp has lost its tension and has to be double-taped wherever she goes.

As the other workers arrive at the high-rise site, the supervisor begins to give them each specifications as to what to do, while she discovers that the machine she has chosen has a creep upwards in amperage that has to be checked constantly. Jackie maintains a rhythm of scrambling back and forth every few welds to adjust it; the only way to stay out of conflict with her supervisor and hold on to her job.

She begins to rise earlier and earlier to check in ahead of the other workers, to secure a different and hopefully the most reliable machine. Labourers drop out like flies, new workers take their places, and the job moves along at a pace slower or equal to one where the work is done properly. It is the cutback method of getting cheap work done fast, but it is not working, and is costing the company and causing the supervisor to drive them harder than ever before.

Because Jackie has become a familiar presence, her supervisor leans on her extra hard. Because she is a female, he orders her to do double the job of men. Having heard somewhere this scrap of feminism, he has convoluted it to throw at her every day as motivation. She grits her teeth, loads a new electrode, straddles the I-beam she is welding and receives an eighty-volt jolt on her ass. She reaches forward to catch herself from falling and grasps at nothingness. She tries to pull off her helmet as she falls. Eleven feet down, she makes impact with a pile of drywall covered with a plastic tarp. The glass inside her visor shatters and she closes her eyes. Other workers gather around her, shouting as to whether or not they should sit her up. Jackie takes off her helmet and rolls to her feet. Without saying a word, she jogs down the piss-smelling concrete stairs floor by floor to the bottom of the building and picks up her cheque at the trailer. She does not even know if the broken machine has made it to the attention of the contractor. She does not even care. She blows the cheque on beer and a body massage and falls asleep on her face.

The next morning, she wakes before dawn. "Early girl, up before the sunrise," she says to herself. "The dark before dawn can be the best time of day for a few rare souls," she remarks, dressing. "Let's hope I'm one."

She climbs inside her car and drives to a bank across the city from her. Letting go completely of her sense of moral worth or social responsibility, she pulls a ski mask over her face, snaps on some gloves, and enters the bank machine area with a card she found a year ago on the street and had saved instead of returned. She spray-paints the sole camera, then rolls her oxy-acetylene kit into the space, and sets it against the wall. Powering up a carbide-bit reciprocating saw, she cuts the machine open in less than twenty seconds, pulling it apart like a hinge. The machine moans in what sounds so like a cry of human rapture, Jackie loses five seconds looking around for a weirdo on the street. Deciding it is her imagination, she sparks the oxy-ace machine up and in another fifteen seconds she has cut through to the dispensing stacks within the machine.

"Easy, lady," she tells herself. "Patience, lady. Easy does it."

Switching off the tanks, she pries the dispenser and cash tray area apart with a crowbar, counting between her gritted teeth another ten. This time, the cry of the steel-and-platinum walls and popping plastic parts is closer to a human voice than a violin is in the arms of a virtuoso. The thermal printer spits a small note, reading an empty balance and the words, "THANK YOU," in large block print.

Jackie takes the note, slides it in her back pocket, and watches the monochrome display flutter and blink off. The bank notes are dropped inside a mailbag she has attached to the back of the dolly kit. She swings the saw over her shoulder and is almost overcome with her own soaking heat.

"Just like butter," she remarks, and her car pulls away from the curb with the hatchback bobbing half-open and the kit lying on its side.

Pulling up outside an unused warehouse, she brings the kit into the front. She puts the volatile acetylene upright before it has time to settle and become explosive. She straps it into the passenger seat. She bleeds the hoses and drives both kit and saw to the storage locker she has rented with falsified identification. Dropping the boots, coveralls, and ski mask into a garbage bag, she deposits them into a dumpster underneath a heap of rotting garbage.

Jackie wheels the car back to her garage, papers the windows, and paints it gold-flecked brown. The money she places behind a panel inside her apartment wall. As the sun begins to climb the sky, her wristwatch reads six-thirty. She scrubs up and calls a taxi, then hops into the work clothes she kicked off the day before. She throws her gear into a bag with a new helmet to replace the one that was shattered. She will not use the car for some time. She tells the taxi driver to pick her up at the same place the following week. As they drive to the B.F. Turner twin towers site, Jackie observes it is six-forty-five. "I'm ten minutes ahead of myself," she grins, "and fifteen ahead of anybody else."

She selects the old machine with the broken ground-lead clamp and is back on the site when her super and the other labourers begin to trickle in at seven. Her supervisor tells her that she is fired and to leave the crew at once. "How can I be fired?"

"Because you fell on your ass yesterday!"

"But I've been working at the site longer than anyone else on this floor! It could have happened to anyone!"

She expects to hear the workers around her volunteering the names of unemployed friends ready to step into her place, but there is silence. Then one of the workers objects, and a second voice joins in, "Let her stay. Let the chick keep her job."

"She probably has kids and stuff. You gotta work to eat."

"Her welds are clean. Let her stay," says another, and finally,

"It's not her fault she fell! These machines are half-busted and you know it!"

The supervisor lets out a sigh. "Okay, back to work. Fair enough, she's twice as good as the lot of ya!" A cheer echoes from the workers around her, and Jackie raises her hands in

a victory salute. She tucks her chin down and nods back into
to her helmet.

"Loyalty—I love that in a stranger," says Jackie.

She laughs and loses herself in her work.

5.

BEN IS DRINKING café au lait on Robson Street with Rudy, who glances left and right as if he thinks he is surrounded by spies.

"I can't believe I went to design school for this, this! All I do is sit on my ass all day and listen to other people. They think I have some kind of promise. And look at me now, Ben, I'm bringing in the Gs. If I told you how many Gs I was bringing in, you would fall right off of your ass! Off of your ass and out of your chair! I'm bringing them in..."

Ben smiles. He knows Rudy wonders. As youth, they had talked about the resistance Ben sometimes meets compared to the way people seem to rush to Rudy, who he has known since they were both boys. For Ben, it's not the cold wall of negation anyone can encounter when they are vulnerable and all their creative torches are lit, it's the not knowing. It's the trying and then not being certain. It's the shadow of racial bias that seems to block the very sun. Ben and his sister were born to a renegade earthwitch who toured and raced motorcycles, children produced through flings with different men. One was a black man; the other was white. Neither man ever materialized; neither had a clue that she was pregnant or that they were fathers. Rudy knows that Ben lives with the psychologically eroding uncertainty of being a young black man in a culture that never acknowledged his reality growing up. Together, as they matured, he saw Ben forced to cultivate a level of maturity that made Rudy admire him. In comparison, Rudy is an emotionally disturbed, passionate splat of panicked paint on a bright canvas. And yet Rudy is suddenly wildly successful.

"How did you land the job?"

"Drawing, baby. Drafting, designing, I'm a good artist ... that's what, that's how I landed it, 'cause I'm good...."

"Cut to the chase," says Ben. "Fourteen months ago, we were working in construction and you were drawing on the side for scraps while you finished your art school. I leave with Wanda for out East, and a year later, Vespa tells me you're building a high-rise building and living in another. So I fly back to check it out. And to visit my sister, remember her? You used to date Vespa, for Chrissake! Yes, she's in trouble again, I think. She's become a failed sculptor who's good at welds. I want to encourage her to come back East. Wanda and me have a nice place outside Toronto now. I wish you could see the new '65 CZ motorcycle I just picked up. New — well, it's from 1965. I brought you a photo." He digs in his pocket. "Sure, I flew out to see my sister, but I also came to see you. And look at us now! Here we are. Getting drunk up in the air. How could you have an office in a Robson Street tower, Rudy? Less than two years ago, you were an underfed, strangely dressed, bad-smelling..."

"If you would let me tell you, do you promise..." Rudy makes a signal with his mouth, a gesture of closing a box and throwing away a key.

"My friend," Ben answers him, "your sordid little life story is forgotten to me already!"

For some reason, this strikes the two men as enormously funny. Coffee splashes from their bowls, causing the waiter to look up. Rudy had bought them martinis earlier and finding themselves together in a restaurant hundreds of feet above the street is making them giddy and boyish.

"I had a studio, in Downtown Eastside...."

"The one where you tormented the landlord?"

"No, no, not the Water Street place, after that. Up along Railroad. It was infested. Mold, mildew, termites, no fireproof doors, rats, roaches, no lights in the halls, no panic bars on the doors, broken hinges, insulation over the windows, pigeons living in the roof, garbage all over the parking, stinkin' all to hell, busted exit signs, no intercom, full of theft, full of piss, stinkin' all to hell..."

"You said that..."

"So..."

"So, what's the rent?" Ben laughs.

"No, Ben, it's gone now."

"Oh, it's gone. Where exactly did it go? Did the firm do something to it? Something a good city does not usually approve?"

"Listen, I had a studio in the place, and was working out-of-shop for an architectural firm or 'drawing for scraps' as you like to call it. So, I redesigned it, redesigned the whole warehouse, all gutted and rebuilt. Then I did a redraw, and even though it was a nice-looking old place, I levelled it, but then rebuilt it with the community in mind. This time I designed an elaborate, harmonic, ergonomic masterpiece, a masterpiece, Ben—a high-class housing development with everything, enough for two hundred families. I thought I'd get a little funding from the city, make a little goodwill for the company. I showed them the chicken scratches one day, and the whole firm went ... berserk!"

"Well, you've never used this term 'berserk,' Rudy. I was always waiting for you to use that term but you never did. Why now? 'Berserk' is your new word. It's a word from your company; it's a word from your sponsor. So, you went over the heads of the other people living there?"

"It was just an idea. I pulled it out one day at a meeting. The tenants never had it together to form their own group." His voice rises to an adolescent pitch. "They were just going to get thrown out, Ben, and the landlord would start the whole thing all over again with some other no-brains."

"But they could have fought to get the place changed without tearing the building down."

"Those people did not have clout. Through the company, I got the zoning changed in just a few days. Of course, it was on the condition that we buy the property from the city after we had the property seized from the landlord. Then, we bought it back, since no one even knew it was on the auction block, for pennies! Connections with the municipality helped. Of course they're scumbags, but they're connected. In a few months, I saw something I had designed on paper rising into the sky."

"What about the people who had been evicted?"

"My point Ben: A terrible, infested, dangerous fire trap was transformed into housing."

"Perhaps some of the original tenants even applied to move back since your masterpiece was low-level housing." Ben watches the sound waves of his voice vibrate in the bowl of coffee.

"Now you know that it wasn't actually in their range. And here is where the company really ran with my idea. Without telling me, they took all of my designs, right down to the play area for children, the atrium, the underground parking, the turf and tree area on the roof—and they turned it into luxury housing—not affordable to anyone in that neighbourhood, and then snapped a wall around it and armed guards. With a beautiful view of the harbour, a beautiful view of the skyline, people bought it up, despite the neighbourhood. The place was sold out before it was built! And I am bringing in the Gs, brother. But my dream, my dream is completely gone."

"Why would you work with them?"

"Why? Because I'm inside now, I'm inside, brother, and I can screw them from their high-security palace. And I will. You have no idea how deep in this thing I am. Do you know what else they did? They hired that contractor—the one that I quit a few years before, and they got the revenues they wanted, and they got the savings they wanted—and do you know how many injuries there were on that job site?"

"Apart from the injury to your pride?"

"Dozens of separate accidents, five fatalities. This isn't a joke, Ben. Remember the glazier that fell off the fifteenth floor? Maybe you didn't read about him. My building. Five guys. The company says, 'Oh, that's not common,' or, they laugh and they say, 'The construction industry—it's full of drunks!' My dream became a great big tombstone, Ben. And at night, I wake up from a nightmare, and it's my tombstone with my name across it in flashing neon lights."

Ben is at a loss for a light-hearted comeback. He stares out the window and thinks that he hates his friend as much as his friend hates himself. The photo of the glowing '65 CZ lies neglected by his plate.

6.

VESPA HAS DECIDED to visit Rudy. But she has not seen her old boyfriend for a long, long, time. She has been boycotting Rudy, because she figured he would get horns and come looking for her. Only reluctantly has she realized he was completely absorbed in his job, and was going to forget her, not to mention himself, if she did not pursue him into his Babel. Her brother had visited him, her little brother Ben who she was supposed to rescue, who seems to be throwing her a life preserver once again. On the phone he said he had not been impressed by Rudy, was too upset to talk about it. Vespa is curious. Is Rudy still the radical-talking punk he was when they were all on the street? After all the revolutionary speeches over midnight candles pressed into the tops of wine bottles, why the change? And as far as she can surmise, Rudy is not interested in any of his past friendships in any way. He seems far more interested in being a hotshot, bigwig, wing-nut bull-dozing poor people's houses, bullying bureaucrats, arranging protectionism, lobbying for privatization, and putting people in and out of business, while he covers the city landscape with high-rises of his own design. Vespa's suspicions are close, but only some of this is true.

Rudy has become a very confided-in, very favourite in-boy with B.F. Turner, the infamous and corrupt construction mogul who is demolishing buildings with his company of the same name. People in the Turner company grumble and are disgruntled by Rudy's rise to power. To others, it only seems as if Rudy has found success and freedom and is living in luxury in a big sunny studio overlooking the Pacific in the upscale West end of town.

It is here that Vespa meets her old boyfriend, his door clicking closed as they cross his rainforest-sourced hardwood. He makes her a drink at his glass and chrome bar, and they sit together on a piece of furniture that is a Brutalist interpretation of a couch. The ice rattles in their glasses and Vespa notices that he is scrubbed and cologne-scented, wearing aftershave and a body spray over top. Rudy has never smelled like this. She imagines the deodorant slapped under his pits like cement.

"Tell me about your work," she tells him, and he answers that he has learned a thousand ways to scare and bribe a politician into complying with a request, whatever it may be. He has learned everything the wrong way around originally, he explains to her, but now he is trying to subvert the conglomerate he works for from the inside out. Instead of saying it in a good-humoured way, he tells her this as if it is a very vital, classified secret, and Vespa feels as if she is in grade four. At the same time, she can see that her old friend is not just drinking to be social with her, but to steady a set of frayed and sparking nerves. She reaches out to touch his hand. He pulls it away. She notices it is trimmed and manicured, not by Rudy, but by a professional trained to file rich gentlemen's nails. She pictures him in the position of getting his nails buffed and it cracks her up. It is not friendly laughter.

"So, what are you really doing these days?" Rudy asks, in an attempt to deflect bad spirit. His voice drops, causing his defensiveness to sound suggestive instead. Vespa, who has just worked for a grubby escort agency doing straight calls to make ends meet, does not get it. She stares. This is the same man who had worked for B.F. Turner as a day labourer. She marvels. This is the same man who fed her grilled cheese and made love to her on a mattress with forty-five minutes of dubbed and stolen music to fuck to before he had to flip his cassette.

"Who's askin'?" She reminds herself that this is even the same man who smashed her antique plates and then glued them back together in apology and sniffles. The result, a framed assemblage piece, used the decorative plate parts as a sky. Oversized plastic farm animals and architectural-model humans reading newspapers sat on benches beside a submerged doll face smiling up from a tree-shaded pond. A plug-in sun shone down on the scene; it was Rudy's apology for his tantrum. A boyfriend struggling to become a gentleman. She still had it on her wall, had always found it quite beautiful, even if it is the last of her grandmother's dishes that he smashed.

He tops off her drink a second time.

"You would love the things I have been doing," says Vespa, lying. "I've been working with bicycles. All the kids bring in parts, but mostly I just work away, changing tires, fixing gears, hybridizing tour bikes with mountain bike parts and so forth. It's funny the things people want."

Rudy picked picks up her hands, and Vespa's heart skipped skips a beat. Sudden intimacy after being pushed away. Dammit. She is still attracted to him, even more curiously because of all his funny new smells. She wonders if he put them on that morning, thinking of his appointment with her and wanting to smell nice. He stared at her fingers. "No, you haven't," he tells her, and he continues to stare at her fingers, turning her hands over in his in a clinical way. "You've grown your nails out, so you've been doing something else. You haven't been working with your hands in that way for months."

She tries to withdraw them, but Rudy holds them tightly.

He brings them to his lips and kisses them. "You have been whoring," he says.

"Some people say so have you."

"For a good reason," he answers.

"For the good reason of making lots of money and turfing lots of people out of their homes?"

"I'm not behind most of that. I'm the moderate in that lot if you can imagine. I'm the left-wing radical."

"I heard you were the right-hand man."

"I am studying the company, like a model, looking down and examining the working parts." He puts his finger to her lips, "In order to disassemble it, but you must not tell."

"Do you have a lot of girlfriends?"

"Some. I don't really have time for anything like that. I don't have time for emotions."

"Do you give them lots of money?"

"Where is this leading?" Rudy asks. He tops off her glass, pushing past her blood-alcohol tolerance levels.

"I stayed out of your way all those months, waiting for you to call me, but every time, it was me that picked up the phone. And you were always too busy. Too busy for emotions. Where should it be leading?"

"You want me to loan you some money?"

Vespa widens her eyes. Rudy's face had not been this close to hers in so long, she has forgotten little things about him. It is hard not to stare, not to memorize all over again the arrangement of teeth and hair and to remember the good way they used to laugh.

His pores are no longer filled with dirt; his skin has been treated by professionals, the little pits and character scars sandblasted away.

"What do you want from me?" Vespa asks. It is a line she has rehearsed.

He smiles at her. "Do you want me to give you some money? I know you have been whoring, why? You are so much better than that. Just like your brother, you could build a motorcycle from scrap. You're talented, a sculptor, why are you...?"

"For money, that's all. Not because I am going to overthrow the escort world from the inside out, or subvert it with my new-found connections to the world of high finance and dirty pricks. It's still me, Rudy, just the same as you."

"It's true, it is still you," he leans forward and kisses her. He draws a long breath. "I want to have you again, here, in my bed, on the bed that looks out over the city. When you wake, you will feel like a princess in a tower."

"Royalty? Okay, and who shall we behead in the morning, Rudy? You? For crimes against romantic poetry? Or me, for being the inconvenient one of your wives?"

"I could tie you, I could take you, I could have you right here in this room."

"I could call the police for help," says Vespa, and she makes a quick grab for Rudy's neon-glowing phone. It falls with a clatter to the floor and Rudy's hand takes hers and gently sets the receiver back in the cradle. She looks up.

She looks up. "If you loved me, why didn't you contact me? I remember you used to speak about love, but for ages you've shown me nothing at all."

"I create visual images, three-dimensional visual ideas, worlds where children will be born and people will fuck and fight and sip drinks looking over the city, and I sell them. Vespa, I sell 'setting' poetry. I create living spaces, animate a human cinema within my own restrictions of lighting and props, and for thousands and thousands of dollars.... That's still poetry, poetry of space and life."

"Beautiful, self-occupied. I wasn't exactly hard to get hold of."

"You could share a part in my future. I'm becoming famous."

"Your future? Your company is famous for killing people. Sure, the buildings are symmetrical, but when the workers fall from the buildings, they still break in messy pieces. Does it bother you that the poetry that lived in their heads spills out of their skulls from the right? Or that their broken hearts are on the left?"

"I think it's time we wrapped this all up," Rudy says, getting to his feet.

"Good, I don't have time for emotions. You don't want to rape me anymore?"

"That was your fantasy, not mine."

He picks up the phone and speed-dials his own security code for the building.

"Are you calling the police?"

Rudy seizes her by the arms and holds her as a security guard peers cautiously into the door.

"Is there some trouble, Sir?"

"Please remove this young woman. Put her in a taxi outside the gates. See that she is returned to Hastings and Main Street."

"That's not my address."

"It's close enough."

"Wait, my purse. I'll get my own taxi." The security guard moves over to her.

She grabs her small handbag from the table. "I don't have time to piss on your floor, Mister, or any of that other funny stuff you asked me to do. Call some other girl, you kinky motherfucker...."

"She's just drunk," Rudy tells the security guard.

"It's okay, sweetheart," the guard says to Vespa. "You girls have a right to refuse it."

The door shuts behind them and Rudy is alone.

7.

JACKIE, HAVING COME to Toronto partly at the invitation of Wanda, has managed instead to get herself into extraordinary amounts of trouble. Following the little heist in Vancouver, the idea of leaving the region appealed to Jackie. Still, she bided her time, working at B.F. Turner long enough to reinforce her alibi and puzzle police before rolling up her small fortune in stolen ATM loot and fleeing in her gold-speckled station wagon for points East. There then followed what can only be referred to as a spree.

Arriving in Toronto, she had found herself making only slow circles toward Wanda, wanting instead to shake her desperation and pull off something impressive before they meet. She became mired in the hope that her life could appear a swirling galaxy of possibility to the one person who might help her, instead finding it had become a cosmic drain, her self-control playing the role of the lost rubber stopper. So, she pulled the chain hard and dropped down into New York State, where the little station wagon became accomplice to a series of ATM robberies throughout the area and into Ohio. She partied as she went, met people who pretended to love her, but her sense of a need to find home also became too great, and Jackie had returned to what she sensed was a glimmer of family and Toronto once again. There she had robbed a deli and been caught, and so, she was once again on the Canadian radar. Wanda had corresponded with her and helped her win parole, and yet ,when she was freed, she had dropped down into New York again to party, meeting people who could situate her as innocent and not involved in any crime. And indeed, Jackie was reforming when she returned from her New York fiesta, only to be picked up in Toronto for something armed robbers had done while she was away. It was poor police work, because armed robbery simply wasn't her style. She hadn't done it, and her New York party friends were the key. But when you are missing basic skills in judging character, strange things can happen.

Jackie did the time, or enough of it, and inside her something hopeful, something Wanda had kindled, grew scared and angry like it never had before. Vengeful rage, buried deep. And now she has finally emerged a wet, hurt creature. She needs to be rescued in ways she scarcely even knows are obvious to others. Bothered by the feeling that someone is watching her, she is playing pool in the billiard room of her favourite downtown hotel when three armed men apprehend her. Immediately, the feeling that just being Jackie is somehow enough of a reason to cart her away sinks heavily into her bones. There is no time to tell the attractive woman she is playing snooker with if she "is someone" or not, and she herself is entirely not certain, despite the badges and the rap, whether these men are under-informed police or merely kidnappers. It is embarrassing to have it happen, and to have them publicly tell her it is "because they know who she is."

The snooker player trails outside to the police car, tears running down her face. She is asking the police just what poor Jackie has done.

"Here we go again," says Jackie. After this, the men press her head inside the cruiser and then the rest of her body. Jackie is now only able to face her own prideful hesitation in reaching out to real friends, represented by the sugar-frosting facade of the over-priced hotel where she had been hiding, and by the sight of a stranger wringing her hands on the curb.

A heavy thunderhead has fallen out of the sky and tumbled down onto the city. It is made up of smaller storm clouds, but they are turned upside down, breasts fallen out of a bra, milk poured slowly into tea. All night, the streets have remained dense with fog. With morning, spirals generated by the activity of a million spoons, have created a vortex of agitated air that pushes the mist to her feet. To Jackie's perception, the head-first cloud has picked up speed, drifts away from Toronto in search of softer earth. People in the processing room at police station comment that it looks as if there isn't going to be a storm, and that no one need to leave home that morning with their umbrellas. Despite this, they all have.

Underground, the downtown court has entertained an indolent series of prostitution convictions, a festive parade of smart remarks, one fart, and two unpursued threats of contempt. Morning is still only beginning. "Jailbird Jackie" is sitting in her cell. The women around her are sensitive enough to appreciate that she is lost in her own world and try not to interrupt her with jokes.

Their new cellmate is thinking about an electromechanical device designed for the issuing of cash. She sways slightly in the holding tank beneath the earth. The women sitting near her have almost vanished in as far as her senses are concerned, in preference to her musings. She meditates on the technology of unattended, online computer banking, imagining herself loading a newly-freed banking machine onto a truck and driving it coolly away. A subway trundles to a stop and then rolls away again from the College Park Station, and the walls shudder slightly. Her arms twitch, her eyelids lower. Across from her, a woman named Mimi stirs, glancing at a woman in a fox-fur coat. They smile, and Mimi motions with her chin at Jackie. It is fortunate that Mimi likes Jackie because Mimi is not only a far more powerful woman than Jackie might guess at, she is one who is destined to redirect Jackie's life.

Mimi grins at the women and raises a brow. Jackie is starting to doze. A loud tap on the bars makes the group jump.

"Your phone call," says the guard. "Best make it now."

Jackie follows him down the hall. Fighting a twinge to pee, she composes herself and steadies. She stares at the phone directory, and then searches for the vintage motorcycle repair shop. Yes, it is there. It has been waiting for her to dial her old friend. The phone rings at the other end. Jackie blows a dark forelock out of her eyes. The overheated density in the guard's station is awash with male hormonal sweat and aftershave.

"Wanda here." Sitting alone at the Toronto bedside of a comatose Ben, who only months before crashed his lovingly rebuilt Czechoslovakian motorcycle, Wanda has been taking calls on her cellphone.

"Hello, love," Jackie answers, realizing she had been expecting an answering machine. "Guess where I have landed. And this time I am certain it is not my fault."

Her heartbeat counts the moments before Wanda's ironic voice responds: "The same type of little lock-up we met in last time?"

Jackie sighs in recognition, shifting on her shoes with no laces.

At the other end of the line, she can picture Wanda's smile at the familiarity of Jackie's voice. Wanda also needs to explain a new situation to her friend. Ben's IV drip glows softly as a chapel window, gathering radiance from the fluorescent lights in the hall. The bible her grandmother had once carried through an alpine windstorm is resting next to his tray. All this she describes to her friend. Wanda is not wondering as to Jackie's claim of innocence. Since the very first day, seeing there was a morality problem in Jackie, Wanda had looked into her new friend's eyes and felt love. And in that first night, she was also certain she had discovered in Jackie a life-changing sense of witchery, a current of what it is to be alive. Wanda was, of course, overqualifying an unethical person, and, at the time, she reminded herself she was also a person easily led astray, something that protective Ben would remind her of if or when he surfaces from his coma, a solo trip to an unconscious realm no one can fathom.

"Take what you need, reach into the cosmos, and if you can survive, Wanda," Jackie had told her, "you can also dance."

Because of her, Wanda had renovated her Catholicism to include a love for things inanimate. Since the unfortunate evening back in Vancouver when the escort agency that promised to connect actors to the movie industry was raided by the police, Wanda had never forgotten meeting Jackie. And in those first days, while she sat studying the strands of life-support wires and tubing that had become Ben, technically recovering, she saw Jackie's thing for machinery was something an ordinary person could admire.

Commendably, despite sensing loyalty, Jackie has never attempted to involve her friends in a heist. She stands inside the battered jailhouse telephone underground and feels wistful for a moment that she had not. Perhaps she might have saved Ben from spinning out his new bike.

At the hospital, Wanda gathers her things. "Because of you, somehow," she tells Jackie, "because of this, Ben will be well."

"I'm not sure I follow your logic on that," says Jackie, but Wanda has already hung up. Jackie shuffles back with the guard, realizing Wanda thinks of her as a sort of visit from the underworld, an underworld that is populated with magic and is holy and revered.

This Toronto arrest, like the last vehicle charge, is based on a copycat criminal who has not only nothing to do with Jackie, but who also has nothing of what Jackie considers her finesse. Because of this, Jackie knows she will be released. While undergoing questioning, she learned that she was mistaken yet again for an amateur with at least one accomplice. Jackie, who never uses an accomplice, had become so interested in solving the case that she had completely forgotten to use her phone opportunity until her transfer to the cells under the College

Park Court. The possibility that they could try her for a crime she had practically solved on their behalf now annoys her and dangles like an ambush. It would be a betrayal of her sleuthing efforts as well as a miscarriage of justice.

Above her, the streets pale. Through the Toronto morning, Wanda races her car past showroom windows, where motorcycles and flashing televisions stare out at wintry streets. All over town, fingers break open bagels, bran muffins, croissants, and apply wet pats of hot butter. Underground, the friendly brown-eyed guard appears in the corridor and motions to Jackie to come. Word has arrived through her state-appointed lawyer that her copycats have been apprehended. As it would take too many hours of phoney legal work to construct a connection to Jackie, she is free to go.

"Because of this, I am reuniting with sweet Wanda. And going to visit a vintage motorcycle shop. Where there is some sort of love. Thank you, copycats. Thank you," she says out loud.

Above ground, a hot-dog man named Gus is cracking jokes with a young man cracking gum, and the flames leaping around his sleeves are three fork prongs away from setting fire to his arms. His arms are muscled like ropes and have old European tattoos on them of interest to both queer men and ladies. He is giddily glad he finally moved East at Swan's urging from Vancouver. He grits his teeth as a streetcar blasts a horn at an absent driver. It is Wanda who has parked her car with flashing lights on the curb, blocking the passage of traffic. One of Gus's teeth is gold, and the backs are filled with silver. The holes are filled with sugar. He smiles as the hot sun breaks through the clouds, and the licorice-wet street before him begins to steam and rise. He is distracted not by the parked car, but by the quickly moving form of Wanda, who has hurried away from the car into the courts. He wants it to be the girl from the Schilthorn, the red-cheeked woman from the Lions Gate Bridge. She has moved too quickly to be certain, yet still his heart jumps in his chest.

Six riders jump off the streetcar: Four men, a boy with jeans on that has a chain leading to his wallet that is knocking against a pocket at the back of his knees, and a girl who wears a toque that says "boy," a statement conveying a range of interpretations. They are all wearing gold goose-feather coats. It is not because they represent something, but because it has recently been twenty degrees below freezing in Toronto, and gold goose-feather coats are a practical and hot look. It is a fashion this winter that a small group of Canadians standing in a snowbank look like lost bees awaiting a message from their Queen. Gus busies himself while the group buzzes around the car and discusses moving it out of the way. The streetcar remains stalled as Wanda has run into the mall. Because they are Canadians, the group of bees call the absent driver "an arse." They shout it together: "Takes a real arse to park in the streetcar lane," and the hum of their shared indignation reverberates back to the onlookers in the streetcar. There is a cheer from within the streetcar although nothing has happened.

The group outside shouts, "One and-a ... two and-a ... three and-a..." while they heave the Honda Civic out of the street and onto the sidewalk. Together, they have the severe expression a crew might adopt while transferring an injured snowmobiler to a gurney. Now the Civic is even more incorrectly parked than before, confusing foot traffic and frightening the street people panning for change.

This time, the yellow bees cheer. They are enormously, extra-proportionately proud of themselves. And the streetcar can now pass. The six gold, goose-feathered friends slap their mitts together and hop back on the streetcar. A great *hurrah* rises up from the passengers who the friends rejoin on the streetcar. The girl in gold announces that the guy who owns the Civic must be one card short of a deck. There is another *hurrah* and laughter.

A relief driver in a grape coat jumps on board to announce that whoever owns that Civic has the kind of hair that grows into his head instead of out. The new driver, who is two suit buttons short of a dress coat since the day his wife jumped onto a westbound car and phoned him from the east side of Halifax, chats to a dispatcher on the phone. From out of the College Park mall, a woman with one regular hand and one prosthetic hand rushes forward, pulling Jackie with her as if she were a toddler. Glancing at the car parked on the sidewalk she declares, "Saint Ciboire! Anyone who would do that must not have both their oars in the water!" Wanda's blue Honda is seven blocks short of a tow-truck operator and fifteen blocks short of a junkyard fine. Her friend stands blinking at the reflected light, at the homeless people wrapped in sleeping bags outside the office towers and department stores, at the snowbanks, and at the new gold goose-feathered coats on the people standing in streetcar. Finally, she stares at the Civic blocking the sidewalk instead of the road.

Jackie has a drawn-out look that is different from the fresh, bright-eyed, fruit-fed passersby, and different again from the feverish, frostbitten people sitting on the ground. Her friend places her coffee on the ground, and together, they shove the little Civic back out of the snowbank and into the traffic. It is a feat of physical power that inspires a whistle from Gus. "Holy foot-longs!" he mutters in a reverent way, an expression he has learned as a member of Toronto's male steam bath community. The cry of exclamation dovetails with his day job without the raising of a brow. He stares at the two women, thinking one of them must surely be Wanda, his beautiful lost girl on the ski hill, as he passes the simulated baçon bits to a boy hooker. Gus and his male distraction are struck in the face by a blast of snow. He turns away, and an eyelash blows into his relish pot and disappears.

When he looks up to flirt, the Civic is gone.

8.

MIMI, STILL AWAITING charges of solicitation, withdraws a neatly rolled joint wrapped in plastic from her vagina. She is glad that Jackie has been freed. She knows that Jailbird Jackie was confident that there was nothing to prove it was her, and a confident ex-con is almost always a right-on one.

The woman with the doob is still imprisoned in the joint, in the holding cells of College Park. She is awaiting trial, floors above, in a courtroom still many levels below the surface of the street, and only a few levels beneath a mall teeming with shoppers. A more naive citizen might suggest perhaps a body-cavity search overlooked her, or that it was never conducted at all. The truth of the matter is that this particular woman has been subjected to many. She has learned the art of transferring contraband on her body in a series of lightning-fast sleight-of-hand movements that are older than time itself. The possibility that uninvited latex gloves will ever recover what is inches away from their grasp is not even worth consideration. It is more ancient, more eye-popping than the most elaborate of card tricks, and it is something that she does extremely well.

The women spark up the spliff. Each take three hauls and passes it to her left in the time-honoured manner, remarking that it tastes a bit like a fish. The third woman strokes the fox fur of her coat and out of protocol says, "I wish I could just walk out of this place right now." It is as if she is speaking to none of them at all.

"I don't see why we can't," responds Mimi, who has a flying squirrel tattooed on her hand. "I am so tired of getting picked up by the same goddamn crooked cops. They're all familiar faces to me. I've been doing this work for centuries. It's my body, not their property. I can do whatever the hell I want."

"You can't walk through walls," suggests a woman in tight tan jeans and white jean jacket decorated in rosettes.

They all lean forward. A good intellectual banter is starting up. The woman known as Mimi can really rattle a woman's cage and she grins cheerfully. "If all our realities are creations of our minds, then everything around us is a perception. And as I'm sure you already know, all our perceptions can be altered...."

Since the woman in white and tan is arguing in favour of pessimism, Mimi is confident she can win. She asserts, "But all matter is composed of some type of carbon-based molecules ... and carbon is bound to other carbons, creating concrete, blood, iron, steel...."

"I am a carbon-based life form..." declares the woman in the fox-fur coat unexpectedly. They stare.

"You most certainly are..." answers jean-jacket.

"A carbon-based somethin'. A carbon-based somethin', she most certainly is," Mimi concludes, and together they begin to catcall the woman in the fur.

A correctional officer behind one-way glass taps on the surface.

"We exist," declares the woman who brought in the joint.

Mimi smiles and remarks, "A grain of sand exists, a feather exists, an electron exists. All of them exist, because we accept them and allow them to be so, and so, we then perceive them to be...."

There is a silence.

"I haven't perceived an electron in some while," the woman in white tells Mimi. The group busts out in laughter.

Beneath the earth, Mimi further digs in her heels. "A drug,

a bug, within the laws of our thoughts, it doesn't matter. A prison. But let's say that we don't believe in their existence, or their relevance to our lives. None of you women in this room could argue that is not true. Then nothing around us is really tangible or true, it is all just an illusion that we have collectively agreed to. If we choose to believe in the existence of a Creator, then we agree that we are more than these material bodies, that we return to the universe after death, and that we can transcend our present form, not just astrally, but by unifying with each other in pursuit of our common destination, our true destiny, to transcend all things physical, to unite and pass through elements sharing the same basic molecular structure as ourselves ... to travel through the non-distance...."

Another silence, this time very electric. All eyes are now fixed on the woman with the joint.

"Therefore, our Gods, Goddesses, and Creators are as dependent on our belief system as a grain of sand...."

"That's why I don't believe in any God," says a woman sitting against the wall. She wears a mass of bleached hair confused in a constellation of ribbon and string.

"For one thing, every time I go to a house of God, 'He's' not there. Sometimes there is a janitor there, sometimes there's a cleaning lady. And who wants a spiritual power watching over them who has a cleaning lady to clean up 'His' house? If God answered prayers, there would be no suffering in this world. Well, there is. I'm about to take the heat for a fifty-gram rock my boyfriend, excuse me, my *ex*-boyfriend, stashed in my apartment, and I've got two little girls. I'm going to jail and he's walking around free. My mother said she might take care of them. Yeah, like she took care of me. I'm suffering right now and I have a tension headache the size of the GTA. Is God helping me? No. Pass the joint, will ya?"

The conversation continues. Mimi observes through a slight shadow in the one-way glass that in the guardroom next to the holding cell, the deep brown eyeballs of an officer of corrections roll upwards under his lids. Above them, the streetcars and the hot-dog man and the swell of humanity rush in all directions. They are expelling a hundred different types of sweats and smells. Mimi feels as if she is able to bob up through the earth and see them there. The guard has been watching her talk, and she stares at him, knowing he is hypnotically drawn towards her in her simple sweater over a T-shirt and a pair of shorts over tights. She takes off her sweater. She has been the centre of the group from the beginning. She draws him into to her group with her mind. There is a group: they are seven, sitting in front of him. And there is only her at the centre. His eyes drift shut again for what seems like a moment. When he opens them, Mimi knows he is horrified. A moment later, he is unlocking the holding cell door, and stands gaping at the empty room. He walks into the centre of the cell, then to the corner. They are not there. Seven women have vanished, and the door to the cell is swinging freely ajar. A current of air from the frosty winter outside makes the many hairs on his body wave in an eerie, spooked-out way. He turns and looks up at the video camera, and the robot filmmaker captures in digital motion the collapse of everything the wet-eyed guard had ever understood about the physical world.

With a slight moan of metal on hinge, Mimi's consciousness leaves the cell, and the door snaps locked behind him.

9.

THE TWO WOMEN are going to meet a man who now has no nipples. He is lucky to be alive. His nipples are at an undetermined spot; a healthy mind would not even dwell on the ultimate resting place of his nipples. Perhaps they are in the stomach of a bird. Indisputably, they are not on his body; there is nothing there now but the form of an abrasion scar, leaving behind the appearance of a manikin who has been dropped into life from a mould. In fact, he has almost dropped out of life on many occasions. His nipples were torn away and stolen from him in a moment of spite by a pissed-off guardian angel responsible for dispensing justice during Ben's various brushes with mortality. They were removed as a reminder to Ben, and as a handy-dandy keepsake to his angels, for keeping keys or for marking pages in his book of life, separated from his body at the place where he once nearly lost everything he had. Many people have had a close swipe with death, but only a few leave a body part at the scene.

Ben has a long history of musk-filled evenings of romance initiated in every case by Wanda, Jackie's one-handed friend, who wears an attractive smell of honeysuckle and Harley-Davidsons, and possesses a power over full-grown men she has neither abused or acknowledged. Jackie, who first met Wanda after her friend was busted for swinging her stiletto from her toe for a Vancouver escort company she believed was leading her into an acting career, knows all about Wanda's feeling for Ben.

"Has he stirred at all?" Jackie asks, staring out at the blur of ditch and weeds.

At the beginning of their romance, Wanda tells her, Ben had a wholesome boyhood fantasy of making love to Wanda before an audience of birds and hooved animals while she was tied to the altar of a famous European cathedral. The way he said it had made her laugh and love. After he confessed this to her, his glasses slipping low on his sweaty nose, he fell asleep, dreaming of nothing but flying through air. Now, his nipples, like two scraps of leather, lie next to a fading single rubber tire burn on the highway. The rubber burn traces a slight register of panic followed by an over-compensated wild angle left towards the dive into certain death below. Wanda's lover had flown with eyes the size of plates through darkness, coloured lights, and the contortions of his rain-slicked motorcycle yet somehow survived.

Wanda tells Jackie that most people about to die in such a way are accompanied by the magic hieroglyphics and dancing rock art of the ancients, ushering anyone on psychedelics into the next world. Jackie responds that actually the way in which he was about to die was the no-frills way that all individuals, having become too fascinated with a prism of rain striking a windshield through a double-hit of acid at a speed of eighty-five miles an hour, can and should expect they will die. They are kissing their rear ends goodbye. Ben had stared headlong into what was certain to be a messy and imminent death.

After skidding along on the shoulder, the inertia of his lovingly rebuilt Czechoslovakian motorcycle had evidently booted his backside bombastically aloft. Not unlike a trick with wires and pulleys in a Shakespearean play, Wanda replies, the man and the machine flew, together, into the air. According to the police who first arrived on the scene, they bounced, much like a rubber ball would bounce, and in a single rebound, were floating off the side of a cliff. Wanda spreads out her arms in the Civic and tells Jackie that she believes that his motorcycle jacket opened out like wings, creating flight. This is where Wanda thinks Ben has gone to in his coma. The flying fantasy must surely be resting in a satisfying and unforgettable way in the back of his mind as now he is waking up again and beginning to lift a spoon. Ben was able to fly through the air with his leather jacket flapping around him like wings, and even though he had just lost his nipples he was oblivious to his misplaced body parts, and so high that the sensation was undoubtedly wonderful. To Wanda, this explained the smile that remains there, fierce, toothy, all-knowing, and so trusting in a higher power that even ordinary people can see a violet aura washing around Ben. He smiles back at them, and the sight of it both attracts and repels.

10.

CZECH LITERATURE is more formal, Wanda tells Jackie, and Slovak literature is more romantic. It is one of the many things the couple argued at length before the crash. As far as Jackie can surmise, her friend is intending to teach her the difference between Slovak and Czech literary styles to her while feeding yogurt to Ben with a spoon. Jackie, invited to look at a partly rebuilt Triumph Trident in Ben's garage, is now trapped in the uncomfortable position of having to socialize with complicated people, in the deconstructed presence of a revered machine. Vespa is coming to visit them, something that has Jackie stoked. Ben sits in a silent posture, not yet his usual self.

Wanda swirls the yogurt. "At the beginning of the Second World War, vast pieces of Northern Czechoslovakia were given away to Germany. Negotiations were conducted in Munich with negotiators from London, Paris, Rome. Now they have fashion shows together. It was piracy! They actually thought that by breaking a small country into a jigsaw puzzle they would save other nations from war ... London, Paris, Rome.... Even today, we are still at the mercy of their ridiculous specifications in clothes."

Jackie takes a long, cold stare at the cradle frame with two pipes running under the engine, the fantastical exhaust system, the mufflers curving out at the back wheel. "I think there should be no borders, no giving away people's land."

"Europe was mutilated," Wanda responds.

Jackie reaches to adjust the spoke tension on the old Triumph even though it has a flat. It is an excellent replacement for the CZ. Even in its condition, it has a spectacular design. She finds that the spokes have been adjusted already, as if someone who had been working on it had then rashly given it away. Undaunted, she begins removing the battery.

"*Agh-ah oogah!*" says Ben.

Wanda jumps up and strokes him on the head.

"Ben just said that the Nazi party also gave Hungary a large portion of Southern Slovakia."

"That may be true, but he didn't say that!"

"He did say that. I'm his woman, I think I know what he says!"

Jackie sighs. "How can you say he said that when all that he said was that one four-syllable word, not even one word or one sound?"

"In theatre, there is a whole school of expression where words become elemental sounds."

She moderates her voice. "Well, maybe he once said all those other things, but just now all he said was…"

"*Arooo ooogah! Zmlknout!*"

Wanda cocks her head, listening to Ben. She breaks into a smile. "True, Ben, true. Interesting point."

With a clatter, Jackie sets down an adjustable wrench. "Classic transference, Wanda. You're projecting onto him things that he can't say. You are unable to accept the rate of his recovery. You are not his translator, let go of your control."

"Wrong. Look at Grotowski and the Polish Laboratory Theatre when Poland was Soviet-controlled. Text prolonged as wails; they toured his plays and made a big hit in free America."

"The idea isn't new," says Jackie.

"*Blahopřání!*" squeals Ben.

"That was 'congratulations,' in Czech."

"Bullshit! You should be in therapy, both of you."

"Wanna bet?" says Wanda.

"*Mir!*" shouts Ben.

Jackie sighs. She remembers the woman in the holding cell, hot young Wanda with the kohl-lined eyes. *Love more,* thinks Jackie, *love your friends.* She changes her voice to a more *sotto* tone. "Wanda, there is no way, considering the accident he's just survived, that Ben could ever be thinking or saying very much more right now...."

"Jerzy Kosiński. A classic casualty of Soviet occupation. State-approved, pornographic slush," says Ben.

The two women stare at him for a second.

"It's true. He always thinks Kosiński is an example of an arrogant writer taking advantage of a gulf in popular culture...." Wanda tells her.

She shovels a spoonful of banana yogurt into Ben's gaping mouth, and then walks over so that she is standing in Jackie's light. "Of course, in Soviet-controlled regimes, a writer was often treated like a criminal. I don't mean a criminal who is not to be trusted, but a criminal against the State. Not that you are not to be trusted because you are not now a criminal. Or not anymore. In all your time in jail, have you ever read...?"

"No," she tells her.

A breath of cool breeze enters the swamp-hot garage as the door opens, letting in bright white sunlight that illuminates the group. Outside, overgrown bushes turned into trees can be seen waving softly in the wind. Ben's sister, dressed in leather boots, comfortable jeans, and a jacket for highway riding, steps lightly into the centre of the room. Jackie notices that she smells of fragrantly crushed flowers, sweat, perhaps motor oil, and spices from places Jackie has never seen. Nodding to them, she crosses the garage. A cry of joy bursts from her throat as she showers her brother with kisses. The yogurty spoon Ben has snatched from Wanda becomes ensnared in her hair.

Ben's sister extends her hand to Jackie as she withdraws the spoon. She gives Jackie a hearty, lactose-lubricated handshake. "Vespa," she tells her. "Good to meet you. Jackie, right?"

Exchanging names, they both wipe their right hands on the thigh of their jeans.

Jackie is staring. And not at Ben. "Vespa! A brilliant machine!" Jackie remarks.

"No!" says Wanda. "That's what her mother called her; it's her real name."

Unable to contain himself any longer, Ben bursts into laughter, spraying the group with saliva and mirth.

"'If the union of a soul to a machine is impossible, let someone prove it to me,'" says Jackie.

"'If it is possible, let someone tell me what would be the effects of this union,' Diderot, 1774," Ben's sister answers on cue. The two women smile at each other with more meaning.

"Vespa, it appears that Ben is talking."

"Talking so soon? That's impossible."

Ben gurgles and Vespa messes his hair, kissing him on the forehead.

"So your mother rode a scooter, and she named you...?" Jackie asks.

Vespa laughs. "No, she rode a Condor. That was the smallest bike she ever had. Swiss Police Bike, 580cc side valve flat-twin Condor. Not too different in many ways from the structure of this Triumph. I told my brother while he was in his coma that if he stabilized I would give him this machine. It's nothing like the thing he trashed, but we'll fix it up all right. Yes, that Condor was the sweetest. The police took it away from her, of course. In Switzerland. They chased her because the Condor was stolen. From them, in fact. They chased her, and they took it away. Long story, long chase, long telling."

Vespa brings down a box of tools from the wall of shelves at the side of the garage and kneels next to the bike. "This Triumph here is just something I picked up. If he can ride it, he can have it, after all he's been through...."

Vespa runs her hands through her own hair a few times, blending the yogurt into her curls. Jackie remains transfixed. Vespa traces her fingers along the length of the large, early model fuel tank and licks her lips. The little hairs on Jackie's arms stand up. Wanda rolls her eyes at them and then gets to her feet.

"We were just discussing the early war period of Czech breakup and describing the post-war annexation," Wanda tells her.

"I know what you're up to," says Vespa. "My brother isn't stable enough to listen to you two arguing about underground art movements. You're only taxing his brain...." Vespa leaves the bike and falls to one knee by her brother. She strokes his hair.

Jackie coughs and looks at Ben's sister. "It wasn't actually me discussing any of these things," says Jackie. "So I wasn't taxing his brain."

"Let him defend himself then. He spoke to me just a minute ago," Wanda snaps.

"He did," says Jackie.

Vespa jerks her head. "He spoke?"

"Slug!" roars Ben. An agitated arc of spittle flies from his mouth.

"Wow!" says Vespa, "He can talk. And I was afraid he would have lost his bad temper...."

"He's back," says Wanda, "and he glows with love."

"Lose it!" Ben shrieks. "It's not a blessing to have a near-death experience. It's not a gift to touch the hand of God, fight for your life, and then surface from a coma to realize you are surrounded by airheads."

They stand staring. Wanda clasps and unclasps her hands.

"*Aroo-aoongah*. And stop staring," says Ben.

Vespa reaches out to stroke his arm. "Wanda's right. You do have a sort of love glow ... and you never had a love glow on you before, Ben."

Jackie watches Vespa, seeing her lips part and pucker and then close reflectively as she stands looking at her brother. She smiles as Vespa's breasts sigh with happiness.

Wanda returns to her seat next to the yogurt. She wrestles the spoon from his hand.

"'The body is an automaton,'" Jackie announces, "'but the mind has free will and therefore lies outside the realm of scientific explanation.'"

"Which is the only explanation as to why he's coming around."

"Descartes," says Jackie, drawing the attention back to herself.

"*Cogito, ergo sum,*" says Vespa.

"Where were you educated?" Jackie asks.

"I am," says Vespa, "self-educated. And an artist and a sculptor, and a chipper of granite and marble and onyx and soapstone, a caster of plaster and silver and bronze, and a collector of Band-Aids and blood."

"Do you write any of your ideas down?"

"I wanted to. To be a real hellraiser of poetry, to write a poem every day. Ben always said poetry was the bastard of painting," she smiles at the Triumph. "It looks like someone's been doing diagnostics.... To tell you the truth, Jackie, it looks as if this whole handlebar assembly...." Vespa looks up, her eyes brightening with surprise. "You did it!"

As if it is a contract for a nuptial agreement, Jackie hands Vespa a copy of the wiring diagram she had earlier placed under the seat.

Vespa looks at her more closely, and her lips part in a silent kiss. "That little continuity check saved me from dismantling the whole brake-light mechanism! There was nothing wrong with it! Now all I have to do is change this bulb."

The two of them lean close and begin plans for an overhaul of the vintage gear works, when Ben roars unexpectedly and attempts to ride up from his chair. "Scarred, defaced, impending separatism, of course it's a metaphor for our relationship. Please, I love you, Wanda...."

"Oh, for pity's sake," Vespa drops a wrench. "Marry him or something. He's speaking and he loves you!"

"*Samostatnost!*" cries Ben. "No one is feeding me with a spoon."

Vespa is finished. The muscles in her neck stand out and her face seems flushed. Jackie is attracted to the mechanism of Vespa. The two women take apart pieces from the turn-signal assembly and set them on an open bandana, their shoulders continually brushing.

There is a long silence while Wanda is cradled by Ben. The garage resounds with hiccups and squawks. A nose blows. Ben makes another difficult attempt to interpret sound.

"He said, 'Vespa likes that demon female,' quote unquote," Wanda tells them.

"He said that?"

She giggles and buries her face in Ben's summer-hot pits, yogurt splattering on the crotch of her dress. She stays there awhile, and Ben turns to them and speaks hypnotically with Wanda cradling in his lap.

"*It is my wish to notify you of an incident involving the metabolic transfer of seven women escaping imprisonment by harmonizing with the sound, Ohm. Employing the same frequency and bandwidth as steel and cement, but with a unified voice of resistance—Ohm being the measurement of the resistance of a current of electricity in response to a measure of power—they have transcended their oppression. Utilizing a female in a brown chamois sweater as means of a conductor, the group has successfully exited in a chorus of seven complete harmonies through the walls of their cell, landing on their cans next to a hot-dog vendor across the street. This is the first case of this sort that I, Ben, am aware of, or have been able to understand since my dendrites went swizzle-side up in a flight through the sound barrier that gave me both the supersonic ability of bats and the occasional ability to read announcements of the psychic variety. This particular news bulletin was posted by the before-mentioned female in chamois. Stay in tune for more astral updates, slumbering hard to bring you the news."*

Ben smiles, his eyelids lowered.

"Did she have a tattoo on her hand that was a flying squirrel? Oh, never mind. I think I know what's going on. C'mon, Scooter," says Jackie, "let's go for a walk."

11.

VESPA, REALIZING JACKIE needs to understand her, brushes her soft body against her and kisses her softly on her fragrant neck. "I've been on my own for a long time," says Vespa.

"How long?"

"Since I was a child."

Jackie runs her fingers, the muscular hands her lovers beg for, slowly along Vespa's torso. "A child?"

"My mother smashed her Husqvarna racer on a lonely frozen river in Sweden," Vespa tells her.

"She was a racer?"

"Mother topped all previous speed records as well as all previous blood-alcohol findings in a single moment of glory."

"And that was it?"

"Since that day, Ben and I have been on our own."

"Who was your father?"

"Men. Possibly men who might have cared. In my case, a very beautiful Russian artist, paid to paint flames on motorcycle gas tanks, made love to my mother on a boat in the Stockholm harbour. It was a party. Vanished the next day. No clue she was pregnant. In Ben's case, an American traveller she met in a bar. An artist, a writer, and dancer. Stayed with her for week, no forwarding address, also no clue she was pregnant. That's why Ben is African American and Scandinavian. Children were not kind to him, and I used to get in fist fights all the time. There are racists and people who are curious beyond the point of comfort."

In her memory, Vespa sees herself as one of two little children left alone on the ice very much like seal pups on a floe, their eyes were large and searching. And although no one had struck them with a club, to Vespa, their helplessness seemed complete. The only relatives in their lives had been an uncle and his wife in Canada, and so the two children were sent there when they were ten and twelve.

She extends herself across her bed and lights a cigarette. "The uncle was Catholic, fascinated by the writings of St. Thomas Aquinas and preoccupied with arguments about the existence of a moral Divinity. I was familiar with philosophical and theological talk and allergic to it at the same time."

Jackie, who spent her girlhood escaping evangelical wrath in foster care, says nothing. She does, however, give Vespa an injured look that suggests the possibility of an enormous, silent common ground.

"My uncle, like my mother, also knew a great deal about motorcycles. That's where their similarity ended, but it was endearing enough to me that I hung around him until I was a fourteen-year-old drug abuser and hooker. I don't think he really noticed the turn my life was taking."

"He could have looked at the earth plane, instead of always looking at a higher one."

"With teenagers, that is wise advice." She pauses, not wanting to be self-absorbed in the way she has just described her uncle.

Jackie laughs, guessing at her hesitation, and takes the cigarette from her fingers. "This isn't oppressing me."

Vespa reclines. To Jackie, she looks very much like a marble sculpture, only her eyes are dancing and full of life.

Vespa explains that the point she turned to hooking and hanging out in galleries coincided with a corrupt moment in the history of Western art, which was almost exclusively appreciative of long, thin females with black clothes and European affectations. This was a matter of taste that made life more difficult for any serious female artist who might be built with a body type that did not conform to the sexual code of the day. Vespa had felt fortunate to be slender.

"Taste," as Jackie agrees, is frequently another word for "cowardice," and cowardice is the foundation of "eugenics."

"Wherever 'taste' defines access," Vespa remarks, "Fascism is lurking in the garden."

Vespa, however, new on the scene, was ardent about her own abilities as a fledgling artist and finicky about which flatterers she actually took home. As unjust social laws go, she soon had a reputation for sleeping with everyone she refused to sleep with.

Although her accent was something people found interesting, at that age, she also had a deliberate-sounding stutter and the problem of repeating phrases in a sort of poetic Tourette's compulsion she could not control or predict. A speech therapist would have relieved her of hours of suffering owing to teasing. A few years later, or in a different circle, performance at a microphone might have declared her an avant-garde poet. Realizing that all the other wispy but apparently successful women were attached to males who defended their honour, Vespa tells Jackie she decided to follow their lead. "I caved in and became involved with a man called Skip Donkely. Skip Donkely was thirty-five years my senior. Since it was his opinion that I was a genius, he set me up with a studio that allowed me to sculpt clay, cast in plaster, and then transfer my casts to bronze."

"What was the trade-off?"

"My soul, almost my life, but at first, it was mornings of contortionist sex in his studio."

"So, you have no soul now?"

"I haven't got the nice untarnished one I started out with. He only asked that I let him care take all of my pieces, photograph them for my portfolio, and that I help him with details such as realist renderings of hands and feet."

"Oh, so it's like Camille Claudel and *The Gates of Hell*."

"Who?"

"One of the best sculptors ever to have lived. She did all of Rodin's details, and was a model for *The Gates of Hell*. Her likeness is quite visible amongst his damned. "

"As I worked with Skip, he subjected me to theological lectures about the necessary existence of evil. It was as if he was trying to warn me of a locomotive I could not see coming down the rails. He was. For a while, I felt comfortable with his lectures because they reminded me of home, and I even wondered if my uncle would approve. Then his arguments began to annoy me, and I offered him an elaborate objection to God."

"I think Skip was far too old for your uncle to approve of him."

"He would've smacked Skip Donkely on the head with a religious statuette. Definitely not given him approval."

"So, did he promote your sculptures?"

"No, actually, caretaking my work seemed to mean hiding it away. As the days wore on, he became more insistent that I model for his, or work on his sculptures for him, and that I put off sculpting and designing mine."

"Creative deferral. Our fucked-up society is built on it."

"At this point, I began to wonder which one of us was the good one in the relationship, and which one was the necessary evil. I already had a feeling I knew which one considered himself the omnipotent God. One night, I drank too much boxed white wine at a vernissage and told him what I thought."

With it, came a terrible fight.

Skip Donkely threw her out of the studio and kept her art. Later, she saw it in a gallery. She was beginning to drink every day. Next to it were other pieces she had done major details on. These were of special mention by the critics. Everybody loved them. All of the pieces had his name on them, something she declared a career-rescuing con job, a life preserver stolen from a drowning artist.

"I could only comfort myself with the idea that my stolen life preserver made of metal and rock must eventually sink even the most buoyant of male reputations."

With very few friends, the thought was colder than the ice cubes swimming in her many glasses of Southern Comfort. She was still drowning. Left without even a photo, and no money to make the kind of expensive sculptures that she had trained herself to make, she wandered down to Gastown, to drink amongst the damned.

"That's where I met Wanda," she announces.

Jackie, who is drifting under the stroke of Vespa's fingertips, but definitely paying attention, responds, "In hell! One-armed Wanda, armed at all times with a prosthetic limb so heavy it floors the most challenging of combatants."

"Yes, and armed with a vulnerable streak and fine-tuned mind, despite her religious side."

"Blessed with a good mind," says Jackie.

Now that she has said it, Vespa thinks she sees Jackie realizing it sounds nicer than she had thought it would. Not contrite, but kindly. Maybe Jackie, Vespa wonders, like herself, spends days wishing she had a little more perspective on basics like blessings and luck.

"It was Wanda who told me that what had happened to me, happened all the time. Wanda encouraged me to go to art school, and I did. To pay for the classes, I landed work with a number of escort agencies. In my books, that gave me complete independence. But the work was not pleasant, often cruel. Then I smashed my fingers with a chisel hammer and had to work with only one hand. I moved slowly toward an arts degree. Of course, I read about Camille Claudel. I resolved to not spend my old age in an asylum, or 'hell' as you put it. I wondered if it could be done. I toured my sculptures. It was hopelessly expensive. Skip Donkely accused me of plagiarism and told me he was getting a lawyer. He did this by leaving my most important opening after having a tantrum in front of the press. With Skip flexing his influence over my life, the galleries, of course, all gave me bad reviews. People said everywhere that my work was a knock-off of a Skip Donkely."

"Someone should have knocked him off," says Jackie.

"Well, Rudy, my old boyfriend, broke into Skip's workshop, found, right where I told him they would be hiding, pornographic photos of me dated before the legal age of consent, And me, the fallen angel, took the old man to court, as well as his fictitious lawyer."

"Fictitious lawyer?"

"His rampage at the art opening, the speech he gave to the press, all made up. Even the lawyer was invented."

Jackie blows out her cheeks.

"Yes, and I was awarded the expense of my arts studies, while the newspapers splashed the embarrassing photos of my juvenile self draped next to the old man's sculptures all over the living section and the arts section pages for days. Those photos that they did not deem overly pornographic, I should say. Something else they went to lengths to mention in the press was how some of them were just too pink for publication. Skip, instead of apologizing, was thrilled to be the rogue in the centre of the scandal."

"Well, after all, it wasn't him naked in the middle of the newspaper."

"You know, Jackie, I actually think he got some sort of amusement out of seeing that humiliation."

"Humiliation? You said you were vindicated."

"There was still conjecture about which claims were his and which sculptures were mine. It dragged. He got to be the bad boy, and I was allowed to remain the exploited virgin, as long as people could see the nudes."

Vespa tells her how she moved on to abstract masses of wires and elaborately welded steel strips, trying to live down the feeling of being a famous old man's pet.

"I loved my metal animals and began trying to automate my welded pieces. I felt happy for the first time, until my closest allies started to criticize my new work. It was Rudy that hurt the most because even though he was a cruel genius, he had been my cruel genius. I should have guessed he was too fucked-up to love a woman without having his penis involved."

"Not all men are like that," Jackie says, "but basic human decency is when caring does not require fucking. So where was your brother?"

"Ben was all hot about his new motorcycle, and his plans for a shop, but there was nothing for me to offer him about my life, except that I had been horribly exploited. Ben had risen above the drag of experiencing racism and was making a brave life for himself, while I felt hollow and useless to him. After we finished laughing about how I had punished Skip, he wanted to see what I had done next. To me, in those days, everyone had the same disappointed look when they saw the wire animals I had created. Like I had lost it or something, or let them all down. Not like I was evolving, just like they were, but that I had really cracked up. "

"You needed someone to tell you it was all right to follow a bliss."

"Rudy would have told me that. Only, almost overnight, Rudy had become someone I didn't want to know. Someone who abused me. So, I came up with the idea that I needed to get out of my head and release something in my mind and really have a breakthrough. Instead, I spent two nights in the hospital after overdosing. I almost died, and it was a total miracle that I got help."

"I'm glad you're still here," Jackie replies.

"And in the hospital, I dreamed of a woman behind strips of steel, caged inside her own desires. Almost at the same time, Ben had the accident with his bike. So, flying out on the plane, I thought the dreams were of me. Then, when I met you, I realized it was your face."

"My face?"

"Your face was the strange woman."

"A woman behind bars."

"Caged desire."

Jackie lies on her back, drawing slow circles around Vespa's breasts with a finger dipped in wine, and listening to a pop song on the radio as if the vocalist on the radio, who will be there when Vespa is not, is the one with whom she needs to feel a bond. They watch the ceiling fan and make love. They are twin engines mounted on the same featherbed frame, racing down a long dusty road patched with sunlight and shadows. Jackie, who understands small motors and knows exactly how to automate any of Vespa's steel sculptural animals, needs to talk to her new girlfriend at the same length as Vespa has spoken to her. Vespa who knows how to bring Jackie out of the cage, where she can love more than only books and machines, needs to wander naked into the lonely places in her lover's heart. Jackie, who had no idea desire could involve caring, tilts her head and listens to the hot words of Vespa's passion, syllables whispered behind an electrical arc.

12.

"EVEN THOUGH I had removed a banking machine with a thousand-notes dispensing coil inside, I went back to my regular day job and was at work a half-hour early the next day. I stayed employed that way, not celebrating my new money but continuing to appear to be the most unlikely person to have done such a thing."

"You just carried on as if nothing had happened?" asks Vespa, a strawberry and vodka mixer in her hand. She stretches herself across Jackie's sheets.

"Only I couldn't stand it," Jackie replies. "I completed ten more days welding for Turner's all-expenses-spared Vancouver Twin Towers project, and then, after seeing several of my cohorts leave on stretchers, I collected a letter of recommendation from my supervisor and bowed out."

"You shouldn't brag about these things. I don't have to know."

"Well, you don't know the salient details, but I trust you. I am taking you into my trust."

"What if you someday brag to the wrong person?"

"Well, I didn't, or I wouldn't be here. If the police ever try to solve it, they'll never prove it was me. They'll never know, and you won't tell them. That's the whole point."

Vespa nods. Jackie is right about her, but it is still troubling. Vespa is the sort of person who wishes she could shoplift or tell a lie.

"I won't tell," says Vespa.

"I know you won't tell, because you believe me. You don't know anything."

"Well, I have to know something about you. Just don't tell me anything I'm not going to be able to handle. You haven't killed any animals, have you?"

"My God! I'm a vegan, Vespa. I can't even kill mice. If you ever eat at my place, you'll see. Everything in the cupboard has been played with by my mice. I don't care, I never care. One is called, 'Slinky,' and one is called, 'Stinky.' They are the grand-mice and they have many children. I wouldn't even move to a new apartment without making certain they get in the box."

"Really?"

"No."

"So?"

"So, I took the cool twenty grand and drove to New York City. It was my first visit there, and I was romantic about the place. I had received a very excited letter from Wanda."

"Wanda?"

"She was getting parts as an extra in art-school movies, but they looked like they were leading to something big. In Wanda's letters, all her female friends were talented, but were all getting treated like sewage. And they were all going to art school by any means they could."

"Well, that was me!"

"Well, I guess that was you. I kept the letters. We can look for them some day. I placed them all in a special folder and read them again from time to time, responding with a post-card of the Empire State building, Mirror Lake in Lake Placid Village, and Prospect Point, Niagara Falls. I continued my life, plucking off outdoor ATM drive-throughs in the resort areas of New York State and Ohio. I enjoyed the fact that it is legal to be in possession of the tools of burglary in New York State. I returned to Toronto and found an automated bank machine actually parked up against a steel door in a busy restaurant-deli with a narrow alley running along its side."

"That's too easy!"

"As far as I was concerned, I was convinced the people who worked there had placed it there so they could rob it themselves at their own convenience. That's the way my mind used to work in those days."

"In those days? How about now?"

Jackie grins at her, ignoring the question. "The next night, I used a new plumbing gas with acetylene in the mix, outfitted it with a cutting tip, and went to work cutting a hole through to the deadbolts on the inside."

"The next day?"

"I never leave luck past the point of spontaneity," she adds, taking the drink from Vespa's hand and sipping. "I found the gas disappointingly slow. Or maybe it was just the minutes ticking off while I worked. I cut through the first layer of steel, and then I found there was a second panel more reinforced than the first. I took out a mallet and began going to work on those hinge pins, heating up the metal around them," she mimes the action, "and punching them up!" she punches an invisible bolt with an invisible hammer, "as fast as I could!"

"Well, you were..." Vespa gestures to her invisible watch.

"Yes! Running out of time! But then, to my complete surprise, the entire door fell open on an angle and struck me—*bam*! Full force on the head!" She points to her forehead.

"My God! Were you okay? I mean, you're here."

"No, I was not okay. I'm here now, but I was not okay. I had a nosebleed, and my scalp bled heavily, and a three-hundred-pound door was angled and blocking my way. I sank to the ground and noticed I was not breathing at all if you can believe that, at all. And my pulse, which normally races, was slowed to a crawl. I dropped the bag of tools, *bang-bang*, and I went to sleep."

Vespa twirls the straw. "You're lucky to be alive."

"Well, lucky, hmm. Lucky. My parole officer would have laughed. He always said I deserved what I got."

"People don't deserve to die for breaking into places, they deserve..."

"To go to jail for that, yes, I sometimes think so too." Jackie sips again, hands the glass back to Vespa, who is sitting up at the edge of the bed, a fiery look in her eye.

"Well, they should go back to the community where they committed the crime and they should apologize. That's what I really think."

"Well, believe me, this was the beginning of a long apology."

"Well, I'm sorry, but that's what I think. I think people should say 'I'm sorry.' And restore the things that they have broken or stolen. That's what I'll always think." Vespa extends her legs again and rests the cold drink against her thigh, her eyebrows high.

"Well, I'm sorry, but I couldn't agree with you more. Anyway, I was younger then, and I didn't deserve to die."

"No, no one deserves to die."

"So," says Jackie, starting again, "I lay there for some time, assessing how I could possibly have come to be there. Finally, out of sheer curiosity I would say, more than an idea or anything, I clambered around it, entered the place, and then fell down in a second blackout on the waxed and tiled deli floor."

"You were totally brained by the giant steel door."

"It gets worse."

"I lay there, inside a restaurant an hour before dawn, in order to rob it in some way. I had no memory of planning the event, only the knowledge that I had never been a quitter. The machine was a small, front-loading bill-dispenser. If I had brought the right equipment, and the door was not in the way, I could have easily scooted it down the alley. In fact, the door was angled in such a way that I could have easily pushed the four-foot high mini-bank into the alley and away from the deli, breaking it out of sight of passersby on the street."

"It sounds like you came around."

"Came around, no! I had no memory of how I had even come to be there."

She notices that Vespa, out of concern for her, is now on the verge on tears. "I'm okay," she reassures her.

"Well, good, because this is the worst thing I have ever done," Jackie says.

"The worst thing? It sounds like you didn't even know when to run. It sounds like it wasn't you."

"Well, that's kind of you because a normal person would have decided to leave."

"But not you?"

"No, I was not making very good decisions."

"Well, who knows? Maybe staying was a good decision."

"No, running would have been it. My eyes, however, were adjusting to the darkness. And there was a strange galaxy of glitter that filled everything. There was a nerve-wracking alarm."

She tells Vespa how it had raged in her ears. Jackie had counted down seconds as she always did, forgetting that she had been out cold for several minutes and not able to make sense of her wristwatch in the dark. She picked up her tools, despite the blood running into her eyes and went back to work. The case broke free with a moan and a shudder, and she encountered a galvanized plate.

"It was not the normal way I even cracked open these things. The machine was front-loading; and I was coming at it from the side, tapping away like a kid with an egg on Easter morning. The problem was, I had not brought an electric drill. But then I came up with a solution."

"What about time?"

Jackie nods. "I only had moments. I duct-taped my hand screwdriver to one of the restaurant's electric blenders and held it up to the screw plate."

"You were innovating."

"No kidding. And there are so many settings on a blender these days, what if it went the wrong way? That's when I realized the ringing in my ears was not an alarm system I had set off, but the physical effect of being struck in the head with the free-swinging door. Not knowing what to do, I stumbled to the meringues in the glass pastry cooler. Suddenly, I found myself preparing to take a nap. Right there, behind the espresso bar. A light was blinking on and off on the eight-inch display screen of the machine. I looked up and saw the deep connection I have with machines was paying off in a way I had never expected. The display screen read, 'JACKIE, GET UP, GET UP!'"

"Sounds like a helpful hallucination. Sleeping off a concussion can be deadly."

"I was certain the display screen couldn't give personal messages to an individual visitor, even at four a.m."

"It's true."

"It's true. 'HELLO,' 'WELCOME,' but never 'GET UP.' I tried to crawl over to it, but I fell back, like this, on my back. I felt a sensation telling me to let it all go. I almost did, and then again, the stupid machine was flashing at me through the haze. Finally, I crawled over to it and propped myself up against the thing, like it and me were old-time friends or lovers at a bar, which is where the dogs and the police found me, dripping with sweat and drying blood."

"But if you had been lying instead of propped, it may have been worse. You might have not made it."

"Exactly. Machines love me. The police took me to a hospital, questioned me about an incident I had not a clue about, not even the remotest memory. I did not know how I came to be in there or where I had planned to go to had I ever left. They stuck me across from a plexiglass wall with a lawyer and that was that."

The delicate details of burglary with intent were explained to her, and she was warned of ten years in prison. Still in a haze, she was behind bars again, and not even because she had stolen anything, although she had intended to eat a meringue. She tells Vespa how people in the city of Toronto began to complain that they were being issued bills spotted with blood, with sad faces on the sovereigns, and the problem circulated for months. When police examined the stains, they found it was not a type they had ever seen before, a sort of type O, mixed with so much oxygen and common sweat that the forensic computers scrolled out a blood type that was 1 sodium atom for every oxygen and hydrogen atom, or an endless series of 1s and 0s. She became known out of sympathy for her concussion as 'The Binary Burglar,' and for days after her arrest, bank machines across the city malfunctioned and refused to issue cash. Jackie's lawyer got her off on charges of break and enter with vandalism, arguing there was no charge for bleeding on a machine designed for the issuing of cash. This, thought Jackie, this was free of charge. Because she had become a darling of bored newspaper writers, and later because Wanda helped her win parole, she got off with a five-month stint in jail. It seemed like a long time, and, although she never did remember the actual robbery, it was long enough for her blurry head to unscramble various yes-no units of information that were fired at her and to bring her data transfer rate up to the normal speed. It was also long enough to recover serial packets of information to her most familiar directories and original file hierarchies where she was used to finding her thoughts. The recovery was an enormous relief. She began to read and cherished every word of every author in the cobwebbed prison library.

"I read fifteen books about young women with different names who each ended up on a street corner before being saved by a male devotee of Jesus and giving him sons. Fifteen. My eyes were aglow at the close of each book, and even the matron worried I would never move on to the Westerns. As I healed from my concussion, I wondered what the hell I had been reading, and an admirer sent me books both by Kerouac and Kerouac's daughter.

"It would be years before I knew that the admirer had been

Wanda. Personally, Kerouac was the healing point, and I was thrilled to have my mind back."

"You must have found that made you more receptive to your own ideas," says Vespa gently.

"Sweetheart, I was a tungsten filament glowing hotter than white. Too pure, and supersaturated, my mind was a little too bright. I was going to freeze at a thousand degrees. I was undergoing a chemical and physical reaction, my energy was vibrating, my crystals were breaking up, my solid structure seemed to be evaporating! Physical state, Church and State, and then, I was pulled out from under the house of cards. I was most suddenly removed."

"Your sentence was up."

"I was released like a rat from an empty sack. I gathered my package of shoelaces, necklaces, and my pawed-through personal belongings. Just when I thought I could not stand it for another minute, I was out on the street, walking without destination, sleeping in downpours, talking in free verse to alley cats and barking out poems to dogs. And just when I thought I would explode from the clatter inside me, I had been cut loose, my body left to fend for itself. I was swinging and sparking in the wind like a broken electrical wire in a storm. I was free, but terrified to talk to anybody, to even articulate a thought. I was absolutely uncertain as to whether I was an anarchist, an Aristotelian, or just a piece of ass. I moved into an unheated garage, fed scraps to stray squirrels, and made friends with toothless old men playing pool on the wrong side of town. I went on a series of fasts because my stomach was turned upside down from jail, and I picked up a job repainting automobiles. I filled my own garage with cut flowers and lined the walls with books and photocopied art. At the end of each cheque, I went to a bar for lesbians, met no one of interest, came home and toyed with the industrial-sized vibrator I had constructed myself. Every night I placed the sexual lubricant back on the shelf next to the chain and gear oil, had a nightcap of whiskey liqueur, and cried myself to sleep."

"How long did this go on?"

"Weeks, then months, while I hopped from job to job, picking up an enormous amount of information with the mathematical, mechanical side of my brain while I patiently waited for my love of literature to turn to trade manuals, and, you know, to escape the hairdressing classes from prison. I even bought myself an arc welding kit and a generator, and anything else that gave me tactile pleasure. I treated myself to chainsaw engines and broken things. I stroked and stoked them, and decided I was not all that different from any other woman who was not getting a whole lot of sex and didn't care. Then, I borrowed a forklift from a warehouse where I was working and drove it through the plate glass window of a supermarket near my house. I tore the four-foot banking machine from its position on the wall and drove it to a van I'd stolen an hour before by jamming a screwdriver into the ignition. I abandoned everything but the money and went home to water my plants."

"What did you do with the money?"

"With the money? I flew to New York and decided to live it up a little. I met a middle-class Russian called Olesya in a bar. We had a fling. When I realized she was politically feeble-minded, I lost interest in her. Then, when I returned to Toronto, I was arrested as an accomplice to an armed robbery gang I had never met in my life."

"They caught you."

"No, they hadn't 'caught' me because it was something I hadn't done."

"They never caught you for the forklift?"

"No. It must have looked too masculine."

"But they thought you were accomplice to armed robbery."

"Exactly. People I'd never met in my life, and much more serious in every way."

"How could you prove that you were innocent?"

"Well, I panicked a little, and then I realized I could contact Olesya. Because everyone saw us partying at clubs in New York. So I scarcely broke a sweat. I just left a voice message and then waited. And then another one, and then another one. All I needed her to do was to come north and testify that I had been with her in bed. I assumed any friend, even an enemy, would fly up the same weekend, and I offered to pay for her flight. I knew I had showed her a good time in bed, and she had seemed eager to stay in touch with me."

"Makes sense. She can easily testify, supported by cameras, bartenders, mutual contacts from that week. So did she spring you?"

"Olesya? No. What she did finally, was to write to me in the form of a postcard that said, 'I'm sorry, but I have my life to consider, and I am not out of the closet.'"

"What? Not out of the closet, when she's the only alibi, so she can't?"

"If only she had been out of my life. Instead, she wrote to me once a week for my entire time back in jail. It was the most irritating thing that I have ever experienced."

Vespa pouts. "What were her letters like?"

"Full of sympathy and invitations to me to come and stay with her once I was released. Then, after a few letters, in the form of grade-school quality poetry, she shared her discoveries in her coming-out journey as a lesbian. They were unsolicited and involved elaborations of Olesya's sexual exploits."

"You must have treasured them."

"I used them as wicks to light my cigarettes or to create bonfires in my toilet after lights out. By the time the authorities realized they had their missing gang member on a security camera while I had been locked behind bars, Olesya wrote to tell me she had met an empowered lesbian who urged her to testify. When Olesya finally phoned me to announce that she was coming to Toronto to deliver justice, I was four hours from release."

"So, she would be the first free person that you would see."

"Well, if I still had not discovered anything helpful to read, I had discovered Gay Pride. I was proud enough not to welcome her up with her new girlfriend. I was post-trauma. I didn't want to risk upsetting her and for all I knew, being sent somehow back to prison. In my politest of manners, I promised I would come to New York sometime and visit her at home. My anger was so deep, it was difficult not to make it sound like a threat. Through long incarcerated days and nights, I had come to hate everything she represented. I had been sending bad-vibe beams at her since before the mistaken bust, and so I was careful to control my voice."

It is difficult for her to tell Vespa all of this, and so they lie in silence in each other's arms, staring at Jackie's ceiling fan and drawing circles around each other's nipples with the tips of their fingers and their tongues.

"Hate's heavy," Vespa says finally. "It wasn't fair of her to pretend to be a friend, and then to be a terrible coward."

Hate is something that has been bothering Vespa over the past five years, while Jackie has been inside and outside of prisons. It had been bothering Vespa since she first sat with Rudy on his lip-shaped couch. It has been hate, and in particular, the intensity with which Rudy conveyed his hate for B.F. Turner. B.F. Turner is someone Vespa has been forced to know all about, and she has pushed him to the back burner of her mind. Here his name and everything she knew about him has boiled with all the things he has done, for all the lives his consortium had destroyed. Even resigned, good-hearted Jackie hated B.F. Turner. Opening the pot only occasionally, each time Vespa finds it is to look in and see her friend Rudy boiling too. Rudy, the man who hopped in of his own free will. Only now when she looks in, she sees a new tremble in Rudy's chin, a lost look in his eyes. She sees the Rudy that she could not forget: A man with eyes that said he could recapture his youth by carrying her to his bed, and a mouth that said he could get away with it if she objected.

She cannot tell Jackie all of this, so instead she says, "Hate's heavy. Hate's a heavy, heavy thing."

They lie in bed together and exchange touches and sounds that express things that are to equal degrees more unexpected and more fantastic than either lover can imagine. They are enamoured with their invention of each other.

13.

AS EVERYBODY KNOWS, B.F. Turner, is in the habit of disappearing for days at a time from his New York offices into the Adirondacks, frequently with a high-calibre gun and ammunition. He has also taken to the habit of scoring the tips of his bullets with an "x"—something he claims to have learned from a Vietnam vet. He explains all of this to Rudy as they drive south together without hunting licenses to blow away unsuspecting deer.

B.F. will have none of it; a man of his stature should not need to ask when and where to hunt, and so, he disregards rules and drives on, heading to a place he has picked out. It is either the deer or his wife, he tells Rudy, and Rudy laughs like a good confidant should. Scoring the tips of his bullets, B.F. believes, will cause the missile to fragment inside the animal, a dirty trick he learned from a dirty soldier, and one that he says he uses experimentally, hoping to prevent a long, drawn-out chase like the hunt that bagged him his only rack. His hound is no longer part of the expeditions. After leaving it tied to a tree next to a locator alarm, the animal had panicked and bitten B.F. He shows Rudy the bite scar as if it is a proud battle wound, then tells him he killed the animal on the spot. It was, perhaps, a financial mistake, to shoot a pedigree hound, but it had never liked him, and so it had never been all that much help.

"It's in heaven now," says Rudy in a chipper voice. He complains of the cold, slips on a set of gloves. He asks if he can examine the scored bullets more closely and the luxury Silverado swerves on the road as B.F. reaches for the case. They already share the same type of weapon. Rudy gets out his own bullets and begins scoring them with his hunting knife.

"Look at you with your little dress shoes and Armani suit? Don't you ever let your crack hang out?" B.F. says and tosses some of his own already-scored bullets into Rudy's lap.

B.F. lets out a grunt-snort of derision and gives Rudy a dirty once-over glance. "I oughta stop at a restaurant along here for a sloppy joe and send you in to get it. With your suit on, the managers will bust a gut!"

"No," says Rudy, in a more forceful way than he intended.

B.F.'s eyebrows go up in interest. They are near a highway truck stop. He cannot resist the possibility of embarrassing Rudy. He has so seldom seen Rudy show emotion or any kind of social discomfort or shame, and now he has him hostage in the backcountry with a lavender tie, B.F. is beginning to lather at the mouth.

"NO! I don't want anyone to see me," Rudy touches B.F.'s hand on the wheel for emphasis. "B.F.," says Rudy in his irresistibly conspiratorial way, "these men will think we're lovers."

"Get out of my truck!" B.F. roars. He then accelerates so that Rudy cannot.

Rudy lowers his voice until it is almost a whisper. "Don't give them something to talk about," Rudy tells him. "Do you know what they do to strangers around here?" It is in the familiar subversive style he reserves for B.F. that always makes B.F. feel he is part of an endless well of inherited masculine brains.

Probably not much, Rudy thinks, looking out at the gravel and trees speeding past him. There is a long silence. It is interrupted when each man clears his throat and adjusts his bass-tone EQs.

Finally, B.F. explodes. "You bastard!" Instead of taking a slug at Rudy, he takes a slug of liquor from the thermos he has by his side. "Why did you have to dress like a cocksucker in the first place? Why? You're not a…"

"No, I'm not, I just like to wear fine suits," says Rudy. To B.F., this answer opens up the topic of how various races of women dress, B.F.'s personal preferences in this regard, and, finally, the wider social problem of whores in general which he expounds on for over an hour. Then he switches to his favourite topic, how the poor and disabled populate cities with no care for what they are doing to the gene pool. Rudy opens his window and is relieved by a blast of fresh air that replaces the smell of B.F.'s conversation. Rudy realizes that B.F. reminds him a little bit of himself, of something unforgivable that he could become. His loathing magnifies.

"What the hell are you doing? Do you have a problem? The air conditioner…."

Just when he thinks he can stand no more and has noticed B.F. is drunk enough to drive into the trees, the truck turns up a logging road and comes to a neck-whipping stop. They have arrived and there is no one for miles. B.F. Has carried in a thousand pounds of extra gear and a cocktail lounge of alcoholic drinks in the cab. B.F. also carries hunting gadgets of every type, including animal urine and skunky odours to mask the smell of his own body. Rudy has travelled with nothing but a light pack and a change of clothes.

The two spend the afternoon prowling a deer trail, B.F., shaking his plastic antlers, grunt-snorting his way through the scrub and slugging at his thermos, convinced he can drive out curious bucks. He stumbles through the brush, shouting, "Come on, ya horny motherfuckers!" and circles the place where a group of does are nervously listening for his movements and disappearing back into the woods.

There is no moment for B.F. where he realizes that Rudy, his right-hand man, the one he had grown to trust, has betrayed him. There is only the appearance of a white-tailed buck, which B.F. sends Rudy to flush through the woods. It is a bad hunting method, always dangerous to anyone who is not firing the gun. Rudy hesitates, B.F. calling him a sorry-ass pussy. Rudy is certain he is drunk, although not as drunk as B.F., who has rambled off to drive the deer toward Rudy. The animal that is running from him is spectacular. B.F. has understated the deer's magnificence. It wears antlers that spread out the length of a man. It is imposing and, despite a harassed look and the catcalls of B.F., it has a fine-tuned sense of the intuitive in the gaze it lays on Rudy, an intimate perception exchanged between two strangers. That is the way they always appear; first there is nothing, and suddenly, there they are, right in front of you, staring at you, not believing that at this moment of grace you would shatter the silence and shoot. Drunken Rudy fires. B.F. falls. The white-tailed buck with the five-foot rack hops away, his majesty intact. Rudy gathers all evidence that he has been anywhere on the scene, arranges B.F.'s gun in such a way as to make it look like he has shot himself, and then hikes in horror from the mountain terrain.

Before nightfall, he shoots a rabbit, recovers the bullet shell, and eats it half-cooked, allowing the blood to run down his face and into the stubble of his new beard. He buries the carcass, washes up in a stream, changes into casual clothes. He walks through the night, consults his pack compass, consults the stars, allows himself to slide slowly back into being Rudy, as he wonders who he is truly to others, now that he is not the man B.F. thought he was in his wildest dreams. It was an accident, but he knows it wasn't. Feeling drained by the enormity of his puzzle, and pulled by the crisis of who he is, feeling overpowered by the charade he still has before him, he walks to the lights of the city.

At the edge of town, he cleans up his appearance, squirts eye drops onto his retina, shaves all but a small moustache. He buys a popular baseball cap, drags it through a patch of grease, and catches a taxi to the nearest airport. By lunchtime the next day he is a clean-shaven man in a six-hundred dollar suit, discussing a development concept in front of twenty company men at a board meeting in New York. Near the close of the meeting, he is met by a beautiful woman who gushes on as the men trail out of the room, praising Rudy for the very good time they have been enjoying these last few days together in Manhattan. She is highly professional; he has used her many times before. She likes Rudy. She may be in love with Rudy. He is the best thing that has ever happened to her, and most importantly, she will fib for him anytime. To both of them, she is his New York girlfriend, the only one he sees. They are very public together, and all her other regulars are very private about their affairs because they are married with wives. She has classic, regular features. Rudy has already researched her; none of her other clients are men he will ever encounter in his business. Besides, her business is none of theirs. He is not a nosy type, but the other men at the New York office are gossiping about her and teasing him when the news arrives that B.F. has gone missing.

Rudy suggests that the last time he talked with B.F., he sounded depressed and talked about going alone to the woods, but no one had taken it seriously. The meeting is hastily concluded, a press release mourning B.F. arranged, and Rudy flies back to Vancouver, pours himself a drink in his studio, and watches the gulls circling over the Pacific. Inside the dark, quiet calm of him, he crouches like a heartbroken, shitkicked girl he once threw out of his apartment, and he waits for the sounds of police.

14.

VESPA IS HOLDING HANDS with Jackie, walking along the soft dirt road where Ben used to race his bikes. Jackie feels the smoothness between her fingers, then finds the grip unmistakably muscular. Vespa has short dark brown hair that is of similar softness to Ben's tight curls. They are leaving dusty footprints behind them; and Jackie is feeling a great wave of joy. Vespa has shown her a way of walking so that her sneaker marks look like a truck track in the dirt.

"Do you think anyone will fall for it?"

"I don't know. They do look realistic." They admire the trail they are leaving behind them.

"Where'd you and Wanda first meet each other, anyway?" Vespa asks her.

Jackie does not want to tell Vespa that she and Wanda first met in jail.

"I could ask you the same question," she answers instead.

There is a silence, then Vespa smiles graciously and appears to give in, as if she knows what Jackie thinks she is hiding. Overhead, trees throw down sunlight in small, moving vignettes.

"I told you. I met her in Vancouver, around Christmas. Way before my brother was even on the scene. He was a boyhood friend of Rudy, and he encouraged him to come out West. Then, for a while, there were four of us. Once she met Ben, after she met you even, then she took him away again, back to Toronto."

"That's where I met her. I was raised in Vancouver, but I moved East."

"Why?"

Jackie thinks about it. "The same as Wanda, I guess. Business."

"You sure are a hard nut to crack. What about what Wanda told me?"

"And what did she tell you?"

"Jail. She was busted for escorting, the same stupid line of work she got me into, and there you were."

"Maybe it's true."

"She was in awe of you. A beautiful girl with disconnected raven hair, overalls, hot-looking. Knew how to fix everything."

"'Hot-looking?' Doesn't that imply some sort of checking out? I mean, 'hot-looking,' that's checking somebody out. I thought Wanda was straight, pious, religious…"

"She is preoccupied with Saints and Catholic ideas. Ben likes it, so she cultivates it. I loathe it. I think that's why she cuts it out when I'm around. But you are in her hot Saint category, as far as I can tell."

"Was she always like this?" Jackie asks weakly.

"We have friction, to be certain. But she's not what you think she is. You'll see. She's tough that one. Wanda was like a mother to me, at one time. A street mother."

Vespa points to a meadow beyond the road, and they clamber over an old fence, thistles snagging their pant-legs.

"Are she and Ben the same age?"

"They are only days apart. I think that's why she was able to bring him back out of that coma. They have some sort of spirit bond."

Vespa smiles. Jackie wonders if Vespa felt a spirit bond with Wanda, too.

"Tell me about the street mother thing."

"Easy. Everyone was talking about home and no one seemed to have one. We heard about a girl showing movies on the walls inside of the big warehouse down the street.

When I walked in, it was completely empty, maybe thirty thousand square feet of space, wide open like the prairie. Or like a winter lake. Wanda had a film projector and chips and flowers set out on old ironing boards. There must have been a dozen of those standing around, Old ironing boards was all the furniture there was. I loved it. And so, instead of hopping to the next party, we sat down on the floor and decided to stick around."

"There were no chairs, only ironing boards?"

"Yeah, that was all. The place had been quite a sweatshop, which made Wanda's main movie of the night a perfect pick. Here we were in this enormous space where people had worked as slaves, and then she showed us the American restoration of the 1927 German movie, *Metropolis*. Have you seen this film?"

"Does it have robots in it?"

"A robot is the star!"

Jackie nods her head. "It's about four hours long. A silent film. There is a worker uprising, and a man who controls the workers and owns all of the machines falls in love with a girl who is a robot replica of the woman behind the revolt."

"No," says Vespa. "The American edit is eighty-three minutes long. With subtitles. Freder was never in love with the robot. He was in love with Maria, the real girl...."

"We must have seen different things in the different versions."

"Perhaps," Vespa looks thoughtful. "But it's much better now. It has sound. It has a little colour. Freddie Mercury has a song in it. Pat Benatar has a song in it. And with the spectacular constructivist images, set to this pessimistic vision of the future, it's a classic statement of the punk aesthetic. And it meant so much to us at the time."

"I have almost everything recorded by Freddie Mercury. I love Freddie Mercury. Take me to the American version," says Jackie, squeezing Vespa's hands. She peers into her eyes.

"Sure, I'll take you to the movies," Vespa tells her. She laughs and kisses her on the mouth. Jackie is dreamy.

"'Love Kills,' 'Fat Bottomed Girls,' 'We Are Champions,' come on, and the guy's named after a car...."

"Mercury is both a planet and a car...."

Jackie sighs. "I know, I know. It's not like I have never slept under the stars at night. Many planets are named after cars."

Vespa wonders if Jackie has ever slept under the stars with anybody else. She thinks not. Jackie's hair begins to prickle as she feels Vespa staring.

Her friend smiles. "That film, that party, it meant so much to us at that time. All of us in that community, about to get kicked out on our butts. Wanda was fascinated by aesthetics. Even then, when she was very young."

"Doesn't that movie have a man with one hand?"

"Rotwang has only one hand. Like Wanda, actually. He is the man who falls from a cathedral. He is chasing Freder, and real Maria, right after they burn the robot at the stake."

"That was sad."

"Not really."

"Why not?"

"Well, he was trying to kill Maria. That's why he fell."

"No, no, it was sad when they burned the robot."

"The mob didn't know any better," says Vespa in a delicate way.

"It still made working people look stupid. And poor Rotwang. They built such a beautiful robot, and then *boom*!"

"I guess I never thought of it that way."

"I'll take you to the four-hour original!" says Jackie with shining eyes.

"Let's go to the re-edit first."

"So, did you and Wanda share a landlord as well?"

"Yes, but Wanda worked as a flower girl later than late. That was why I had never met her before, even though we lived only a few blocks away, because she was out every evening, and then slept into the afternoon. She kept a gun by her bed, a real gun, along with a few other things she had locked away inside a small sleeping room she had built out of drywall. It was all torn down a few weeks after the party. The rest of the time I think she roamed around the warehouse, which was being emptied and then prepared to become condo space and studios for the very rich. Her rent jumped from forty cents a square foot to twenty-two dollars."

Vespa raises a brow at Jackie.

"Wanda built the room herself? So, she had both hands then."

"No," says Vespa. "She had a prosthetic hand, even then. Rudy went in, into her room later, and we started to talk, and that's how we got to know her. How did you get to know her?"

"In jail," says Jackie, trapped. She looks closely at her friend. "How come you always say, 'we?'"

"I was hanging around with a little crook named Rudy. Interesting how we met our landlord." She tells Jackie about the night they had heard the steam clock chime thirteen times, and how they had run through the streets shaking their rattles, accepting an offered wallet from a terrified man with combed-over hair.

"It didn't end there. It turned out the next morning he was our mutual landlord. He had been stumbling home a few blocks away, too drunk to recognize us, but we recognized his name on documents in the wallet and had to return it to him. Very awkward."

"Did Rudy often rob people?"

"I don't think so. It was because we were shaking rattles. He hid the wallet in a nook near a switch plate to keep it safe and the next day, he arranged for a friend to give the wallet back. For Chrissakes, Wanda loved him. We all loved him. I don't know if he took the money out first or not, but Rudy moved on. He moved on and he moved up, never looked back, and then the business world took our friend."

"So, a crook's reflexes, but a human heart!" Jackie is privately searching through her memories to see if she can turn up any mention of a man named Rudy. She turns to Vespa.

"You should hang out with honest people," she tells her, and kisses her new friend gently on the mouth.

"Well, I hang out with you, don't I?" asks Vespa, the question hanging a moment too long. The part of Jackie that changed in prison stirs within her.

"You hang with me, so why don't we go somewhere truly fun for a change?"

"Like a romantic vacay?"

"Exactly!"

"What's better than here?" asks Vespa.

"Nowhere is better, and everywhere is perfect, when I'm with you," answers Jackie, "it's just..."

"Just what?"

"Don't you want to experience New York?"

15.

THE POLICE ARE in Rudy's New York office, going through his things. Rudy's lawyer is with them, a company lawyer who is watching that nothing is meddled with, while Rudy sits in his studio, sipping herbal tea and eating sushi. They are apologetic; they are simply going through the steps. Because B.F. had made special arrangements that placed Rudy in his position should something happen to B.F., now that something has happened, Rudy is seen to have motive. The position Rudy finds himself in is not face down, with his arm around a deer-shooting rifle lying inches away. This is how B.F. was found, as a family of skunks paraded past him in horror, and many prize white-tailed deer, including the buck with the superlative rack, stepped silently in their pussy-ass way over his form.

The position Rudy finds himself in is as head of the company, information that has now been released to B.F. Turner's consortium by a series of digits, which have been given to four of B.F.'s lawyers and that have been combined to open his safe. It is nothing Rudy could have known, and B.F.'s documents state that he did not want Rudy to know as this would have changed the dynamic of his power role and contradict his tested and true managerial style. His lawyers have already remarked, how could Rudy have had motive to dispose of B.F. since he had no idea that his friend, his boss, had made these provisions.

But, evidence that Rudy was in B.F.'s four-by-four has been collected by the police. This is fine, though. There are many witnesses that saw Rudy being hurried into B.F.'s car and driven to lunches at private clubs in the few days before the week of his disappearance. They also saw B.F. driving around in the lux Silverado, and parking it in the garage under their offices, next to the car. Rudy admits that he has been in the cab of the truck. The fact that the fatal bullet was fired from a gun of the same type and make as B.F.'s, and that the bullet is in fact one of B.F.'s own, scored on the end in the same way all the other bullets he was carrying in a bullet bag on his person were scored, seemed to close the case for many of the small-town investigators that had first arrived on the scene. It was announced in the papers that police were ruling out foul play, something Rudy read carefully before rolling the paper into a ball and firing it into a seagrass basket beside his desk.

So, B.F. had taken his own life. All his papers were in order, but as those close to him knew, all of B.F.'s papers were always in order. B.F. was most certainly loaded on alcohol at his time of death. At the time of death, in as far as anyone can prove, Rudy was leading a seminar in New York City.

As the police continue their search, Rudy calls his pharmacy to arrange for valiums to be brought to his studio loft. The police respect that Rudy is in mourning. They are puzzled at the angle of the bullet, as it seems that B.F. must have shot himself while holding the gun out some distance from himself, and yet still reached the trigger, despite no gunpowder marks on his clothing. The bullet, which should have nearly passed through him at such a close range, has not just lodged but is shattered inside him, making it extremely challenging to determine the distance from which it was fired. A police hypothesis is circulating that B.F. hooked the gun around a branch, and then pulled the trigger in this way, with the gun slightly away from him. The gun would then have immediately fallen to the ground, landing where it was discovered next to the body. The crime photographer, a local newspaper journalist, sold his film to the medical examiner's office only after they had determined the cause of death was a probable suicide, and has given the newspaper the photographer worked for the scoop. Other evidence of gunpowder around the shot sight are obscured by seven days of decomposition and the clumsy work of local police who not only moved the body but zipper-bagged it before thinking to mark the spot where it had fallen. The local cops who found B.F. are hunters themselves, and are not too fond of B.F., best remembered for threatening one of the locals with a handgun and mistreating a dog not too many seasons past. Local police handled a downed B.F. as similar to a downed white-tailed deer, going about the business of transporting him, weighing him, and identifying him, long before they thought to comb the kill site for signs of foul play. Ballistic experts spend hours with B.F.'s 30.60 rifle, impressed by the bullets that shatter on impact but unable to find a feature that distinguished the fatal bullet from the others. They are surprised that the gun gave off such a weak charge, since the entry point seems to show signs of a bullet discharged from more of a distance than the hooked-branch theory suggested. When forensic experts arrive in the area, they trace every deer path in sight for signs of footprints, or evidence of a second party. Rudy had worn gloves to fire the unregistered 30.60, later dropping it miles away into a river. As a caution, he had hiked out to a sideroad and changed into a pair of mass-produced rubber soles for the last few miles, shoes that called no attention to his tread.

Later, at home, Rudy mixes a featherweight valium with a hammer of a martini and sucks the olive until he falls asleep and almost chokes. The night before, he had been kept awake by police, and he was in a very sober mood about his inebriation. Having anticipated the conversation for days, he was able to provide a seamless, emotional explanation of his whereabouts and actions during the week of Turner's disappearance. He took the opportunity to describe B.F.'s life and his character, breaking down in tears during personal anecdotes, such as the way B.F. always said he went hunting to shoot deer instead of his loved ones. Rudy clearly cared much more than the other members of the company who are interviewed before and following Rudy, and who vent their spite for B.F., as well as possessing their own motives for killing B.F. and having much less of an alibi than Rudy. The woman who Rudy dates in New York was anticipating being contacted by the cops and knows what she wants to say. Rudy is one of her livelihoods; besides, he is her friend. They talk for some time while Rudy sweats it out. When the detective re-emerges, he is smiling from ear to ear. "She's funny…. They don't make nice girls like that every day," says the officer. "I would marry her if I was you. Cut out on everything and make a family with that princess in New York."

Rudy remembers her mentioning something about getting a start in life at a telephone sex line and makes a mental note to send more than flowers for her kindness in the cover-up. The police are sympathetic, friendly, courteous beyond the call of duty. If there is anything more for them to discuss with him, they will approach his lawyer first. And they did call before visiting him at the office. And B.F.'s death was ruled a suicide.

Rudy knows he killed B.F. Rudy is not afraid. He pours another drink. Rudy is in the shade.

16.

JACKIE AND VESPA are in New York, and they are intent on having a real experience. They have been having an intense couple's talks and decided moving there for a time may be the best way to get to know a city. They also have convinced Wanda and Ben to come and join them for a few days so that they can celebrate Ben's recovery and enjoy the city together. Unfortunately, Jackie's version of New York involves Olesya, who was thrilled to learn she was coming, and hoped Jackie could stay at her place, now that Olesya is out-of-the-closet and repentant. She even cuts her a key. Jackie and Vespa sit with Ben and Wanda together in a Manhattan café and for a moment, complete peace hovers above them. The New York skies are clear and the day is warm and welcoming. A few hours later, they have ditched their things at Olesya's apartment on 108th Street and gone apartment hunting as a group.

The building Olesya lives in is fairly new, and it is, without question, a design of B.F. Turner, although definitely not one of Rudy's. Jackie does not know who Rudy is, and she is tired of hearing his name. Olesya is with her girlfriend, Alaska. Jackie explains that they are shopping as a group and the girlfriend wants to know who Jackie is. "Jackie is an old friend," says Olesya, and then, "Hey, why don't we come shopping with you?"

The six of them set out on the sidewalk, and Jackie and Vespa find they are continually being bumped to one side by people who will make room for Ben and Wanda because they are a heterosexual pair, and for Olesya and her girlfriend because they are dressed in trendy clothes and look important, but not for Jackie and Vespa, who look like life has knocked them around so why not knock them again since they clearly need a lesson. At least, that is the way Jackie sees things, and because of this, Jackie is getting more and more irritated. Ben also seems to snaps at her, while his lover has made a wonderful bond with Olesya.

"That's a nice name, 'Olesya!'" says Wanda. "What does it mean?"

"Defender of men," says Alaska, and they laugh.

Jackie doesn't know what the hell is up with them all. She didn't expect Olesya would want to hang out. Although she told Wanda what she thinks of Olesya, now the two of them sound as if they are prepared to share many personal intimacies, including the entertaining story of Jackie's miseries in prison. The two women seem to squeal every time they pass a store display that has expensive things they can't afford, until Olesya's liberated lesbian girlfriend Alaska makes a noise that means, "On the streets of New York, squealing is taboo unless I protect you with my aura of cool." Sadly, by mid-afternoon, Jackie is consumed with a heavy, cold, hunting, calculating wraith of resentment. Olesya has become the representative of everything that has oppressed Jackie. She is going to oppress squealing, privileged, middle-class Olesya right back again, and she knows it now. She wants to see Olesya do time. Criminal time. She feels herself changing into an uncaring, emotionless machine. A motorcycle, an automaton, a steel animal. She will perform a series of tasks required to take away her hate, which she has now affixed to Olesya, even though the hate has arisen from her own soul.

Another passing pedestrian bounces her off the sidewalk while Wanda attempts to lead the group of them into a shoe store. Olesya's girlfriend is not coming. As Jackie smirkingly predicted, Alaska is gazing longingly down the street and glancing at her phone as an excuse.

But Jackie has not been listening to the conversation. Jackie has been too busy getting bumped into the gutter on Vespa's behalf. Now she looks at the retreating back of Olesya's girlfriend, stalking away in the crowd. "Hot one, huh?" says Olesya, zooming in uncomfortably close to her ear.

"I think she is stuck up," Jackie replies.

"That's too bad. She's on the board of several of the big art committees here. She could pull a deal for Vespa's sculptural work."

"Vespa can pull her own deals. Thanks anyway."

"Sometimes I wonder if you even like me," Olesya says as she drifts into World of Shoes with Wanda and Ben. Ben is already having his feet sized by a store attendant. Jackie knows he has no intention of buying shoes.

"It looks like they are going to be a while," says Jackie.

"Well, I'm going to get something to drink," Vespa announces to the group.

"Look," cries Wanda, "fetishwear boots!"

She takes Olesya's hand as they disappear in the direction of kink at the back of the store. Ben puts his shoes back on and says he will join them for a beer as well. The smell of his feet dissipates through the store. The three leave Olesya and Wanda with the salesperson and cross the street. A chanting is heard a block up; some sort of picket. A ragtag group of protesters are marching in a circle.

"What is that all about?" Jackie asks their server.

"What's what all about?"

"A big noise down the block."

"It's a shopping protest. Big corporations pay street people to march around waving signs with corporate logos on them, demanding to purchase their products. It's a marketing stunt. At the end of the protest, the marchers are paid twenty dollars each."

"Sounds offensive to democracy," Jackie says.

The server has no idea. A pitcher arrives and Jackie downs several pints in the blink of an eye. The three of them look around and realize they have emptied the jug. They order a second.

Outside, cars are blaring their horns. Jackie feels a buzz go through her body, and lets the world around her become irrelevant, far away. She realizes she has not had breakfast. She gets up a little unsteadily and walks to the counter, looks at a menu of food. Perhaps this is why hate is unravelling itself inside her psyche. But hate, which is in control, doesn't need nourishment. Hate just needs to perform the action that will send Olesya to the torment her cowardly unwillingness to step up and testify on Jackie's behalf subjected Jackie to. Hate wants Olesya behind bars, receiving months of insensitive, jolly messages from the same people who could spring her—cold-hearted well-wishers enjoying their free lives, while she grovels for their help. Because this is what Olesya did to Jackie. And now, Jackie smiles robotically, sees the server, and needs nothing. To cover her tracks, so no one can see her coiling to strike, she orders a plate she doesn't intend to eat.

Ben smiles at her. He is enjoying being back out in the world with his mental health and well-being returned to him. He tops off Vespa's glass, then his own, and the two siblings explode into peels of hilarity. It is good to hear them laughing together like this, when a few months ago all Vespa could do was sit by Ben's bed and crack jokes into a silent room. Jackie snaps her fingers and another pitcher arrives, her steaming lunch arriving with it. "*Nudle s tvarohem!*" Vespa cries in delight, and Ben takes her hand. They begin to browse a menu that suddenly carries a version of every dish they imagine their departed mother ever cooked for them as kids.

"Time to take action," says Jackie, and she gets up from the table. She weaves across the street, presumably to tell Olesya and Wanda where they are. Instead, she turns into a subway station, sees a series of lockers, and gets hit on for change by a drunk. "Whaddya call a gay lawyer with indigestion?" the man asks her. Jackie quickly runs out of the station, hurries back up the steps, and turns into the door of a gallery, thinking it is the door to the World of Shoes. Jackie walks to a display case labelled "Canadian artifacts," brimming with "found" items. The "found" items look to Jackie like stolen ones, acquired from another culture under the guise of artifact collection. They include toy dolls, hand-carved talismans, hand-knapped spearheads, hide scrapers, bones carved for fishing or fleshing, arrowheads, and the fragments of handles from various tools.

"How much are these?" Jackie asks, when an irritated-looking man in a blue sweater appears from behind a divider.

"All of these were dug up by Canadians," says the man.

"From graves?" asks Jackie.

"Who knows?" says the man. "Some can be dated from grave sites because they were found with bones and other archeological items."

"How much for real human bones?" Jackie asks.

The man brings his hands together and smiles. "It depends on how much you are willing to pay."

Jackie sees that the hide scraper is priced at almost four hundred dollars. She laughs in a grim way and retreats to the shoe store for a breath of leathery air. It is clear now that on certain days that the people of New York are willing to sell their mothers at a marked-down price.

In the back of the shoe store, Wanda and Olesya have completely commanded the attention of the owner. "An erotic treat," says Wanda, "all this black leather. Yes. Just yes."

They are surrounded by opened boxes of pumps—buckled, velvet, vinyl, cut-aways—ballet slippers, zapatillas, high-heeled penny loafers, and embroidered mules. The salesperson is placing a boot with sixty eyelets on Wanda's foot, while Wanda is extending her leg in a way that will piss Ben off endlessly. At the front, Olesya has piled her things, including her purse and her trendy tangerine spring jacket, in a place where anyone could take them away. Jackie does, and no one notices. Olesya is modelling a pair of sandals in a foot mirror with her back to the door when Jackie slips back out.

"It's time," says Jackie, "to do it. To do the thing I came here to do."

She walks for a block and approaches a bank teller, demanding money in a hoarse European accent from beneath the scarves and tangerine spring jacket that she has removed from Olesya's things. She tells the bank teller she has a gun. Even though she is behind bulletproof glass, the woman gives her a fat envelope full of hundred-dollar bills in a sympathetic way, as if she has been looking forward to a diversion.

"Thank you," Jackie says in her thick, put-on accent. She turns on her heel and dives into the traffic, crossing a street jostling with hundreds of people waving signs. Jackie places the money in the subway station locker, rolls Olesya's tangerine jacket into a ball and forces it into the purse with Olesya's scarves. An alarm is going off at the bank when she re-emerges, but no one seems to be paying any attention. She looks around the street, holding the jacket-stuffed purse under her arm and carrying Olesya's wallet, a fat address book, and a small pepper spray in her left hand. Slipping on gloves, the tangerine jacket, and throwing the hood back up over her hair, she covers her face in scarves and pops on the pricey sunglasses she found earlier in Olesya's pocket.

"Grave robber!" she screams at the hypertensive man with the "Canadian" art. "Expect to see more of me, until the day you stop robbing graves! I am Olesya! The avenger!" Unable to bring herself to point the thing, she fires a short blast of the spray uncertainly over his head and he falls to the floor, hacking and pleading for mercy. Jackie coughs in an accented way, keeping the scarves close to her nostrils, and she steps back out, rolling Olesya's things back into a ball. She walks calmly into the street. People are beginning to shout about a bank robbery, but inside the shoe store the atmosphere is innocently unaware. An air conditioner hums over the door. The salesperson and Wanda are hidden behind piles of tissue paper. Hapless Olesya is somewhere in the back with the kink. Jackie dumps the tangerine spring jacket back where she found it.

"Hey!" says Jackie, and she wades into the store. "People are wondering about you."

She realizes Wanda is allowing the salesperson to lace every one of the sixty-plus eyelets on a set of boots she has pulled from a top shelf. Wanda is also reclining in such a way that the shoe salesperson can see up Wanda's minidress to the overheated underwear squirming inches from his face where she is seated in the now sweat-slippery try-on chair. Jackie grimaces. She has known Wanda so long. She wants to be a good friend to Ben, but the moment is ideal. She claps her hands together.

"Olesya, why don't you step out onto the street with me, and these two can close the shop for a moment or two while they decide what they want to do."

"What they want to do?"

"Well, it is obvious what they want to do, and I think they need some privacy. I am certain Wanda will see the Pilsner umbrellas when she feels she is done with here."

"Understood!" says Olesya, "We'll stall Ben. I'll be back in half an hour to buy the things I have set aside."

"I'm sure we won't need a whole half an hour."

The salesperson ties Wanda's boots more energetically. They are four hundred dollars, and Wanda is not going anywhere. Jackie helps Olesya into her tangerine coat, spinning the sign on the door.

"Okay, just snap the lock, like this?" she asks them.

"Perfect," calls the shoe salesperson with a growl.

A second later, she is in the street with Olesya.

"Oh, look Olesya, a gallery...."

Jackie hears many male voices talking in serious tones on the inside. They step in, and the man in the blue sweater, who is now sitting next to a water dispenser, is drinking cup after paper cup of spring water and blowing his nose with paper towels. His rescuers have turned on the air conditioner and opened the windows, and he is being comforted by a young woman with fashionable, intelligent-looking, non-corrective glasses. He looks up at Olesya and shouts, "You!" before falling back into his chair.

"What does he mean? Does he know her?" Jackie asks the young woman.

"He was attacked. What does he mean? I don't always know. He has fits, sees ghosts, sees all kinds of spirits coming to get him...."

"You! You!" he shouts again and begins to rise from his chair.

"Oh dear," says Jackie.

"He'll be all right," says the young woman.

"We'll come back," says Jackie.

The two of them sweep back out into the street, Olesya in her tangerine coat, followed by incoherent shouts.

"Do you have any money?" Jackie asks her.

"Only a banking card."

"I thought so," Jackie glances across the street at the beer umbrellas rocking in the wind.

"There is a small bank a block down," she tells her, as if she is giving orders to an officer of the military. She gives her a friendly punch in the arm. "They will be fucking like rabbits in that store, so you go get money while I go keep the beer drinkers occupied. Whatever you do, be sure to kill a little time. Don't come directly to the bar , or else the two of them may come out looking for Wanda."

"You've handled everything perfectly," says Olesya. "Isn't cheating what life is all about? I think so!" She blows Jackie an unexpected kiss.

"I will see you in a while then," Jackie answers, and dashes into the street. "After you have finished killing a little time," she remarks to herself.

At last she sees what all the noise is on the bar side of the block. The police have told the unemployed and homeless people who have been hired to carry corporate banners in this faux protest to get off the street. But because they are temporarily employed and have no fixed address, and because the official representatives of the corporation that they are carrying signs for are not there, the police have no one to take aside. The homeless people continue to march. Each one has ten of a promised twenty bucks in their pockets for an hour of chanting and waving signs advertising trendy new Internet shopping. The police have brought vans to carry these people away, and they are beginning to scatter in fear just as the corporate reps arrive back with their megaphones and the rest of their promised money from a late martini lunch.

"You can't arrest them, we rented this sidewalk!"

The police shout at the protestors to break up the picket, while the PR men shout at them to stay. There are clearly going to be some arrests. The media has been called ahead of time to photograph the whole thing.

Jackie walks back into the bar where Ben and Vespa are discussing the day their mother led the Swiss police on a cross-country motorcycle chase before she was arrested for possession of an unregistered 500cc Condor in a small Swiss village by a lake. Now everyone outside on the street is getting arrested, it strikes Jackie, everyone except Olesya. Striding past the bank where the protestors have created a tangle of traffic, Olesya is spotted by the bank employees, who smoke cigarettes and discuss the recent robbery. They are watching the corporate picket campaign and the media snapping pics. Finally, one of them reluctantly tells an officer who is on the scene in response to the alarm.

"Look! That's her!"

Olesya stops and looks about her, wondering if it was wise to leave Wanda alone. She regains her step, and decides to head back to her apartment to get the other bank card in her other purse. How long will it will take Wanda to have sex, she wonders. She breaks into a light jog, something she is used to doing only on the treadmill at her gym, and three police officers break into a trot behind her. It is difficult to lose anyone dressed in a plastic tangerine jacket with green and yellow scarves. Olesya almost runs by her apartment—it is such an everyday trendy place, built almost overnight by B.F.Turner Consolidated, the politically incorrect construction company. As she has said before, she can never figure out why politically incorrect things are always such a big deal. She pauses, realizing that she also has the keys to her girlfriend's apartment. Olesya realizes she is in love. More even than with shoes. Her heart is suddenly aching, a surprise-feeling, because Olesya has always told herself she can bail out if she gets too emotionally involved with women, and go back to non-emotionality with men.

From the other side of the potted cedars at the foot of her building, four male police officers watch as Olesya nibbles her thumbnail, pondering the new emotion. Many floors above their suspect, an African violet begins a slide from its vinyl plant-mat to the street below. The plant picks up speed as it plummets. The officers following Olesya divide up and begin to prepare an arrest.

Jackie, feeling flush, orders a plate of *Nudle s houbami* each for Ben and Vespa. "Didn't I just bring you a plate?" the server asks. Apparently, the group has not even noticed she was gone.

The African violet strikes Olesya on the head and she hits the pavement. The police cuff her and call an ambulance. The spores of the violet disperse explosively into the dirty New York City spring air at the same moment as the shoe salesperson gets his horn deeply into Wanda. The violet finds an inventive place to plant a seed while the police load Olesya onto a stretcher and pop her into a security ward with seven money-stubborn junkies and an ad rep concussed by a slap and a megaphone blow on the head. Ben looks up from his finished plate with a self-satisfied look just as Wanda wavers across the street to the terrace of umbrellas, lurching into the dark, comforting atmosphere inside. She is happy, but slightly off balance, having drunk champagne deeply from a hundred-dollar shoe.

17.

"FATHER," SAYS RUDY, "I have slain thee." He has escaped them all now and set up his next phase of operations deep in the Adirondack forest, where no one can ever come. Soon, he will overthrow the patriarchy, but first, he must process what has come to pass. He gazes down at the rack of a magnificent white-tailed stag. Since white-tailed deer are not in the habit of looking up, it is easy to observe them from his platform in a tree and to watch them as they come and go, along with the other animals and birds that live in the forest. A family of chipmunks live at the foot of Rudy's tree, and he realizes they are the most delightful and energetic animals he has ever seen. Long before he was able to see them, he would hear their sound in the morning, a low repeating cry like a woodwind instrument being struck against a fallen log. He has been in this treetop perch for over a week, unravelling. The disappearance of B.F. is weighing most heavily on his soul. The game that B.F. played the most with Rudy was that of intimidation, threats, and ridicule. Rudy has to wonder why he had slipped so far into Turner's pit of games. Even though it was never mentioned between them, one of the largest games in the boardroom had been Rudy's art of sales talk that ultimately won the envy of his colleagues. He was tuned in to the needs of B.F, became able to sense things long before the others. This emotional charade between them had suddenly snapped with the firing of the gun, and now that he was able to contemplate it, he was forced to face a tidal wave of emotions he had carried with him since the day he had been hired, long before he found the inside track.

"Wasn't I the voice in the boardroom that asked non-violent questions, the investigating questions? Yes, I was. I wanted to know if it would be necessary to frighten or intimidate another politician or developer in order to push a plan. Not that I wouldn't do it. I just loved that clarity. Just loved it."

A chipmunk leaps through a dapple of sunlight and runs vertically up a neighbouring maple, as if it is listening and is suddenly invigorated by what he had said.

B.F. knew every man's hang-ups and intimate weaknesses. It was an Old Boy's Club where Rudy played the role of the only other adult in the room, while Turner was the furious father. The men around Rudy had been handpicked and would carry out orders to the letter, even commit what came close to murder. A sense of belonging was more important to them than their own dignity. Their vulnerabilities were something B.F. did not directly torment them with, but everyone knew he kept a blackmail file on each man a mile thick.

B.F. Turner had liked that Rudy challenged his big-crime bluster and considered Rudy a shot of fresh blood. He knew that inside Rudy, a small, shy child was simply satisfied that he had beaten his own monsters for another day and won the approval of the dragon.

Rudy had survived only by being an intimate disciple and slave to B.F's moods. And the reward system he enjoyed was seeing B.F. lash out at another instead of lash out at him. Finally, like the others, thinking he was above the charade, he had become only another subservient son. Now that he has killed the father, Rudy has lost all guidance. He knows he has committed the gravest sin. Even the hand of God will not reach out to comfort him in his terror, he is certain. And he knows he has to pull himself together. He watches the chipmunks and pens a poem in his notebook:

With each familiar passing
The arranger of order and grace
Displaces the structure of chaos
And leaves fallen leaves in their place.

It is all that he wants to write for now because of the scold-
ing sound that the animals and birds make, and the suddenly
curious faces of the whiskered creatures that live around him.
He is aware that he is the newcomer again, and these animals
do not approve his arrival. It's not a very good poem, but the
idea that destruction has a place appeals to him. He has been
studying the writing of Zen monks and their disciples, and it
seems to him that they wrote short verses that had great signifi-
cance. Despite his negative feelings, Rudy derives pleasure from
the realization that everything on the forest floor has been put
there within moments of his eyes falling upon it because some
creature, insect, bird, or incidental action of the wind placed
it there and nowhere else. He makes it his business to notice
these beautiful arrangements if it is their wish to be seen. In
many of the Zen Buddhist poems he is reading, he encounters
the word, "indulgence."

"I am indulging in the forest with my senses," he tells himself.
And, he is reading other poets. In fact, that is almost all that he
has brought with him to read. He reads Kerouac, who spent
sixty-three days in a mountaintop shack as a fire look-out,
surrounded, like Rudy, with bears and chipmunks and deer
and endless marching miles of rock face and trees.

"'A blade of grass jiggling in the winds of infinity, anchored
to a rock, and for your own poor gentle flesh no answer,'"
Rudy reads aloud. He decides Kerouac wrote with an obliga-
tory tone because he felt that he had to record his experience
of isolation, not because his isolation brought him revelations
that he had to record. He uses Kerouac's text to start his fires
in the little portable stove he has brought with him up on his
perch. Rudy has eaten many things; his staple being the sprouts

that he is trying to grow in jars housed in a cupboard made of crates. He gathers berries, reads about edible plants from a wild-crafting book, and writes to himself day and night. He contemplates his murder of B.F. and resolves that he acted with his wild, natural human side, which he embraces as much as his good side, a side he has seen very little of until now. After ten days, he resolves to focus only on his good self, having passed through the flames of self-torment that occurred a few days after he was cleared in the shooting death of his employer. He reads Thoreau and copies into his book a paraphrase of a sentence that intrigues him: "'I find in myself an instinct towards a higher, spiritual life, and another towards a primitive and savage one, and I reverence them both.'"

Rudy is comforted. He is trying to release his spirit from the three passions: greed, anger, and ignorance. He lies awake at night staring at the stars and contemplates the four great wisdoms of Zen Buddhism. Then he contemplates rising above the conceptual area of the profane and the sacred, outside of arguments based upon differentiation. He is living a simple life—a life structured around chants that he invents himself, things that he reads in ancient poetry, and more contemporary poets that strike him as relevant to his search. When a family of birds break through their shells in the tree next to his own, he is able to recite to them a poem of Patti Smith's, one that ends with pretty stars. Kerouac, whom he hates, mentions that stars are "'the words,' and all the innumerable worlds in the Milky Way are words, and so this is the world too."

Kerouac thinks that no matter where Rudy is, he will always be in his mind. There is no need for solitude. Rudy disagrees. Thoreau tells him, "This whole earth which we inhabit is but a point in space.... Why should I feel lonely? Is not our planet in the Milky Way?" Rudy thinks Thoreau is much tougher than Kerouac. Hemingway recommends Baudelaire, another man, but so does Wanda, someone he has almost forgotten he ever called a friend. He reads *Les Fleurs du Mal*, and stumbles upon, "*Mainte fleur épanche à regret / Son parfum doux comme un secret / Dans les solitudes profondes.*" Rudy thinks of Wanda again, and shrugs off the sensation that he is a star with a dangerous comet flying toward him.

He is struggling to reach a sense of peace with the composition and decomposition of all things. He begins to wonder about the question of God because he has only ever encountered a work-harder, reward-later, punitive God. He sits and meditates, and waits for a new idea to challenge the part of himself calcified with punk cynicism and distrust of any form of power greater than the ones he can sense.

Twice a week, every Monday and every Thursday, he picks up his cellphone and talks to Camelia. Camelia has been at his side for a long time. Rudy trusts his life to her dry, reasoning sense of humour, and he has placed her in his office while he is away. Most of the other people at Turner think he is fishing or with his family. Only Camelia knows that her boss is on a personal retreat. With the help of an elaborate series of codes Rudy has established with B.F., he begins the process of dismantling the Turner empire from within.

Camelia need only type in numbers and names, so certain crooks are paid off and their obligation to Turner is finished. Rudy knows, almost universally, that the phone calls and the money represent an enormous relief to the various deal-making politicians and underworld agents he has been involved with—people who can now live free of the blackmail and personal coercion involved with his boss. They can now forget a man who bullied their every move. They can now forget all of it and get on with their crooked lives. He also drains the Turner empire by sending some of Turner's loyal employees to other companies or, if they were extremely destructive, to early retirements, like an ownder swapping baseball players in big-league teams and then forgetting their names. Again, according to Camelia, the backlash was small. None were angry, and they were universally pleased at being sent to greener dollars.

Rudy wishes Camelia well and tells her they will speak again next Monday. He reads *Leaves of Grass*. "What is grass? ... / And now it seems to me the beautiful uncut hair of graves." He writes another poem to himself, a haiku style, to complement his obsession with Satori:

Slipping out from cover
find in this pale place of blue
the moon is rising.

Rudy does not know what the rising moon represents, although he watches one from his tree every morning, but he hopes it is the influence he is playing over the housing hierarchies of the big cities where Turner Consolidated has always called the shots. The change in the urban sprawl is about to throw the high-rise housing market into convulsions. He is pleased with himself and spends the day throwing berries at small grey squirrels. The next day he writes:

Break, hunter
The incomprehensible you chase and chase
Has itself raised her white tail and raced
Towards a higher surrender.

Rudy thinks the poem smacks of mortal playing God. He supposes that's what a poet is: an observer in an uninvolved state. The more Rudy's senses become aware of the cycles of death and birth around him, the more he feels an acute sense of other senses that have been dormant or asleep. He feels them there, but grasping at them is like grasping at air because he is certain that these other senses want to convey information to him about a state of natural order that he is not equipped to understand. There is no master; there is no friend or group of friends to express his feelings to. There is only Rudy, the wind, and his little platform in the trees. He busies himself penning verses and finds them no less dangerous to his state of well-being than an injured deer is secure in the dark of a night forest.

He reads Doris Lessing's poems and thinks about reversing the destruction he has colluded in by faking a friendship with, and then taking away, Turner's life. He pens in his book: "Striving to achieve what strange reversal," a quote from Doris Lessing's *Briefing for a Descent into Hell.*

Strange, thinks Rudy, ignorant of his arrogance and with no master there to guide him. *Strange, I thought I had just climbed out of hell, and am emerged.*

An uncomfortable nudging tells him a danger is approaching him, and there is nothing he can do.

He closes his eyes, and he can hear the wind playing through the trees all around him, birds rattling the leaves, ravenous chicks calling to them in fights and flights of rapture. He picks up the cellphone and calls Camelia again, his trusty satellite dish transmitting the call to her desk.

"On a Wednesday!" She is happy and surprised. Rudy needs to talk to someone anyway. He is spooked by his higher perceptions, and Camelia is a grounding force. She is wired on lattes and dressed in nylons and silk, and she is sitting behind a red oak desk with a dress pump swinging off her toe a thousand miles away. Rudy specifies the coordinates of six downtown sites in her city, which swift-minded Camelia notes are Turner properties. He wants her to buy as many of the condo units as she can and then strike a deal with the city so that low-income families can move in. "You realize that will devastate the ambience of our buildings. In all fairness Rudy, our original buyers will sell and move out...."

Rudy pulls the scales free from a pine cone, tossing them spinning into the wind.

"The more vacancies the better. I want all the units in those six sites filled with families earning less than twenty thousand a year within three to six. A minimum target."

"Rudy, are you going nuts?" says Camelia.

"It's a little favour I have to do for somebody in a high place," he says, smiling at a sparrow. "Besides, we must face the music, and it will make the company smell like a rose."

"Holy mixed clichés," says Camelia. "Are you normal? The only way you're going to make this company smell like roses is to rip it out by the roots and plant something new."

"Camelia. One more thing," he tells her.

"You want to buy a free hit of heroin for every junky in downtown Vancouver?"

"I want Turner to get busy now, moving low-income families into our developments under a rent scheme through the city. If the city doesn't believe our goodwill, here's a hook. I want you to price the top three properties you'll find listed in my Speculations and Bidding folder, file five. Once we get a price on them, we come, we see, we conquer, and I want to proceed with a very old design plan you'll find enclosed in file eighty-five, folder four. Oldest design I ever came up with, the first one that made B.F. think I had promise. B.F. turned it into an exclusive place with gates and guards. But the original plans are all there, and that's what we're moving on now. Just gut the old buildings, leave the skeleton standing, but gut and reinforce. All the new contractor lists are under folder four. If people are leaving the developments, others will stay on. We will integrate rich and poor into the new system, and it will be a place for children to thrive and grow."

"I cannot do this all by myself," says Camelia.

"Certainly not. No woman is an inlet. Just start the bidding. I know when something is hot, and these properties are hot, hot-hot, sizzling..."

"Rudy, if I may, you wanted to buy the properties in file five. Two of them we already bought. We already built there, Rudy, we own them and they aren't for sale."

"That's where we save money. We do the same thing as we do to the other ones. We gut and rebuild. Anyone with inside information knows those buildings are as stable as a donkey's arse. They're built on metaphorical sand, Camelia, on sand."

"But we built them. You built them."

"And there's nothing wrong with them according to the old Turner philosophy, with their outward appearance. But they aren't fit to live in for more than another five years. After that, the outsides will be falling off too. And we don't want the outsides to fall down and kill somebody. Of course, we could just demo those two entirely..."

"No, wait," says Camelia. "Let's start with the bidding on the other property. The one that just needs gutting."

"'It's not easy to achieve freedom without chaos.'"

"I can't believe that's you on the phone."

"Actually, it's Anais Nin," says Rudy, scribbling in a book.

"After we get the bidding started, then you can demo your old sites."

"Great start!"

"Rudy? Are you okay?"

"I'm better than I have ever been before."

"Then we are turning old Turner around?"

Rudy smiles and watches a sun-dappled squirrel so close he could reach out and stroke it.

18.

JACKIE AND VESPA will have to take care of Olesya's apartment while she is in jail. A video of Olesya spritzing the gallery of the grave-digging man with pepper spray and saying, "I am Oleysa! The avenger!" is on three television stations and the cover of *The Village Voice*. The woman who knows a whole lot about art is begging back Olesya's love. A number of other women are begging it for the first time. Alaska is also coaching her on what to say to the media. Olesya is still in the prison infirmary. She remembers nothing but agrees that the woman in both the bank and the gallery video is definitely her. She is discussing appropriated art, and she is more articulate on the subject with every interview, with Alaska coaching every moment at her side. Olesya is now so well-versed on her topic that Jackie feels her first moment of real shame while she and Vespa watch the television and Olesya says, "When the white man reintroduced the horse to North America," causing Jackie to blurt out, "I didn't know that! I thought there never had been any horses!" and Vespa to whisper reverently, "Neither did I."

Olesya is discussing social differences between the discovery of unmarked grave remains in postwar Europe, and the same discoveries in North America when the little telephone rings by her bed. Vespa remains fixed to the screen.

"Call before you dig," says Jackie, and throws herself, stomach-wise across the bed to answer.

"Jackie? It's Wanda. Ben and I want to leave the hotel and come over there. What do you think about Oleysa on the television and her little talk about her friend who spent time in prison, preparing her for her ordeal?"

"What did she say?"

"Don't you have the television on? She just mentioned the whole thing. It is obvious she looks up to you, Jackie. Didn't you hear her?"

"Hey, she just said some stuff about you!" says Vespa.

Jackie covers the receiver. "Press 'Play!'" Jackie calls out.

She wants to hear what Olesya says, but Wanda is nattering in her ear. "Now she's moved on to some commentary about Indigenous artifacts."

"Is she talking about Indigenous artifacts?" Jackie asks.

"No, she's talking about you," says Vespa, reclining on Olesya's fun-fur couch.

"There's a bit of a time-lapse.... She's talking about me, and Vespa's hitting 'Record'...."

The opening credits of a Rossellini movie blast the room.

"Turn it down! Turn it back!"

"You said hit 'Play'!"

"I said 'Record,' so we could play it back, Wanda, I gotta go."

"It's all over," says Wanda. "She only talks about you for a second. Then she moves on to..."

"Vespa, she talks about me!" Vespa is thumbing through Olesya's video recordings.

"She also says some very interesting things about stolen grave objects."

"Rossellini. Olesya is much more erudite than I had thought. I wonder if she *has Ladri di Biciclette!*"

"Vespa! I said turn it back!"

"Jackie, for heaven's sake, I can't turn back the time," says Vespa, "and it's probably over by now."

"*Ladri di Biciclette* was De Sica. All the characters were amateurs, it wasn't real!"

"You're back on the air again," says Wanda. "They keep running the clip where she talks all about you."

Jackie strains to hear Wanda's newscast through the receiver.

"Well," says Wanda, "I guess that was all there was. Just a little clip. Too bad we didn't tape it. Can Olesya videotape TV in her apartment?"

"Yes, that's what Vespa's fooling with right now. She's looking at her tapes. She wants to watch Rossellini and De Sica, instead of watching me. I don't enjoy De Sica. It's not even real filmmaking. And it's got goddam modern things in the middle of black-and-white things.... When I watch a film..."

"Of course, it's real filmmaking. It's Neorealism," says Wanda, suddenly in her element. "How could you say it's not real? That's why they hand-pick everyday people!"

The New York news station is discussing the release of a killer whale back into nature that has been trained only to kiss girls in bikinis in exchange for tossed fish.

"Listen, I'm on the television again! I mean, Olesya is. I'm here, and I'm on television. I'm three places at once."

"Now that's Neorealism," says Wanda, "And a dash of the surrealistic. If you've studied the forms. Travelling through time, three places at once."

The whale is followed by a clip discussing the use of homeless people to advertise Internet shopping. Jackie is seen bobbing across the street over to the Pilsner umbrellas. Olesya is running out of view in her tangerine jacket. A journalist on camera moves in front of the scene to discuss the police reaction to the picket.

"I have to go," says Wanda. "I know this whale."

"What if the whale is attracted to places where there are bikinis?"

Wanda hangs up.

Vespa leans back and scratches her head with the remote.

"Well, I guess that's all there was."

"What do you mean? She was talking about me."

"She was talking about a lot of interesting stuff, Jackie, if you had listened nicely instead of talking."

"I was listening, as a matter of fact, and I think Alaska, her coach, is very intelligent and she is telling her what to say."

"I bet Alaska doesn't have Bergman in her video collection."

"It's probably on loan from her," says Jackie.

"What do you have against Olesya, anyway?"

"Sometime, we should talk."

"No time like the present."

Jackie warms up. "Bergman as actor or screenwriter?"

"Writer, of course. The opposite of Brecht."

"Bergman was a pessimist. He created films like a factory creates boxes of chocolates. I read Brecht in prison," says Jackie, sitting down next to her girl. "The Nazis tried to nail him down, and McCarthyism tried to bust him here in America. But he was too smart for all of them. He was smart like a fox."

"Thea von Harbou, is that a woman? Wrote the screenplay for "M.""

Jackie is unresponsive.

"Where the underworld organizes to catch the killer, and hold a kangaroo court. All the criminals circle around Peter Lorre, and he says he can't help who he is..." Vespa explains.

"I know. I've seen it. Peter Lorre was one of the most brilliant actors of that time. A talented homosexual, and then he killed himself. Because no one understood the difference between what Peter Lorre was and what his character was in that film," says Jackie.

"I wonder if that's what Olesya feels like. The homosexual surrounded by hostile criminal elements," Vespa continues.

"Stuff it," says Jackie.

"Why do you hate her so much?"

Jackie says nothing.

"Bergman then. Don't tell me you haven't seen *Autumn Sonata*."

"I was in prison. They show get-a-job movies in prison."

"'To you I was a doll that you played with when you had time.... You shut yourself in and worked, and no one was allowed to disturb you.... You were always kind ... but completely preoccupied.'"

"What was that?"

"That was *Autumn Sonata*.... "

"I'm like that?"

"Sometimes. You do have several sides, Jackie, several sides. I think there are parts of your personality that won't talk to me. Healthy feelings you don't show."

Vespa throws her arm around Jackie and they settle back on the fun-fur sofa. Alaska's cat, which is staying at Olesya's because it is shedding and Alaska is trying to carefully paint her passion for Olesya in oils, leaps up onto their laps and deposits a sweater's worth of hair onto their clothing.

"I love you," says Vespa.

"I'm easy," says Jackie. She throws the cat onto the floor.

"We should go to the bedroom."

"Why?"

"People in this city spy in windows like this one. Besides, the couch is lumpy."

"It pops out."

"Yeah, well let it pop out for some beer. I'm taking you to the bedroom."

The intercom buzzes. "Paparazzi," says Vespa.

"Is that another filmmaker?"

"No, it means...."

"I know what it fucking means. Paparazzi ... it's a type of pop-out couch."

The intercom is more insistent.

"Ignore it," says Vespa. She unbuttons Jackie's shirt.

"What about the paparazzi watching from the windows across the street?"

Vespa throws her leg over Jackie's hip. Jackie unbuttons

Vespa's jeans and slides her hands across her warm, smooth stomach.

The door rattles.

"It's me. I came to get my cat!" Alaska laughs and the cat jumps in alarm. "Just kidding! Hey, what are you kids up to?"

"What are you up to?"

"Can't sleep in my apartment. Too full of fumes. I'm giddier than a glue-head in a glider factory."

Alaska stares at the two of them as if there were certain parts about them that she would like to paint over and correct. "I just need somewhere to crash," she tells them. Her tone has a kidnapped-sounding quality. She turns on her heel and goes to the bedroom, quietly closing the door. From inside they can hear her saying Olesya's name softly to herself and sobbing like a child.

"Well," says Jackie, moving the cat across for a second time, "I suppose we should pop out the couch."

19

RUDY WAKES with the slow rocking of his tree in the wind, and the creaking of branches around him. It is Tuesday again, and he calls Camelia to discuss a New York property that continually resurfaces in his head. He has dreamed of it twice, and in the second dream, he was Freder in *Metropolis*, the movie Wanda had rented so long ago. In the dream, the streets were burning, and he ran to West 108th Street with Vespa's hand in his, and there was fire raging in the street. He turned back, but Vespa was inside the building he had helped design, which became Cubist, distorted, corrupted, and there was no way to get her out. A crowd had formed and things were falling, slipping from the many inch or more off-angle balconies and falling on people's heads. He was Freder, and the answer was to fly, take flight, like Ben had once dreamed of doing. Rudy knew he was capable, but he had not the wildest idea how to begin.

He calls his satellite dish, which phones his company and tells Camelia to quietly have Olesya's building inspected and repaired or else demolished to make way for a new multi-level play park with indoor soccer, a swimming pool, and a rink for urban kids.

He sits in his tree and stares at his hands. His books are full of sketches, but his mind is full of the shame and the torment of his deceit. He is walking alone through the desert of the father betrayed by his son. Nothing will comfort his spirit, and he is not eating anything that he does not stumble across, too sorry now to kill even a squirrel for his food. He feels that many eyes are watching him, but he does not want to believe in a God watching all of them. Any form of hierarchical thinking gets him down. He is confused. He has nothing to say to B.F. Turner. There are crowds of dead around Turner when he sees him in his dreams. He cannot reach him. He wants to comfort him, to hear him joke about raping teenage whores again, to be forgiven by a man who split his wife's lip for overcooking a salmon. He doesn't know where he is going anymore, and he wonders if he should hang himself from the tree. He wants a larger hand to hold his own, and then realizes he has wanted it for so long that his hand reaching out is not a man's hand at all, but a tiny child's hand, injured from fooling with picklocks and trying to jimmy the back trunks of cars. He wonders at it, stares at it. It is scarred already from fighting with boys twice his size.

20

NATALIA, RUDY'S NEW YORK girlfriend, is sitting in her apartment on West 108th Street, staring at her long, and according to Rudy, expensive legs. She can't help but feel as if her whole world is sliding from her. First, she lost her African violets. And now, the women above her, who ignore her in the lobby, have started a campaign. First it was to get the woman who was accidentally struck with Natalia's violet out of prison. But the woman who was in prison had every reason to be there as the television news showed. Before pausing underneath Natalia's building, she had robbed a bank downtown. She had then pepper-sprayed the operator of a small gallery, a man who could have been an asthmatic or a person with a delicate heart. Now, the woman refused to come out of prison; she was on a hunger strike and talking on the news with more airtime than the killer whale. It was as if the killer whale, the issue Natalia really did care about, was only able to come up for air for a few seconds and then was pushed back under the surface by the debate of this woman's actions. As if everyone was forgetting that she had robbed a bank, as if appearances did not matter anymore. Rudy, in the midst of all this, had asked her to fib for him, to say that they had played in New York for four days instead of two. Then he had stayed with her, and he had paid the tuition for Natalia's attendance as a student in the dance school she had always wanted to be part of. Before leaving, he had put money into her bank account so that she would have time to attend the class, practice the moves, be coached privately, and still carry on with the other interests in her life. Rudy had said that he would have a private investigator follow Natalia and make sure that she pursued her studies, tossing it off as a sort of paternalistic joke. Now the building is surrounded with photographers, and Natalia knows, from lying in Rudy's arms and being a confidante to Rudy's fears, that his company has the corrupt money and power to take away people's lives without retribution. So, the man who may or may not be following her, may be doing it for her safety because she knows that she has been seen with Rudy. Or he may be doing it to ensure that she does not tell the police she was only with Rudy for two days before the day that B.F. was announced as missing. In other words, if he has hired someone to follow her, the individual watching her movements could be an assassin. But Natalia is not afraid of assassination. She is afraid of losing Rudy. Via a deep-woods radio and satellite system, Natalia has received a poem a week. Some say things like,

> The animals that surround me
> Are not trained in artifice
> They live acutely for survival
> Contented just with this
> Without concern for buildings
> That will stand a thousand years
> They trade no lies for bricks of gold
> That will fall around their ears.

Natalia likes it when Rudy sends her poems he has written himself, but it disturbs her when he adds at the end:

"What ... fills this city? The pleas to end pain? The cries of sorrow? On the assassin, or assassins, I call down the most vile damnation—I will avenge him as I would avenge my own father."

Natalia, who is feeling paranoid as a result and stops smoking cannabis to put herself to sleep at night, stays up late reading until she happens upon Rudy's quote in *Oedipus Tyrannus*, which is being shown at a theatre in the Bowery district. When she goes to see it, she realizes that it is a play about a man who kills his father. Also that the actors are all wearing recycled plastic packing material and automotive parts as costumes. Despite the nudity and the endless minor notes of a collection of keyboard pieces squawking from three different tape players placed around the room, she is able to understand what Rudy is saying. She suspects that he continues to suspect foul play in the death of Turner. Whether it is a reasonable fear is not important. She sees now that he related the old man Turner to his own father, a man who died early in Rudy's life. In *Oedipus Tyrannus,* the death of the father by the son results in a curse, and ultimately the tearing out by the son of his eyes, which in the Bowery version is demonstrated with paint-filled sponges and hand-held paintballs that squirt outward. Natalia leaves intensely grateful, invigorated, and grossed-out. Fortunately, Rudy is not sleeping with his mother.

She calls his mother in Etobicoke, intending to tell her Rudy is in danger. Instead, she asks her about Rudy's father, the one who had died when he was young.

"Rudy didn't take that very well, I must say. Now I think Gary went just the way they said he did, by falling in the river all liquored-up and drowning. He was a fool for the bottle, something I tried to protect Rudy from. But after Gary died, I couldn't protect Rudy from the rumours. He was up to some mischief before he died, a part of a bad crowd. Rudy always believed that they had killed him."

"Do you mean the safe-cracking? And being in with a gang that specialized in picking locks and breaking into businesses and banks?"

Rudy's mother was surprised by this woman who knew

intimacies about her son's life, and, at the same time, pleased by the directness and frank concern of the younger woman's manner. She herself had remarried and had not talked about her previous husband much in the past thirty years. It had been forbidden in her house. The manner of Rudy's friend was kind, relaxing, and her phone voice was so calming that Rudy's mother realized she had words and pent-up emotions that had been trapped inside for years.

"It was a very hard time for our family, Natalia. All I wanted was to protect my son and keep him from a life of crime. Rudy did not mourn or act like a boy who was in mourning as I thought he should. He would sit at his father's place at meals, insisted on keeping favourite articles of his father's clothes when I just wanted to throw everything away. And the other things I wanted to throw away ... Rudy was too fast." She dabbed her eyes.

"What other things of his father's did he keep before you could throw them away?"

"You know what sort of things. His father was his model, but he was a criminal. Rudy," his mother told her, "is by comparison a very honest boy. It was a great pleasure talking to you, dear. I hope he marries you if he has told you he will."

"He's on a retreat right now," said Natalia.

"Oh, they run away, but he'll be back. You seem like a very nice girl."

"I mean, he's gone off to the woods for a while to collect his thoughts about life."

"The death of the Chairman. He told me all about that on the phone. He's been put into a position with a lot of responsibility now."

"Yes, he has, and he's running it by remote control. I'll have him phone you when he is out of the mountains. I'll have him call you as soon as I can," says Natalia. She believes this woman, this caring mother, might have been a good person for Rudy to do something else with besides brag to over the years. If Rudy is not killed by assassins. The word is stuck in Natalia's mind.

Animated, take wing with the spirit of wonder
I climb weightlessly high and fall shamelessly under.

It is a poem Rudy has written about young hawks he has been watching as they begin to fly.

"I will show unto thee the judgment of the great whore that sitteth upon many waters," he adds.

Less charmingly, he follows with, "'Where we are, / There's daggers in men's smiles: the near in blood, / the nearer bloody.'"

This time, Natalia knows the last bit is a quote from the death of Macbeth. There is a production in the East Side with vocalists projecting the words of the play from behind screens, while the actual parts are acted out by power tools, concluding in the death of a reciprocating saw at the hands of a twelve-amp grinder and a five-foot orbital sanding machine. Despite the promise that sparks will fly, Natalia chooses not to go. She studies *Macbeth* instead, looking for clues in the conspired death of a king. There may be several assassins, and if Rudy is in danger, she certainly wants to be in the know.

The next mail comes only a day later and opens with "'Had he not resembled / My father as he slept...'"

He follows with his own haiku:

Look further
Hawks grown to feast and murder
Yet a grace on the wing.

He then sends his best wishes and tells Natalia to have no fear. A living dog is better than a dead lion.'" It is a quote from Ecclesiastes.

Empowered by the talk with his mother, she writes to Rudy's secretary Camelia, using the encryption device Rudy has installed into Natalia's computer and told her no one else could understand.

"Hey? Emergency, answer back!" she writes Camelia. She writes it a second time with a new encryption to scramble the words, then a third. Camelia will have the technology to unscramble it, she tells herself, then retires with a book about the assassination of Abe Lincoln. She has settled in with his prophetic words: "Corporations have been enthroned ... an era of corruption ... working on the prejudices of the people..." when a *gong* on her computer notifies her that another email has arrived.

It's Camelia, pissed as hell, wondering what Natalia meant by, "Askance? Scenery, enemy herb!" not to mention, "Keen? Hymen, brace necessary!" and, "Wench? Beg, sneaky creamery!"

It has just made Natalia sound like a whore, which she is. She rambles around her apartment, then lights up her "enemy herb" and stares out at the city. That is when she has the herb-enhanced memory of Rudy installing the encryption. It does not take her much longer to realize that the letters from "Hey? Emergency, answer back!" have convoluted into those three anagrammed and unsolicited insults she then sent off to a woman she has never met. Which means that not only was Natalia unable to communicate with Camelia, except in the form of an apology from an unhacked-with computer, but that Camelia was also not able to read or translate her communications with Rudy. So, Camelia would have no inkling of any assassination talk or premeditated murders that may be in the works. Natalia put the roach out. She had told herself to quit, and paranoia is the last thing she needs if there was a threat.

21.

THE NEIGHBOURS in Natalia's building have had an incident. They had been getting along well—a friendship lubricated by drinking—and they have just returned from a movie. Because she is high, Natalia realizes she has seen this before in a neorealistic movie. The movie is about three women who watch in drunken dismay as their imprisoned friend's over-amorous cat pitches from the balcony and falls harmlessly six stories into some shrubs. In the movie, the innocent cat slides slowly on a spilled drink and some ice cubes. There is also a slow-motion sequence, which provides plenty of time to pick up the cat before it goes over the edge. Alaska is surprised by the over-amorous cat and thinks that it should be able to catch its own bearings in life as she did after losing her lover to a jail sentence. Jackie was a little too loaded to believe that the cat was falling sideways. As far as she was concerned, the whole building was doing some pretty interesting stunts with gravity, a theory which, when the building inspectors finally arrived, proved sound. Vespa had just smoked herself up and was certain that the sliding of the cat was somehow a replay from the film, not realizing that neorealism is called neorealism because it has just really happened, or it is about to really happen to you. The cat walks out onto the balcony, Jackie spills her drink in surprise, and the animal begins to slip on the ice. Rather than hesitate as the women in the movie had done, they break with the script and leap forward to prevent a yet-to-be-proven harmless fall. Failing, they clutch at the balcony railing and look down with tragic faces at the cat spirals away from them on the wind.

It is Alaska who immediately feels guilty. Jackie is transfixed and is still staring bug-eyed over the balcony at the social dysfunction of it all, while Vespa and Alaska appear on the lawn, wandering through the security lights, calling out the pet's name. Didactica, the cat, has fallen into a soft hedgerow of decorative shrubs, is thrilled to be the centre of attention and is not injured in the least. To be sure, they take money from Olesya's defense fund and taxi the animal to the vet at midnight. The vet puts a tensor bandage around the animal's left foreleg and a Hendrix-like white scarf around its head. He charges them one hundred and seventy dollars.

Natalia tries to avoid them after they recount this to her in the elevator.

The next day, a press meeting is held and a full-scale campaign is launched to activate the people in Olesya's building, so unsound that both an African violet and a cat have fallen from the balconies, resulting in expensive damages in both cases; or, three if you love plants. The woman upstairs, who owned the African violet, appears to be avoiding the women on the sixth floor, but she is so friendly in the elevator that they cannot imagine why. It is frustrating their campaign, and since she lost her African violet, they would like her to be involved. Alaska offers to coach her so that she can talk to the press. The other tenants in the building have stories of cans falling out of cupboards, magazines sliding paranormally from tables, and one semi-retired gentleman is willing to testify that a carpenter's level slid across his hall floor as he was watching television and struck his miniature Sheltie in the ass. He hesitates to reveal his name. It is Alaska's hope that they will all sign for a class-action suit, hoping they can win damages from B.F. Turner without having to actually move.

Lawyers make Jackie nervous and she is haunted by dreams of a falling cat superimposed by a second dream of a powerful, menacing-looking flying squirrel. She also feels uncomfortable around Alaska, who is in love with Olesya because she feels nervous about what she has done to Olesya.

When Vespa makes love to Jackie her deep, intense eyes burn into Jackie's soul, and she is beginning, for the first time in her remorseless life, to experience regret. Jackie goes to Ben and finds solace there. Ben has discovered a month-to-month studio rental which is basically a cheap garage.

"It's New York," says Ben. "People are everywhere scrabbling to find apartments to stay in, but this little garage, because it's unheated, it's been waiting here unrented. I think it's cute."

Like Ben, Jackie has always enjoyed garages. She throws her money at the rent the same afternoon. While Wanda tours galleries and shops in SoHo, Ben sits in the quiet of the garage studio space, contemplating his recovery. "I was outside of my body, and now that I'm back, I can't decide how to move forward with my life. My reputation in vintage motorcycle repair is something I can salvage, but I've changed, changed in some ways I can't yet understand. I love Wanda, but I don't always know if she sees me."

"You'll need some money," says Jackie, who thinks easy money is the solution to all ills.

She finds Ben's company is uncomplicated compared to his sister. They hang out in the garage while Wanda is off shopping and exploring the city, often with Alaska, her new bff. Together Ben and Jackie begin designing an ultralight device shaped like an animal, one that glides without sound. They are both fascinated with flying, or at least, Ben's obsession and the dream have drawn Jackie in.

"In the coma, Jackie, I was astrally suspended outside of my body. My whole life, cruel people have tried to tell me that the physical form of a black man makes me not worthy of a full, free life. I tried to choose people who loved me. I had a boyhood friend, someone I loved, so you see I am capable of loving a man equally to my passions for a woman. I had to face this in myself. Society is not kind to that sort of passion. He was one of several men I have felt love for, physical love, and Rudy hurt me, and then he took up with Vespa, and also hurt her. I saw that I had to stay close to Vespa, who has cared for me selflessly from the start. I wanted to build something for her as well. For everyone. I saw the full extent of it, and while my body healed, I healed my mind with it. I felt love for myself, for the first time, I guess. Love. Maybe it was that. My body letting me back in. Nothing is going to stop me now, Jackie, nothing."

Jackie rents torches and has tools, machinery, and steel and aluminum parts dropped of. She consults the blueprints with Ben. A flying animal. When Alaska or Vespa visit, Jackie says it is a sculpture of little Didactica, and that it is going to be a publicity mascot for the group. Jackie is lying; it is Ben's flying obsession becoming ultralight, it the reoccurring dream squirrel coming to life.

At the building, Natalia is unsure whether to join the safety of the tenants' committee, or to go into hiding. She is certain she is the only tenant who knows the condo unit zoning is about to be trashed by Rudy and the entire place altered, perhaps demolished entirely, to make way for a more organic look.

From his perch, Rudy wants to complement local *fin-de-siècle* architecture while providing a complete gymnasium for children who are registered in nearby schools and wish to bring their own guests. He also plans to install an indoor park and a wave pool, as well as facilities geared to help long-term homeless people have shelter that is so responsive to their needs they will never want to leave. If they do want to leave, and then come back, Rudy wants to make sure they can. Natalia has already seen drafts of the atrium with its waterslides and its lending library.

"It's possible, Rudy, but won't it inconvenience the people already living here?"

These are now combined with sketches of other features less fantastical and closer to those found in the fixed-income housing of more progressive countries. She wonders when the place will be inspected properly as Rudy has ordered, and when the tenants will be paid off if it must be demolished for flaws. Her email *gongs* as she is cooking a linguini. Strangely, when she later removes the pot, the linguini has migrated from the centre to the western side of the oven.

It is a Rudy poem.

Like father like son with every door picked apart
Five rooms one mind one four-chambered heart
I have not killed my father but my mourning is dead
His windows are broken his spirit has fled
With my father above I will face down my death
Breaking open all doors 'til my very last breath.

It's cute, thinks Natalia. She is glad Rudy did not kill his father; it's something he certainly never mentioned to her. Neither did his mother. He was only fourteen when he lost his father and he wasn't involved. Now, with a tear in her eye, Natalia thinks Rudy, poetic as he may be, is losing his mind. Not allowing for assassins, she has been afraid of losing him, but not in this way. Maybe that is why all his new apartment buildings are designed to house street people and the homeless.

Rudy signs off: "'I have done the deed. Didst thou not hear a noise?'"

Another quote from *Macbeth,* she knows it now. She is glad she finally caved in and went to see the version in the park, where an obedience school walked through the roles with microphones and woofers hooked on to canine collars. She is no thespian, but Natalia recognizes the quote from the performance, and the meaning is clear as a contact lens on a dinner plate. "I have done the deed," can only mean he has begun the orders for the inspection, and the possible demolition of the building at West 108th. He is way ahead of the tenants committee, and she has no one to tell.

"Like a thief in the night, she breaks into his heart..." she types, thinking it is an original poem and then realizing it is a song by KISS. She erases and types, "Call yer ma!" instead, accidentally hitting the key that encrypts it and sends it to head office.

The next morning, there is a note on Camelia's desk that screams, "Creamy All!" in large, bold-faced letters.

Oh well, thinks Camelia. Why not go to New York and meet this hottie? She has heard from the New York office that Natalia is an extraordinarily delightful woman, perhaps even the mastermind behind some of Rudy's progressive changes. It's good to have her alliance, but her emails, particularly calling her a wench, have been more than a bit demanding. It is against her professional and personal policies, but if Rudy won't come out of the backwoods, Camelia wouldn't mind getting a little bit of that cream herself.

22.

WANDA AND BEN have returned to Toronto to assess the bike repair shop and decide what to do with their lives. They are making love, and he is breathing in the new tantric way that Wanda has taught him to. Distracted by the half-finished glider project and the possibility of setting a lucrative new repair shop in New York, Ben can't keep his thoughts focused. He is fighting the urge not to visualize the male server at the New York Pilsner bar when a souvenir plate of the Statue of Liberty that hangs over their bed falls from the wall and strikes him on the head. He collapses into Wanda's arms, and Wanda, delighted with the sudden intimacy, holds him tenderly, until she notices the blood trickling from his hair. The plate, like all good souvenir objects designed to celebrate freedom—and commemorate the first thing immigrants and tourists see upon their arrival to New York—is made of a heavy-duty ceramic similar to the cermet chosen by NASA. It does not shatter but falls like an Olympic discus onto the hand-hooked rug by their bed. Ben moans in such a spectacular way that Wanda is not alerted to the fact that he has just been knocked unconscious, causing all the precious neurons they fought so hard to remaster to suddenly go on the blink. She is enjoying the feeling of his more sensitive muscles relaxing in, and on, her body. But the weight of him is getting to be a little too much. When she sees the blood, she rolls his body slowly onto his side, hoping to look into his eyes. Instead, he slips from her embrace and to her dismay, rolls to the floor. The fall is three feet.

In a heartbeat, Wanda is at his side, slapping Ben once across the face. Determining he is unconscious, she calls an ambulance to rush to their home. Unsure what to do, she reaches for the little watering can that she keeps by the window and waters Ben frantically with a vitamin-enriched plant fluid. To her surprise, he begins to stir, a smile beautifying his face. She pops a small device in his mouth that measures the pH balance of his soil.

It hangs from his lips like a cigarette and Ben begins to speak: "I saw it all so plainly, Wanda. I was wearing a backpack full of math books, and Rudy was at my side. We had borrowed some things from his father, some things Rudy always wanted but never had the nerve to take. He wanted his father to pay more attention to him. His father had been involved with the men he did business with, taking late calls, running off to meetings, and drinking like a fish for months. He was obviously involved in some big scheme, but no one in Rudy's house knew what it was. His father was sworn not to discuss it with anyone else. I was the only one outside their house who even knew something was different, who knew anything, and that was because I had promised. In some way, I think you're the key to all my memories of that time. At the time, my God, how we feared his father.

"I still remember picking out special gloves so my fingerprints wouldn't be found by Rudy's Dad! Because his dad had fingerprint dusters, special chemicals, explosives and wires, and putty, all kinds of things you expect only a cop would have, a cop and not a crook. Now, I figure his father was mixed-up with both of them, but at the time all we knew was that we had boosted his precious pro lock-pic set. We took it for our own use, vowing it would be back before he was home that night. The leather of the thing smelled beautiful. The order and precision of all the picks, the logic and the language behind it, this was a language of adults that both impressed us and frightened us.

"It was Rudy more than me who didn't want to understand. Rudy wanted to act out against his father and to look into his father's world. We turned the lock-pick set over in our gloved hands, smelled the stolen-wallet smell of danger. But the desire for the know-how was pure adrenaline, and it appealed to our frustrated teenage lives. At the time, we were so young, we felt like we had a hundred years on our hands.

"That night was cool and full of the cries of night hawks and bats, and we were in the illegal possession of lock picks to open and start the ignition on any Ford Mercury or Thunderbird, any Lincoln Continental, any Dodge Dart or Plymouth Fury, or any Chevrolet car that caught our fancy.

"Our eyes fell on a '70 Chevrolet Chevelle SS, and we both said, 'V-8, 450 ponies,' and slapped hands.

"It was parked outside a little restaurant, just a diner, with two cars between the front of the place and us.

"Rudy and I hopped inside and started fooling with the ignition. We left the driver's side door wide open, and Rudy's legs sticking out into the parking lot.

"That's when a couple came out of the place and got in the car parked closest to the restaurant window. Rudy saw the couple and pulled the door shut, but when he tried to draw his leg in, his knee caught against the dash and the door caught his foot.

"We were pressed close. He looked into my eyes and gritted his teeth from the weight of the door crushing against his running shoe, counting off the seconds for the people to drive off in their car. But they didn't drive off, they stayed there, kissing and talking together, as if they were going to discuss the whole damn menu and what a miracle it was that there was a diner open at night.

"I remember the sweat breaking out on Rudy's face, and the little fuzz-face of a moustache he had at that age, and I felt like passionately kissing him, even though that was something that neither one of us was wired to ever do. As if he had read my mind, Rudy winked at me, and then he opened his sulky mouth, extended his tongue and licked it across my lips.

"His eyes were black as coal briquettes. The moment hung between us. Then he started the car, pulled in his leg, and gave the Chevelle all the power it had, without caring if the couple in the other car saw us or not.

"We burned out of there laughing, cruised around town, stopped for some ice creams, and called out the windows at every female we passed, asking them if they would like a ride. Finally, we drove out to the Scarborough Bluffs, left the car, and walked along the beach looking for a party on a Tuesday night.

"Of course, there was nothing but the waves breaking against the bluffs and the wind moving in the trees above us.

"We pulled up weeds and whipped each other with them mercilessly, and I whipped Rudy so hard through his T-shirt that he actually started to bleed. Then we climbed straight back up the bluffs, right up the cliff side, still laughing like two wild dogs, and circling around for the car.

"By now the sun was rising, and we hustled the thing back to town, doing a hundred miles an hour on the straight stretches and making plans for another day.

"Finally, we ditched the automobile and walked back to his house.

"When we got in, his mother made breakfast and told Rudy that his father had been home, had rummaged around, left again, stinking drunk and driving the family car. We slapped hands again, thinking we were lucky to have escaped his wrath.

"It was only two days after this that Rudy's father finally made one final and unforgettable appearance, and when he did, it was in Lake Ontario, floating face down near the docks. It was evening. Rudy and I were eating pickle sandwiches by the television when the phone rang. When the police told Rudy's mother, we heard her scream, and we picked up the basement extension line. We heard them ask her if they could drop by and examine the house. Without speaking, we threw everything we could find that Rudy's dad might own, including the contents of a small safe with a tumbler lock and the coveted lock-pick set into a bag and we tore out of there at double speed.

"We hid it in the chimney of my uncle's home ... my uncle who raised Vespa and me after my mother's death. He was a very religious man and prone to rant on about fire and brimstone, but he had sealed that chimney long ago and converted to oil heat, so there was no danger of the thing catching a spark. Rudy wasn't even acting like a kid in mourning. He was just acting like he was doing a chore, a job that could protect his dad. I don't know when Rudy mourned really, only that I spent that whole summer and important parts of the next few years like a brother to Rudy as he followed in the footsteps of his father, going places even I feared to tread. Unlike his father, he didn't brag, he didn't join a gang, and I was the only one who knew anything about it at all.

"The police questioned him that night, and he didn't even let out a whimper, and I know they told him that it wasn't an accident, and whoever got his Dad could get him too.

"The worst part was, I just knew he thought that the car-lock pick combination set we stole was somehow the reason that his dad died. He knew that his father came home that night, looked frantically for the lock-pick set, and then left in his own car, without the ability to either access something or to transfer into someone else's car and escape being followed. Not having the lock-pick set killed him. It was clear.

"When I tried to tell Rudy that his dad was no small fry and could probably start any car he wanted with his bare hands, Rudy just sank deeper into being a crook. Mostly, he was fond of finding places he could pick open and then using the tools he had at hand to crack a safe and make off with the money. He was methodical and liked a ritual and a souvenir at the same time, complete with a little flashlight for dramatic effect.

"Never, never did Rudy get caught, and he did it for years. Many a night I would be working late fixing one of my uncle's stupid American motorcycles and wondering if my friend was going to get caught or kill me for ratting. I never ratted. I think Rudy knew I was in love with him. Since the night he licked my lips, I was in love, and I stayed loyal to him. Even when we duelled with weeds and he whipped each other until we were bleeding, Rudy was always in control, but he always pushed things as far as they would go, and I didn't know if he would someday decide to methodically push me off the face of the earth. We stayed friends. Only one thing bothered me as I was sorting through Rudy's 'Get Well' cards during my convalescence. I was wondering where the photo of my friggin' CZ had gone, where I had put it. The only one I ever took."

"Umm, Ben, there's a lot of blood, and the paramedics are here. Should I let them in?"

"What do you mean 'let them in?'"

"You're naked, Ben. You don't have anything on."

"I'm not ashamed," says Ben. "When you have been in a coma for weeks, nothing can ever embarrass you again."

Wanda jumps up and opens the door, and two uniformed men hurry in with a wheeled stretcher. Ben tries to sit up and winces from the pain.

"A plate fell and it struck him quite hard...."

"Where is the plate, the plate that struck him?" The medics seem suspicious, as if Wanda had struck him with a baseball bat and then called for help.

They lower the gurney and begin lifting Ben onto the surface. There is a clatter.

"Oh, there it is," says one of the medics, holding back a smirk. "It was stuck to his ass."

"He fell off the bed," Wanda adds helpfully, "and must have landed on it."

"Shut up, Wanda, this is embarrassing," says Ben.

"Really, pussycat, you're lucky I was there."

"Was this a domestic?" says the first suspicious paramedic.

"No, it was a decorative," she tells him. "We have other plates for domestic purposes." She picks it up and puts it on the gurney next to Ben.

"I love you, honey."

"I love you too," says Ben. "Please ride in the ambulance with me."

"She can't ride in the ambulance until we get this sorted out."

"Says who?"

"New rule when in suspicion of a domestic dispute."

"But you'll be there. It's not like I can suffocate him or something," Wanda says.

The gurney starts to roll.

"Why can't she come with me?"

"She may not have hit you, but then again, you may have amnesia and not remember that she hit you."

"With a decorative plate?"

"Your blood and hair are on it."

"So are my ass-prints! Wanda?"

"Yes, Ben?"

"The photo?"

"Yeah, the CZ. You only had that one shot."

"It's in a safe, in Rudy's mother's house."

"In a condom?"

"No, in a locked box. And the combo..."

The gurney begins to move down the stairs.

"The combo to the safe?"

"Is written inside your first prosthetic hand, the one you wore when we first met..."

"The big heavy one? It's in a box of my things!" says Wanda. "I'll bring it!"

"Just wear it, baby, just wear it!"

The gurney disappears into the ambulance and the ambulance pulls away, followed in minutes by Wanda in a taxi. The next morning, after being watched by nurses and interviewed by a psychiatrist, Ben is able to go back home. There is a large bandage around his head. Wanda has forgotten to bring him any clothes. Arriving on a small, single cylinder Jawa, Wanda asks Ben to negotiate a blanket from a nurse, and then insists on driving him on the awkward vintage motorcycle back to their home. Ben clings to her back like an infant. When they arrive, the small blanket has blown away and Ben is wearing nothing but a wristband with his health care information on it, and a small green gown that barely falls to his waist. He wraps Wanda's leather jacket around his middle and hurries up the stairs to their second-storey apartment.

"Let's go!" says Ben, transforming himself from hospital escapee to man.

A short quarrel later, they emerge in full leathers, hop onto Ben's fully restored Triumph, swing out into the traffic, and begin weaving through the Don Valley Parkway, into the Gardiner Expressway snarl to Etobicoke, where they park outside a small diner that has become a landmark to Ben. Parked nearest the door, there is a couple kissing passionately in a 1975 Le Mans. Otherwise, the lot is empty. Ben and Wanda order two plates of French toast and a large poutine for Rudy's mother, to go. In a jiff, they are back on the Triumph, the wind blowing through their hair, fried potatoes in the panniers. The feeling of a powerful and well-tuned bike between their thighs once again gives them a sense of control over the mixed-up world around them. They pull in to Betty's house, situated at the top of a meandering suburban hillside. It is surrounded by blossoming flowers, roses, climbing vines, and things that his Rudy's mother has allowed to seed because they are wild, but beautiful, like Ben remembered her boy. Betty seems to have aged little. She invites them in, slamming the door behind them fast enough to nip Wanda in the ass. Wanda hands her the poutine.

"Hello, Betty," says Wanda. "I am Wanda, Rudy's Vancouver friend." Betty asks them if they know Natalia and then seems disappointed that they don't. She asks them if they are in some kind of trouble with the law. "No, we aren't here because of us," says Wanda.

"Well, I can't tell. People in biker jackets always look like they are in trouble."

Ben reminds her that he has fixed the alternator on her car and is Rudy's boyhood friend. As they bend over to set their helmets by the shoes, Betty sees the bandage and Ben's shaved scalp.

"Is that from your accident?"

"No, I'm all healed up now. This is from a plate."

"A brake plate?"

"No, a decorative plate that we had over our bed. It fell down."

"Oh, I get the picture." Betty swings her hips back and forth, miming the movements of a fucking man and then throwing up her arms in fear of falling objects. Finally, she falls limp at the knees with her hand on her imaginary dick, staying that way until Wanda begins to laugh.

Betty straightens up. "Seniors' Theatre Circle," she says with no attempt to conceal her pride. Wanda claps and Betty offers her a gravy-soaked fry.

"It wasn't very funny at the time. I was in the hospital all night, with nurses staring at me."

"They weren't staring at you, they were admiring you."

"They were staring."

"That is true. He didn't bring any clothes," Wanda tells Betty.

Betty puts her hand on Ben's arm. "A very special woman who will love you to your dying day," she tells him. She goes to the refrigerator and gets them some pina colada punch. She returns for a bag of ice for Ben to put on his head.

"Please, I'm okay," says Ben.

"It's bruised," says Betty.

"I know, but they put ice on it all night. I don't want to have a frozen central nervous system. I could go for a beer, though," he says, swinging their familiar old door open with a smile.

"No!" says Betty, reaching out to stop him. "Keep out of the fridge!" Until that moment, Ben had not actually looked in the fridge, but now he glances into the little bulb-lit box with surprise.

A stack of plastic-wrapped fifty-dollar notes extend from the stuffing end of a small turkey jammed in Betty's chiller tray. There is also a large collection of what looks like quails, half-wrapped in paper banknotes and piled against the inside wall of the fridge. There is no sign of beer. Ben quickly slams the door. "I'll take frozen peas, if you have any of those," says Ben, "I just find ice so lumpy."

"Go sit, go sit," says Betty. "I probably have beer somewhere. I don't know."

Ben shudders to think, but Betty ushers him to the living room with Wanda. Once seated, Ben takes a look around the room. It has become much more expensively furnished since the last time he had seen it, —now, the room boasting boasts a wide screen television and a stereo system with four speakers, two on marble stands and two mounted on the wall. A glance at Betty's music collection showed her CD's to be perfectly aligned with the taste of a fourteen-year-old girl. Her bookshelves are full of hardcover travel books, interesting amateur acting trophies, and porn. Betty returns with king cans of Bud and joins them with a smile.

"So, what the fuck do you want?" Betty asks. It occurs only then to Ben that Betty could be carrying a gun as her first late husband often did, hidden and nowhere in sight.

"Just to see you, just to show the old neighbourhood to my gal," Ben answers.

"Bullshit."

"Betty," rescues Wanda, "do you know where Rudy is? We haven't seen him in ages, and Ben misses him, even if he has gone kind of corporate."

"Kind of."

"Your house is nice. Has Rudy been sending you money?" asks Ben, throwing the conversation back into unknown waters once again.

"No, none at all. The little panty-waist, he thinks I'm shacked up with the man who killed his father."

"I have to pee," says Wanda.

"In the basement, just down those stairs," says Ben.

"Oh, thank the sun and stars!" cries Wanda, and she runs to the basement door, crossing and uncrossing her legs.

"There's a new one up here," says Betty, "A new one I put in myself. What a lifelong learning disaster that was! It took me three weeks to get the tile glue off my furniture."

"Just let her go."

"Young lady…" Betty begins to rise, but Ben touches her arm.

Wanda has found the light switch and has raced down the stairs.

"When she has to go, she really has to go," Ben tell her. "So," he continues, "have you seen my uncle since he moved into retirement?"

Downstairs, Wanda has removed the heavy old prosthetic and is peering into it with a flashlight. This is something she has never done before, but Ben has done it, and there, just as he promised, are three sets of digits, down inside the mechanism, sheltered from wear and tear. The safe is exactly where he had told her it would be, next to a bookcase full of legal manuals. Wanda pops the prosthetic back on, using her old, familiar, heavy hand to turn the dial on the box and open the lock. Inside, she find, the manila envelope Ben has mentioned and some books of poetry Rudy had written himself. She slips them inside her sweater and relocks the safe. There is another envelope of writing in a hand different than Rudy's, and she leaves it where it was. She feels a frisson of fear raise the hairs on her nape.

"Never could get that damn thing open. How do you do

it?" says Betty, standing at the top of the stairs. She looks at Wanda credulously.

"It's just my magic hand, it knows, and opens thing compulsively..." says Wanda.

"Knock it off," says Betty. Wanda holds out the heavy prosthetic for the sake of veracity. Rudy's mother walks across the room and feels it. She can also see it is a club. "Nice weapon," says Betty, reaching under her sweaters. "I only have a little derringer 22 caliber, tucked here," she withdraws it, "under my breast." She points it at Wanda.

"You know I ought to slap you for meddling with my things," she hisses.

"I can never slap anybody," says Wanda, raising the heavy prosthetic limb.

"I know it's phoney. It isn't a real hand at all."

"It's in very good condition for its age," says Wanda, attempting a conversational tone.

"The pistol or the hand?" Betty says, glaring at the safe.

"It's a very heavy hand that has knocked the lights out of very many people," says Ben from the bottom of the stairs.

"But she broke into my safe. I haven't been able to break into it ever. That's insult to injury. Hell, that's break and enter. And there's something I want in there."

"Wanda, open the safe."

"Lock picks," says Betty. "Rudy put them in there and I want them out. It's the whole set for Fords from the seventies. He won't even return my calls."

"You can buy those online if he doesn't call back," Ben tells her. His voice grows necessarily comforting, like a trained negotiator in the cockpit with a terrorist. "I'll buy you a beautiful set if we can't find them in there."

"But these ones belonged to my original husband. That, and there's a little 1975 Mustang parked about a mile away, one that is daring me out of my mind."

"We were after the GM set, but they weren't in there at all...."

"Oh, you can have those. My new husband has them already. It's the Mustang," says Betty, "I can't stop thinking about it. I want it. Or at least, to drive it. It just sits there, night after night, like a lost kitten with no mother."

"Did you see a Ford lock-pick set in there?" Ben asks.

"Ben, she's got a gun pointed at my head. All I can do for the moment is pray to heaven and repeat the damn combo."

"I'm sorry," says Betty. She lowers the gun.

"Well, let me show you what the hand can do," says Wanda. Ben switches off the lights.

"Switch those on at once!" scream the two women together. Betty has once again cocked the little pistol.

The prosthetic hand turns the tumbler-lock three times, and the safe falls open. Ben turns on the lights.

"Turn those off," says Betty, and she leans over to Wanda, throwing the arm that was not holding the gun over her shoulders for a moment in an unexpected gesture of reassurance. They shine their flashlight into the opened safe.

"Well, I'll be," says Betty, "letters from Gary. Leave the light on, Rudy, and quit foolin' with it for the love of Pete," Betty snaps.

"My name's not...."

She reaches in and recovers documents that had been written before her husband's death. "These are of great value to me," She stands, smiling. "Your phoney hand did that?" she asks Wanda.

"It can open almost any type of tumbler or wafer lock, simply by sensation," she tells Betty.

"But only in the dark," says Ben.

Together, they climb the stairs back up to the kitchen.

"Well, I'm indebted to you, young lady," Betty says. Then, she opens one of the letters, now crisp with age, and reads to them aloud.

"'My Dear Betty, I know I have been terrible company in the last few months, drinking, pacing, dulling my normally unrivalled sexual performance....' Hum, hum..." says Betty. She skims for a few paragraphs, then picks up her king Can and takes a slug.

"'I have become involved in some extremely serious business affairs. In a very few days, I will be opening the trunk of one Ford Fairview car and depositing the body of a certain member of my circle of criminal acquaintances. Please forgive me, I will be in Reno for several days, then return to you with a great deal of cash. I remain your faithful husband, championship bowler, and loving father to my son. I certainly hope that my recent sexual performance...'" Betty hums aloud once again and sets the pistol by her hip.

"'I hope this to be my last illegal act, but I doubt it knowing me. We must get Babyface out of our business as soon as possible or our whole family could suffer the consequences of his stinkin', finkin' flap and rattin' mouth. Our whole family, right down to our very dear Rodney, the apple of my eye.' Oh, he called him Rodney. His name was Rudy."

"He must have been distracted in those final days," says Wanda helpfully.

"I'll say," says Ben. "He was drinking like a fish."

"'I have gone for a long walk and to feed pepperoni to a guard dog at a nearby printer that can process some government mint quality paper that has fallen into my hands. The counterfeit plates are with Babyface, but Babyface is our snitch. I will only return to pick up my lock-pick set, and then I will be gone. I am leaving this note where you will find it, in a small envelope underneath the basement telephone that the boys always eavesdrop on. If I do not return, you will find the combination series to this safe jammed inside your red bowling shoes at the toe.'"

"Oh, how long does this letter drag on!" says Ben, remembering stealing off with the vital letter at the direction of his boyhood friend.

"Hushy-hushy!" says Wanda.

"A note at the toe of my bowling shoe.... Jesus fuck! I wondered what that scrap of crap was!" Betty picks up the derringer, walks to the refrigerator and brings back two pina coladas on a tray for the couple, a king Can for herself.

"'If I do not return in seven days, I am dead, or I have hooked up with a woman in Reno who is a better bowler, in which case, *c'est la vie*. Goodbye, baby, I have left these poems for you to publish as a sentimental memory of our love.' Poems! I don't want to read any stupid poems! That's what his son was always doing. Tennyson *this*, tennis elbow *that*. I don't have time for such things. And look at how many there are." She holds up the fat stack of papers, and then something catches her eye, and she starts reading again. "'All of them are about you, and I was just joking about a girl in Reno. I love you, baby. You are my heart's desire. I sure hope my recent sexual performance ... *hum hum hum* ... and I hope to be in your arms soon!'"

Betty slams down the king Can and bursts into tears. She tosses the loaded gun onto the floor as if she was tossing a chicken drumstick.

"I have to thank you, thank you, you flower-power hippos, you hippie bike and rollers, you have safe-picked your way into my heart and healed my haunted past. There must be three hundred poems here, and all of them are all about me."

"I'm sorry it didn't work out."

"Are you kidding? His penis was the most dismaying part of his personality, which was flaccid to begin with. My new husband is wonderful, doting, and he doesn't like to bowl. But now I know that Rodney had his lock-pick set on the night of the murder. Which is what snuffed old Gary instead of Babyface and his flapping mouth."

"Rudy, he's called Rudy, Betty. You called your son Rodney."

"We had better go," says Ben. The envelope is starting to migrate out of Wanda's sweater and into the front of her jeans.

"Yes, you had better...." She picks up the little gun again

and points it their way. "But why didn't you tell me you were going to break into my safe?"

"I thought you would be angry at me for wanting the GM seventies lock-pick set."

"Ben, you know me better than your own mother. Who is she? Who is she, Ben?" Betty asks, waving the pistol.

"She's a little Grand Prix that has just been sitting there for months, and I thought..."

"For pity's sake," says Wanda. "When a woman with a pistol invites you to leave her home it's considered good form to do it."

"She's just jealous that your first love was not a woman," Betty snorts.

Ben looks at Betty with surprise. He has no idea she had guessed his boyhood feeling for Rudy had a romantic element.

"Well then, good luck with the Mustang," he tells her.

"And good luck with your muscle car mistress."

Betty sees them to the door and embraces them through their jackets. Ben feels a small shoulder holster under her sweater.

Wanda is beginning to make a crinkling sound as she walks. "It was nice to meet you," says Wanda. "I'm glad you are happy with your new husband."

"Happy? He's the hottest thing at the Theatre Circle, and he's only heating up when we hit home! It is my belief, God rest Gary, that this is the love that God intended me. Otherwise he would not have walked into my life, at such a needy time." She smiles to herself. "A lot of the ladies call him Babyface, because he's so...."

"Gotta go," says Ben and Wanda, and they close the door swiftly behind them.

23.

SINCE THE FALL of the cat, Jackie has been unable to get the idea of a glider out of her head. Why can't Ben and Wanda move to New York? It might be fun. Jackie thinks a fresh start for them all could be the answer. The new garage she has set up with Ben and the magic beginnings of a flying animal glider is louder for her than the chatter of Alaska and Vespa planning the class-action suit against Turner, or the sight of people walking in the streets below, carefully crossing the sidewalks when they approach their building. The newspapers in their hands carrying the story of the mysterious mood-swinging mogul B.F. Turner, and his ultimate suicide by rifle. A long discussion of manic-depressive illness is carried on into the "Living" section. The Turner company has avoided any sort of public discussion of who is taking Turner's place in the conglomerate or how the company will be run following his demise. Shareholders have not been affected, and an official press release will announce the company's restructuring in a few months. Turner's widow is in mourning and tells the press she has moved to their winter place in the British Honduras, which no one has told her is now called Belize. That's it for comments on B.F. Turner.

Where Rudy is in all this is anyone's guess. It is bothering Vespa a great deal and she loses her temper every time Jackie tells her to wonder about something else.

They decide to have a private date with each other and so

they wander into a film about a dog that runs away from its American owners in Greece. Vespa says the film is for children and does not want to see any more. Jackie has never been to Greece and stays after Vespa has run out, then remembers, it was a date. Finally she finds the theatre that her lover has run to. It is not filled with children. United, they kiss passionately through the second half of a Greenaway film in which a wife serves her dead boyfriend's remains to her husband in a feast.

They both feel a little sickened by the equation of their sexual desire with heterosexual cannibalism, but it is the only theatre that is not full of children cheering for a dog. Returning to Olesya's apartment to make love in her bed, they find Alaska is back.

"Well, that somewhat concludes our date," says Vespa.

"Don't change plans because of me," says Alaska, sprawled on Olesya's bed.

Vespa redirects Jackie by drawing. Vespa draws beautifully and has filled pages of Jackie's workbook with pencil illustrations that would look stunning in a gallery.

"These are beautiful," Jackie tells her, snuggling close.

"Thank you, Jackie." Vespa looks up at her and the look conveys she is still in love with Jackie.

But then Alaska comes out from the balcony, deliberately interrupting. "What are you two up to? Oh, sketches ... let me see them...."

"I'm not sure if Vespa is ready to share," says Jackie, but her lover is already looking at Alaska with an overly-open, an approval-seeking gaze.

"Well, they're all right. I'd call them a bit overly formalistic. Definitely masculine."

Instead of telling Alaska to fuck off, Vespa turns to her and asks her what she would change in the design. Jackie grits her teeth. A rubber alligator dressed in Spanish moss falls unexpectedly from the north wall, and Jackie takes the crash as her cue.

"I'll be in the studio," she tells Vespa, without saying how much she'll miss her.

"It's a garage, not a studio," says Alaska. Vespa and Alaska laugh and Jackie feels the old coil of hate surfacing towards Olesya's friend before she remembers the talks about love she has had with Ben.

"Come with me?" Not waiting for a response from Vespa, Jackie picks up her own sketchbook blueprints and heads down to the studio, where she has a cot. There she sets to work adding Vespa's designs to Ben's concept.

It is an aluminum hang-glider in the shape of a cat, using two chainsaw motors and sporting a devised muffler system that not only redirects exhaust but surrounds each engine with insulation similar to the sound attenuation of a recording studio. She works until she hears a tap on the door and Vespa arrives with two coffees. Jackie is in the middle of her welding, experiencing a deep connection with her machines. Startled, she burns a hole in the light-gauge aluminum she has chosen for Vespa's design.

The aluminum has increased in tensile strength through heat treatment and is still incredibly light. It is true to Vespa's sketches, and so she assumes Vespa can see Jackie is true to her love. This connection is not necessarily the case. Preheating with a brazing torch set to a low temperature flame, Jackie transfers to a heavily fluxed electrode set at a DC reverse polarity and only 100 amps. With a nod at Vespa to shield her eyes with the protective helmet Vespa is cradling on her hip, she strikes an arc and begins a near vertical pass in a straight line.

She has shaped the joints by hand so that they fit together snugly. Despite a back-up plate, Jackie begins to burn another hole. Even though she is doing it for Vespa, it causes her to slip into one of the states Vespa finds almost impossible to communicate with.

Jackie has also not greeted Vespa physically, but she cries,

"Oh, ah, baby, poor baby," whenever she burns the aluminum model.

"You are working on my model, but you don't want me here," says Vespa through the shielded helmet. "My spirit but not my person. My muse, but not my..."

"Mouth," Jackie interrupts.

It is not true. She has been hoping Vespa would come and visit her with all her heart. The arc, which is extremely difficult to keep alive at such low amperage, gutters out and dies.

"I think it all looks very moody," Vespa finally says. Jackie snaps off the power to the arc welder and lifts her visor so that their eyes can meet. She smiles at Vespa. "I think it looks very faithful to my love of your original sketch."

"But you don't want me around?"

"Who says I don't want you around? Only you think that." The holder-cable winds around Jackie's foot and she almost trips as she steps toward Vespa. They both look at the machine.

"But maybe it doesn't want you around," Jackie says.

"If it doesn't, then I'll leave you two lovers alone."

"It's not my lover, it's an arc-welding machine." Jackie's eyes travel over it and she brushes some dust from one of its dials, but Vespa recognizes the stroke and is jealous. "Baby, I was hoping you would follow me here. Where have you been?"

"Alaska and I went to every door in Olesya's building, and we also created lists of all the other Turner properties we can find. Olesya's lawyer says that she is interested in helping us with our case. It isn't her speciality, but it looks like it could be a high-profile thingy."

"How's Olesya?"

"She ate an asparagus and apricot energy bar yesterday and a cabbage and cranberry energy bar in the afternoon. Today she drank a mocha-almond rhubarb and bee pollen milkshake and consumed at least half of an algae and wheat germ smoothie."

"Does this mean she's eating?"

"Her lawyer says there may be an amnesia loophole that could get her off the charge."

Jackie loses her self-control. "There is no amnesia loophole. If that little bitch finds some freaky New York State amnesia loophole and walks away from this one...."

Vespa looks at Jackie darkly. "Did I remember to say the work is very passionate? I think I'll go now," she tells Jackie, and she leaves quickly, tossing the helmet with a clatter behind her at the door.

"Well ... we won't let that bother us," Jackie tells the welding machine, and instead of pursuing Vespa, she removes slag with a light chipper hammer, then strikes the difficult arc again and nods into her helmet.

AFTER PHONING FROM Toronto, Ben and Wanda are returning to New York. They are riding in on Ben's rebuilt Triumph 750V Trident and they are having the time of their lives. In a apologetic attempt to win back Vespa, Jackie has traded the use of a rare Gilera Speciale Strada with a yuppy journalist for an exclusive interview with *The Village Voice* describing her amnesia incident and her correspondence with Olesya. It was a bribe and she accepted. She even allows herself to be photographed as the reformed ex-con.

Vespa is ecstatic and in love with her again while Jackie's face is in *The Village Voice* as a previous felon for the sake of Olesya's amnesic loop.

Feeling angry and wild-blooded, she binges on a weekend in an expensive hotel near Lake Placid. Wanda and Ben join them, and they watch the moon rise over artificial water while she holds Vespa's hand on a midnight walk through a members-only golf course in her biker boots. Jackie has now outed herself as a struggling artist who is also a semi-notorious criminal. She has a strung-out, three-sheets-to-the-wind feeling that an FBI agent will make a sound-bite match of her interview style with the way she screamed in the gallery and robbed the bank. She kisses her lover, feeling unable to make a good judgement about anything emotional anymore that is not Vespa's body. She fears that by caving in to the interview, she has just set herself up for a devastating replay of her previous time behind bars.

On the bike, Vespa is thrilled at the speeds Jackie achieves, fully confident in her mastery of the bike and her control and handling of a stranger's machine. Jackie is shocked to realize that she pushes 160 klicks an hour almost the whole way, awed that her passenger is happy and calm.

When they picnic in the mountains, Wanda suggests Ben undress so that the women can sit clothed around the picnic basket like a sexist Manet. The two begin to discuss war and Degenerate art, and Ben mentions Paul Klee as an influential image-maker, complaining he was torn from the walls of Dresden and Düsseldorf by German censors for having a primitivist sensibility. Wanda becomes furious because Klee was quoted as saying that the feminine world was intellectual and emotional with no sense of humour. Ben remarks that Wanda's inability to perceive satire makes Klee right.

Wanda cites Joan Miró's *Person Throwing a Stone at a Bird* as a much more threatening form of Surrealism, and to prove it she throws one. The bird flies away; Ben does not laugh. Vespa and Jackie go for a walk.

"I know that you got this bike for me, for this trip, and I know that you have to give it back."

"I might buy it," says Jackie in a shoot-from-the-hip way, because she has no idea how else she would acheive her plan of chopping the beautiful Speciale Strada and hybridizing it with the power of Gilera track racers without telling the person who lent it to her what she has done. If she does, she will have to pull money out of various places she has stashed it over the years, and if she does it without telling them, it will have to be enough to mend the broken heart of the owner. If she does modify the borrowed bike as she feel compelled to do, and give in to her limited impulse control, it is going to be an extremely expensive social *faux pas*, made worse by her scary new, hot off the press, public persona of Jackie, the Reformed Crook.

"I want you to promise me that you have retired as a criminal," says Vespa, kicking through leaves. "Ben had a brush with that through Rudy long ago, and a lot of people are going to be talking about you. I want you to promise me that you will not steal or rob things anymore. If you can promise this, I think I can save your reputation."

"Okay, I promise," says Jackie, lying. "But what about stealing something like a big, sweet plum sitting on the top of a fruit bowl when no one is around?"

"Jackie, if you promise me, I'll do what I can to salvage your reputation as a serious artist, a person with a vision, a person people trust...."

"No problem with salvage. Together let's go to every salvage place in New York State. We can trade buy an old pickup and go from here to Ohio looking for interesting pieces of bent, distorted, and hopeless warped-out-of-shape steel."

"And aluminum, you have such a sensitive touch with this medium. I can't wait until Ben sees your work on the glider cat."

"Yes, I'm good with it. I could weld a house of beer cans, a canoe out of flashing."

"You drive like my mother used to drive. Very, very fast. When I am with you, I feel like I am rocking in a cradle."

They reach the end of their path and the trail winds off in two directions at once. Vespa looks up at Jackie, her eyes flooded with love.

"Let's turn back, back to the primitivist degenerates."

"Good memory," says Vespa. "I was just going to call them the babes in the woods."

Instead, she takes Vespa in her arms and kisses her, the old trees whispering above them. "I love you," says Jackie.

"I love you more," says Vespa. "I wish you could see how bound to you I am. It's hopeless for anyone else to attempt their charms on me. If you hurt me, I will pull away, but I think it's too late for you to lose me."

Jackie brushes the hair from Vespa's eyes. "I will always love you as you are right now," says Jackie. "Such soft shadows under the trees, you, so beautiful, so desired by others, choosing me."

Vespa smiles. Her eyes admire Jackie's squared jaw, the frightened, tough, unquenchable spirit in her eyes.

They make love, and later, they ride back into New York in a mood of fulfilment and tranquillity, the engines humming beneath them as Vespa and Jackie swap spots. Jackie begins to ruminate on her desire not to lose her life, and something stirring in her about her own mortality makes her think perhaps she isn't the morally corrupt person she used to believe she was.

Vespa continues to push the Gilera Speciale Strada up to 180 klicks, passing and then waiting for her brother and Wanda, who snail along at 125 klicks for most of the journey. The gun up to 150 klicks for a straightaway chase with Vespa as the countryside opens out around them and the wind presses against their faces until they are forced to grin.

They are both ticketed as they enter the suburban areas that surround the city.

"Jupiter and Saturn did play," Jackie tells the police officer, but since she is only a passenger, he dismisses her explanation. They stop and inquire as to whether or not the restaurant has noodles and cheese, and Jackie is tempted to playfully impersonate Olesya's voice and order a wheat germ smoothie. She realizes this is something she must never do.

25

A MAGAZINE HAS TAKEN photos of Jackie's *Didactic Aluminum Cat*, presenting it as work she has done for the Condo Owner's Association of West 108th Street, and Vespa has made the photographer focus on the fine weld work and elaborate interpretation that Jackie has made from Vespa's sketches. The magazine profiles not only Jackie, but a collection of Vespa's other metal work, even publishing a few photos of the stone sculptural works she won custody of after she sued Skip Donkely.

The photos she had shot were all she had left of her stone sculpture, and she had sold the sculptures at the time for the price of a hydro bill. Donkely's name is not used to promote Vespa, and Vespa is not particularly used to promote Jackie.

It isn't everything, but it is a start.

Hang-Gliding Cat is sold to a gliding club, on the agreement that it may be used as a mascot for the Condo Owner's Association, who receive a small gratuity every time someone pays to try the glider and it is seen as a cat ethereally falling through the skies above the club. It soon becomes locally famous, and Alaska acquires a collection of article clippings with photos of the flying machine that she sends to Olesya.

Olesya has been determined to have had a nervous breakdown, after her amnesia argument was rejected by the court. Her lawyer has quit the case after declaring her specialty was real-estate disputes rather than criminal law. Olesya's mental health is being reassessed in an infirmary, which Olesya declares is a Soviet psychoprison.

Her most memorable statement is that if any of the doctors around her were put on Haloperidol for a week they would be twitching, drooling, convulsing, and they would be unable to rest or to sleep.

None of these things have happened to her—she is not even on drugs—and Wanda is furious. She tells Olesya to read about the use of neuroleptic drugs experienced by protesters and dissenters of the Soviet system who were submitted to this abuse. She sends Olesya collections of Natalya Gorbanevskaya's writings, a poet who was imprisoned after protesting the Soviet invasion of Czechoslovakia, and one of hundreds diagnosed with a psychiatric condition when they were only challenging the State.

"Be careful," says Ben, his voice echoing in the workshop. "I've made a bath for the aluminum. I want to braze these pieces together once they are perfectly clean."

Ben and Jackie are working together on a new glider: A folding Squirrel that can carry over four hundred pounds and snaps together like a kit for kids.

"Isolation, that's not good," says Jackie, who has been reading everything Wanda dug up on the topic of totalitarian abuse. Ben nods his head.

"Being out of control of your body is equally frightening, I think," he tells her.

"How do you know?" Jackie asks. "You have never been incarcerated! You have no idea what it is like not to have any control over how people are going to behave towards you. Believe me, in prison, you have to figure out the whole thing by yourself, understand someone else's idea of punishment and reform, and all out of sight of everyone. If they kick you, if they hurt you, if you hurt yourself, it is out of the view of the bourgeoisie. There is an eye on you all the time, but it is a punitive eye, and an eye that judges the concealment of your spirit as a sign that you are rehabilitating."

"Are you saying people are born with destinies, or are you saying people are born free and then they fuck-up?"

"I would never say that we are born fated. I think that is a philosophical concept that serves the State. And I don't want to get into one of your theological dialogues, or your uncle's 'existence of God' arguments that rattle around in your head. I am how I am, and yes, I fucked-up, but unless you are very wealthy and well-connected, the time in a prison is generally considered a descent into Hades, not a rehabilitation. It's a retaliation for the abuse other people in society have heaped on the warders. And to those who appeal for help, many people will say, 'Well, it's not supposed to be the Hilton, you know. It's meant to deter.' As if society is not creative enough to come up with productive ways to deal with people who break laws, besides trying to break them in spirit."

Ben gingerly sets down the piece of metal he is rinsing before applying a weld. "Trapped inside my body all that time, I made connections to freely associated ideas, incarnated my own primitive images, and touched the places where the spirits within our mind ignite life. Because I had nothing much else to do, lying there presumed vegetative, I travelled around in my unconscious and, over time, I got to know it like a taxi driver knows a town! When I began to speak again, you were in my garage, doing a check on my brake mechanism like a real pro. But I really resented you when you looked at my spasms and they made you discuss me like a damaged machine. In front of my face. I wanted to throw you all out on your asses, to tell you the truth."

"I saw that, Ben, and I feel ashamed. I was uncomfortable because of your physical condition. I'm sorry," Jackie says.

"You were horrified! My convulsive movements made you feel like I was not 'all there' as people like to phrase it. That's a scary feeling of not being in control."

"Maybe because some of them you now admit were hostile

and aimed at me. Maybe you picked that up. But I also saw grace in you. I actually wondered why society so often takes real battles, like yours, if you'll forgive me, like mine, and hides them behind walls. I wasn't in the best condition myself at that time if you recall. But I didn't call you a broken machine!"

Ben laughs, shakes his head, and picks out a brazing rod for the aluminum.

"I didn't know you would recover like that. It was different than anything I had seen before."

Ben takes his aluminum, and dips it in a pickle liquor bath, then rinses it, and repeats until the surface is perfectly clean. Like Jackie, he is methodical about good work.

"Where art seeks form, it finds the human spirit," says Jackie.

"Who's that a quote of?"

"Me." She starts up her grinder so that conversation is impossible.

Both Ben and Jackie have spent whole days working together in near silence. Neither one will tell the other that they have been tormented by images of their work partner's suffering each night as they sleep.

Jackie lets the grinder moan down to a stop and consults the blueprints she and Ben have drawn together. Next to them lies a newspaper with Olesya quoted in the middle section. She is drifting out of interest to the public.

"We should get her a proper lawyer," says Jackie.

"Why?"

"Ever been struck on the head and ended up rigged and framed for something you don't even remember doing wrong?"

"I guess a bike accident is like that. I've never been to jail," Ben says.

"Bullshit," says Jackie.

"Never. Rudy and I must have stolen a dozen cars at least and parked them in unexpected places. We never sold them. Never bragged. Never caught. But there was more. Rudy used to safe-crack, break locks and find his way in. Never made a mess. Never got caught. Always acquired the most interesting things."

"Isn't Rudy Vespa's old flame? The one who is up with B.F. Turner's Conglomerate? The sellout Rudy?"

"Same. But he's left behind some very interesting scraps, which is pretty sloppy, and not like him at all. I don't think he thought I was going to pull through my coma with my wits. Either that or he thought I would never challenge him. I am."

"What do you have?"

"Some papers I safe-cracked from his deceased father's safe in the basement of his old family place. Went in and had a tea with his mom."

They look together at the envelope Wanda had earlier hidden down her pants.

"So, Rudy has never been caught?" Jackie asks.

"Over a hundred break and enters, over thirty grand theft autos. And something to do with the benign presence of the new man his mother married after he lost his father."

"Who was that?"

"The man who killed his father. Big-time criminal. Police fink. Protected. Same man his father set out to kill. Night of deceit that took a twist. Mama never had a clue."

"Was Wanda interested in this stuff?"

Ben cautiously pours a collection of receipts, frayed-looking, and time-stained papers and notes across the table.

"Nah, she was hoping it would be money."

"What is it?" Jackie turns away, displays disinterest, the opposite of what she is feeling.

"Mementos. Even if he didn't leave with the money, he always left with something of value to the place he broke into. Receipts, chequebooks, must have bugged the life outta them. The only thing I wanted in this package was the photo of my '65 CZ, unmangled." He shows Jackie the photo, evidence of Rudy's affection.

Jackie smiles. "Were they mementos or a collection of blackmail devices? Bombs waiting to go off?"

"All of it, certainly. All of it he could have blackmailed the owners with. You can see he stole fudged books and good books because the real accountancy was always in the safe. But as far as I can tell, I don't think he ever blackmailed anyone. Of course, they are now something that Rudy could be blackmailed with himself."

Jackie turns to the pile on the table, examining the scraps Ben has poured across Olesya's spread in the newspaper.

"Yeah, fudged versions of the books and the real accounts, dated the same days: 1997, 1999, 1991, 1995, all paper-clipped together. Any auditor got their hands on this, he could have put the whole operation out of business, and there are dozens. And other kinds of insider files and records of company tactics, secrets and tricks of the trade, and notes on the competing companies, some of which were stolen by transferring secretaries and paying people off."

"Dirty business school from the ground up."

"I don't know if it was over his head or what, but he certainly was primed when he walked into Turner's office. Vespa always said Rudy was bad to the bone, but he couldn't have been that bad if he never capitalized on this."

"Probably afraid."

"I guess....." While Jackie looks on, Ben scoops the material back into the envelope and puts it into the bottom of a tools drawer, shrugging in a way that means he does not want to discuss his relationship with the owner of its contents. He sweeps the newspaper clean again.

"What do you think Olesya meant by 'psychoprison'? You think she's alright in there?"

"Ask Alaska. She sees her often enough. It's not as bad as she describes. She's not drugged, but I'm sure she's not all right. The last time I got out of the can, I was so surprised at how isolated people are on the outside because I had been so lonely inside the walls. And I really started to think about it. I mean, we need our communities or we're nothing. Not cliques, not destructive little cults, but the unity of contact and dialogue with many ideas, many people. We may have our own power of one, but a person can become divided on the inside, and even once they are free, divided they will fall."

"So, what's 'wall therapy' all about?"

"A psychoprison term for isolation."

"Fitting, but not too poetic. I suppose that could mean a long time, looking."

"It was a punishment they used when someone had done something that angered them. They left them alone to look at the walls."

"Yeah, and sometimes they were wet-wrapped them, and insulin-shocked, and...."

"Ben, I read it same as you. I just don't want to think about it all day long."

"I thought you were thinking about cats and flying squirrels all day long."

"No, all night. It's just that, reading the testimonies.... "Well," she sighs," torture is wrong. We should get Olesya a decent lawyer."

"We don't have money for a decent lawyer, remember?"

"I always have the way to get the money," Jackie growls. She starts the grinder again, bringing the conversation to a close.

26

THE PLACE BEN AND JACKIE have chosen is a large, picturesque gun shop and gallery in a quiet little town along the Hudson. The sublime hill that approaches the town is broken by a scenic cliffside and its drop of two hundred feet. Next to the gun shop is a glass and lens-making factory. A jog over is a storage container company. The roof the gun shop, factory, and storage container company share is a flat piece of pitch over two-thousand-feet long. It is a superb landing spot. All three are surrounded a ten-foot fence—except at the front—and which is in no way scalable, thus denying access to the roof. Next to the storage company is a junkyard; any unexpected wind could set the glider down hard enough inside its gates to usher in terrible injury.

The night is very dark. Clouds have moved across the moon, and the two friends assemble the Squirrel in near silence, their preferred method of respect for each other's private thoughts. The glider snaps together easily. Every surface has been machined within a hair of their own preplanned specifications. It is a sort of dance, each of them dressed in clothes that are as close-fitting as possible, that allows the cool air, which is steady at five knots, to pass through the first layer of weave, while their sweat vaporizes through the bottom weave, absorbing their anxiety.

Jackie snaps the airspeed indicator next to her right shoulder and puts on the yellow night-vision goggles that she insists improve her vision. Ben, riding shotgun in a sling behind her, insists on infrared to direct the Squirrel.

The dark surface of the gun shop has absorbed more heat than the surrounding surfaces and stands out to him in radiating thermal colours like a candle in the dark. There is less than a mile between the shop and the cliff. Jackie will have to crab into the wind in order to maintain a straight line, and then land the Squirrel as soundlessly as possible on an unknown surface.

Her entry to the landing spot must be within twenty feet of their chosen target, and her wind drift correction must be perfect before the final landing. There will be no opportunity to run a test flight over the area and see if it is suitable. If the gun shop has money inside, there is nothing else Jackie needs to know. She expects to bounce once, and then come to a rolling stop with less than two hundred feet to manoeuvre within.

Her only brakes will be Ben's running shoes, provided he does not forget or fall out of the glider. She has adapted rudders onto the Squirrel and a simple aerobatic design that is her only defense against crosswinds, downdrafts, updrafts, wind shear, and the possibility of going into a spin. She cannot handle the Squirrel if it should invert.

She cannot foresee any of the usual turbulence caused by building obstruction, and even though Ben claims it is thermally glowing with absorbed solar heat, she cannot imagine the roof itself causing her difficulty as she sets down.

The wind has raised itself to eight knots by the time their craft is ready. Her airfoil angles have been designed with a minimum of camber, and, like a real squirrel, with a dependence on tail drag, so that they can avoid pitching, with an emphasis on stability above speed. The horizontal tail is covered in long phoney fur that Ben has combed and combed so that it responds effortlessly to the wind. It is equipped with a rudder. The two kick off and are airborne over the town. Jackie does not look down at the escarpment below her, only at the little sleeping city she is approaching as her craft is buffeted by winds.

As they move toward the target, Jackie makes a sharp turn to battle a draft blowing her away from their landing. She crabs in at a very slow airspeed, requiring an angle that frightens Ben. "Nose up! Nose up!" he shouts when she finds she is higher than she wants to be. Jackie noses down.

Moving once again in the same direction that the wind is pushing her, she is suddenly much closer to the landing surface than her drop in height had indicated. She lowers one wing, then straightens seconds from impacting with the roof, and not on a ninety-degree angle.

She ups two of her three squirrel flaps in the direction that the wind is pushing her and lowers three on the other side. At the same moment, Ben moves the rudder away from the crosswind, causing a levelling effect as the glider hits the roof. It is still aiming at the corner of the gun shop, bouncing in a diagonal instead of straight on, quite different from the landing they had calculated. Ben drops his feet while Jackie pulls an emergency lever that raises the Squirrel's tail in the air, breaking wind.

After a few more bounces and a terrifying roll, the thing comes to a stop within inches of the edge of the roof, which is trimmed with foot-high decorative flashing.

"Holy crap!" says Jackie, and Ben exhales a sigh of relief. He moves his legs, pushing the wheeled Squirrel backwards, and when they are safely away from the precipice, they jump out of the beast and snap the assembly into parts.

Together, they move with the sort of efficiency grim fear of capture has put into their limbs.

Ben rappels down the inside wall, against the bricks and inside the fence, and finds the window he wants to enter by. It is not set with an alarm, as no one in their wildest dreams would enter the gun shop of this small town, especially through this particular route. He pops a frame and then opens it by reaching inside. They already secured a blueprint of the heritage building's layout, while Alaska, Vespa, and Wanda were busy obsessing about Turner developments in New York.

Masked like a Wild West cowboy, Ben walks through the empty halls, looks into the windows of closed rooms, and finds that there is a small shooting range, reinforced for sound, while the rest of the floor is dedicated to museum-type displays of arms.

He finds displays dedicated to firearm manufacturers such as Remington, Winchester, the Springfield rifle carried by Union soldiers during the Civil War, and shrines in devotion to Samuel Colt's early revolver and the Horace Smith and Daniel B. Wesson pistol. He descends a set of stairs and is suddenly surrounded by displays of contemporary automatic weapons.

He has struck a showroom, although it still has that small-town museum feel, complete with its Buffalo Bill trimmings. Ben hurries down the steps, which creak as heritage buildings will do, and arrives at the first floor.

A large sign is directing him to a basement shooting range, but the first floor is dedicated to only the sale and pawning, and not shooting, of guns.

He opens the tumbler-type lock on the door of an office with a Confederate flag. With twice the speed that Rudy demonstrated to Ben, even in his most agile and adolescent crazes, Ben finds a safe by a large oaken desk and kneels down. Using the putty and explosive compound refined by Rudy, he blows open a seam around the lock mechanism. To his partial surprise, the entire gun shop does not explode in a fireball of gunpowder.

Reaching in with gloved hands, he taps the door open on its hinges and withdraws printed payroll accounts, as well as a stack of money received for transactions throughout the week, each set into deposit envelopes ready to be dropped into the bank the next day.

The remainder is in bills from twenties up, and Ben suspects it has to do with the pawn business and not the over-the-counter trade. He bags everything and runs past the pawn area where there is a camera. He draws in a sharp breath as he comes unexpectedly face to face with a life-size poster of an NRA recruiter holding her Colt .45 like it is a jaunty toy. She is looking so intensely peppy that he assumes at first she is a nightwatch employee who is tripping on dangerous drugs. When he realizes it is just a poster behind the window glass of a door, he composes himself, hurrying up the remainder of the creaking stairs.

Ducking past a mesh of camo-netting designed for ambience, he re-emerges through the window and pulls himself back up to the roof.

Looking supernaturally calm, Jackie has completely dismantled the Squirrel and wrapped it with ropes inside a tarp. He helps her lower it quickly onto the lawn. It rests behind trees and hedges. It remains there, waiting silently while they complete their descent.

Ben is the last to come down. Jackie has already charged the engine of a postal van in the front of the building and loaded it with gear when Ben arrives.

Together, they drive the van to the edge of town, where they have parked a '73 Firebird on a utility road and out of sight. Ben claims he borrowed the Firebird from a friend. Piling the gear inside, they push the responsive little muscle car to a comfortable 150 klicks. Their adrenaline drains now, as the rosy fingers of dawn begin to poke through the horizon.

"How much is in there?"

"I don't know," says Ben irritably. "Did I have time to count?"

"Do you think we're doing the right thing?" asks Jackie. Ethical issues nag at her priorities these days. She worries that the town will not find their postal truck and people will not receive their letters on time. She worries that someone who works at the glass-and-lens shop next door will not be able to park because of police.

"Of course, we are doing the right thing. Didn't we agree to get Olesya out on bail, even get her a lawyer, and get her out of the joint?"

"Since when do you call it 'the joint?' You've never been in jail, so since when do you call it 'the joint?'"

"That's what everybody calls it," says Ben.

"I hope you are never in the joint. I feel incredibly guilty already."

"I am an adult and I made an adult decision," says Ben.

"Adult? Your face was lit up like a kid. If anything happens to you, it's all my fault."

"Nothing will happen. Thank you. And yes, I'd like to avoid that, too. In the American justice system, while I am culturally a European, I am a Black man in their eyes," says Ben.

"I have asked you to promise that I am responsible if anything goes wrong," says Jackie.

"Jackie, while I appreciate your political sensitivity, it's just that kind of self-loathing, white- people awkwardness that really gets me down. I appreciate your awareness, but right now, the reported number of giant squirrels landing on American gun shops is hovering at only one. Can the guilt for God's sake, and let's get on with the task," says Ben.

"Count the money," she tells him.

"Seventy thousand, more or less," he tells her.

"That's all?"

"That's all? What do you mean, *that's all?*"

"I mean, that's a lot, but if they're pawning I guess they have to.... What kind of a business was that place running? Loan sharking, what?"

"They had a lot of vintage weapons in there, but it looked like a cross between a museum and a supermarket. The kind of place you would stroll around and load up on sentimental firearms for your loved ones."

"So, they still do a brisk turnover. So that's not bad. I thought we would still have to sell our mothers."

"I don't have a mother."

"Okay, neither do I. Sell our motorcycles maybe. Or borrow or whatever other people do. Seventy grand. Do you think we can park this thing back at your friend's house before they get up to go for work?"

"I'm sure of it," says Ben. "For one thing, they aren't my friends. For another thing, it's been sitting there for weeks."

Jackie accelerates the old Firebird into high gear.

Back at the studio, Wanda is looking for the man she fell in love with, the man she kept vigil for during his coma, the man she feels guilty about screwing around on while she was cloistered in the World of Shoes. But the place is almost empty, as if an evacuation has occurred.

Many of his most-loved tools are still there, as are Jackie's welding kit, her jacket, and her things. Forlorn, Wanda begins to cry, feeling this is a sign that Ben has left her for Jackie. She tries to reason with herself. She reminds herself that Jackie is a lesbian who once asked her why anyone would want to sleep with something that looks like a board with a hot-dog nailed to it. Then she thinks of all the time the two of them have been spending together, and she moans, sinking to the floor against a red tool cabinet on little wheels. Wanda wants to kick it with her foot. She wants to knock it to the other end of the workshop, or throw it over on its face. She wants to dump everything inside it on the floor. Ben and Jackie have been very careful not to tell anyone else about their plans. That includes Wanda.

She looks in drawers. They are full of plans for models, animated and not, gliders and metal imaginings that walk. They are wonderful. She could not think of two more upstanding people than her missing friends.

But why is Wanda left here, left out, seated on the floor of a glorified garage?

Who is she besides Ben's companion, Besides the vigil at his bedside? Where has her purpose gone, after the last spoonful of yogurt has been pushed away?

Alaska is trying to help her sell her writing, trying to push her film and art critiques, what is Ben doing? She moans, mechanically clumsy, an intellectual, a woman with a big brain, a woman with a half-finished Communications degree and no one to communicate with.

She pulls open the bottom drawer, pulls out an envelope and pours the contents across her knees. She stares for a moment, then separates each piece of material and examines it, as if she is an auditor for the government. It is the most incriminating collection of documents she has ever seen. She has never seen it before. Before her is Rudy's fucked-up adolescence and early twenties, represented in every memento from that time that he ever felt passionate enough to keep.

Clearly, he was a passionate burglar. It is her answer. And it is powerful enough to restore Wanda to her senses, because Rudy, who the newspapers now say is the new CEO of Turner Consolidated, is the key man in her campaign to win money for the Condo Owners at every development Wanda has researched, where there are universal complaints.

Now Wanda has something private, something powerful, something that will put her back in control of events in her life. Wanda is going to bite back hard, and Wanda has something called "threat of disclosure" to attend to.

27

NATALIA IS WORRIED about the people in her building. They are all trying to sue Turner, and if the legal action is successful, they will destroy any plans to destroy the building and end up winning their legal right to live in a luxury palace that is about to fall down. She wants Rudy to marry her, and she wants him to come back to work before the company gets out of hand.

Camelia came to New York and asked to see her, and when they met at an upscale restaurant for coffees, Camelia pretended to drop a spoon and then ran her hand up Natalia's leg.

As the day wore into evening, Camelia took her to a dinner club where they sat together watching a production of *Hamlet* expressed by watercolourists on large flip sheets of paper. It appealed to Camelia's boardroom sensibilities, but Natalia did not like. Later, she took her to a bar and invited her to dance to a song called "Suck My Kiss." It embarrassed Natalia, as she was being trained for ballet and she did not know how to move her body to the time of that music. As far she could tell by Camelia's cues, rubbing together was the way to boogie down. Camelia ended up getting very drunk on Manhattans—so drunk that Natalia had to drive her to her hotel.

Since it was an expensive-looking place, she left the people at the desk to walk Camelia up to her room, telling them that she had been drinking bourbon with dry vermouth and cherry bitters, and should be left with a fresh pitcher of water in her room.

Clearly, Camelia could not handle everything Rudy was telling her to do. As far as Natalia could surmise, Camelia was experiencing a breakdown and needed bedrest more than deskwork and communication by long-distance phone.

She writes a short letter telling Rudy to come back to New York and be with her to take proper command of Turner before Camelia collapses. She asks him whether he was ever coming back to take on his responsibilities or if he was going to live in the forest forever. Now that she doesn't have to drive anybody home, she pours herself a drink, and settles in for a speed-read of *Hamlet*. It was quite a bit like the watercolourists are performed it, and now she had abstract images to attach to the prose. Her email *gongs*. As she suspects, Rudy is up on a Saturday night.

> Better stop short than fill to the brim.
> Over-sharpen the blade, the edge will soon blunt.
> Amass a store of gold and jade,
> and no one can protect it. Claim wealth and
> titles, and disaster will follow.
> Retire when the work is done.
> This is the way of Heaven.

It is a quote from Lao Tzu's *Tao Te Ching,* one of the oldest books in his collection. It isn't right for him to be quoting it, all by himself in a tree. It is the sort of thing people read to each other in encounter groups, or after yoga, or in bed when they were cozied up to the one they love. How can he know what is going on in New York?

She has been trying to tell him in quick emails, but there is no way to fill him in on the events that are affecting their future if he is not there. Her Manhattan, set in a slopped pool of bourbon, begins to slide away from her at her desk. With the grace of the dancer she will someday be, she catches it, wondering why gravity is such a problem in her home.

Camelia finds a letter the next morning by her email remote requesting a meeting with her in New York. It's from "a woman who was once a female friend of Rudy." She assumes it to be Natalia, forgiving her for her drunken behaviour by pretending that Camelia is not yet in New York but only just arrived.

She writes back playfully announcing that she is now in New York and invites the "female friend" to meet her in the cocktail lounge of the hotel where she is now staying.

A few hours later, after a two-hour shower alternating between hot and cold taps, Camelia is made-up, dressed attractively, hesitating over lipstick, and eating Tylenols like they are jelly beans.

She paces the restaurant waiting for the arrival of Natalia. She has just taken a seat and ordered a tea when a noisy motorcycle parks outside. A piratey-looking woman strides in and calls her name.

Camelia is glad she subdued the lipstick and feebly raises her teacup in a salute. Wanda walks to her table, sits down with an envelope in a hand that to Camelia's bugged-out eyes does not seem real. But then, nothing about this woman seems real. "I have to be fast," says Wanda. "I wouldn't give the valet my keys."

"I know how that can be," says Camelia. "I don't even remember how I got back here last night."

"Silence!" says Wanda.

"Are you with Natalia?" asks Camelia, not one to be daunted by a gruff manner and a scuffed jacket.

"Is she a West 108th Street tenant?"

"That's where she lives, but I was hoping..."

"Yes, Natalia is one of us."

"Uh-huh," says Camelia, thinking "one of us" is a euphemism for queer. Then, because no one else is saying anything, she adds, "I was hoping as much. I was thinking I may be one of those as well."

"All we want to know now is where to contact Rudy."

"Why?"

"Because he is not doing his job, and because our lawyers want to speak to him at once."

The valet is tapping on the window.

"This is a legal matter now?" Camelia asks.

"You don't have to be involved in any of this. It's Rudy's problem. We are all past the point of no return on this one, and he can't hide forever. Look what's happening to us all."

"I am entering quite a big decision in my life around this area. But certainly, I know when my feelings have been stirred." She glances shyly at the saucer. When she looks up, Wanda's hand is outstretched, palm up, open. Feeling lonely, Camelia takes it.

"Rudy, where is he?" Wanda persists.

Camelia scribbles an email address and some coordinates on a napkin. She is hung over. She notices the napkin is made of linen. She passes it to Wanda, who releases her hand.

"Thank you," says Wanda, and she smiles. Camelia realizes that the gentle hand that embraced hers was made of rubber rather than skin. Outside, Wanda mounts the chrome-polished bike, winks at the valet, pulls into traffic, and is gone.

Camelia goes back up to her room to have a nap and pack her things. She leaves a note on Natalia's machine, telling her she had a very nice time, but she is not yet sure if she is "one of them," and that Natalia's friends are certainly rougher trade than she thought they would be.

The next morning, Natalia rises and reads Rudy's quotation once again. She thinks to herself he is being influenced in the wrong direction by these great poets, because he knows so little about what is going on and is not with her in the big city. Natalia writes, "Awareness bias in *Taos*," mistakenly encrypts it, fires it off, and goes to her balcony to meditate in her garden of small rocks. Some of them have slipped from the edge. Entertaining Camelia has been a long, tuckering ordeal.

In his treetop perch, where he has only just started considering reuniting with Natalia in a low-profile way and adapting himself slowly, through therapy, back into society, Rudy receives an anagram that reads: "Beware Assassination."

28.

FOOT-LONG GUS and Swan have been in email contact with Wanda, and they are coming to see New York. They are bringing a baby. It is Swan's. It is the five-month-old infant of their friend Celeste, born during a past-life regression session with the famed Dr. Tetons Popair. The men are enjoying carrying the little Arnica Montana everywhere they go. They are looking greatly forward to seeing SoHo, Little Italy, Bowery, the small theatres of the Lower East Side, the large theatres of Manhattan, The West Village, The East Village, The Gay Village, the Greenwich Village, the Flatiron building, The Chelsea Hotel, The Manhattan Bridge Arch, The Chrysler Building, The American Museum of Natural History, The Empire State Building, The Hamilton Fish Park, and all the islands and ferries that are available. They have obviously never been to New York before. Wanda tells them that it may be difficult for them to stay at Olesya's, but that there are many hotels in the area, since the baby is too young for a youth hostel and they are too old. The three visitors arrive on a Wednesday, and book into the Carlton Arms hotel on E 25th Street, with a four-poster bed and a room that is decorated with a fresco of two women making love. It is not what they wanted, but it is queer and the only vacancy they can find. The halls have also been decorated by local muralists, and the stairwell is painted to look like a sky, with floating hats and chairs decorating the blue.

They proceed on Thursday morning to the Metropolitan Museum of Art. Edgar Degas and his paintings of girls engaged in ballet studies bewitch little Arnica and send her into fits of squeals. Gus believes in having a disciplined orientation from an early age, while Swan is of the mind that if Arnica is excited by the images, she has a right to express her reactions, even if they are louder and in a sharper octave than the hushed sounds around her. Swan takes her into the men's room and changes her wet pants so that his childrearing principles will not be shot down by his oblivious boyfriend.

Gus is gazing at *Woman with a Parrot* by Gustave Courbet, which Cézanne had a photo of in his wallet, and is wondering why it had pissed off Émile Zola. He moves on to *Les Demoiselles de village*, which Courbet divided into sky and hill. Within the composition are three well-dressed women; one holds a parasol, and one looks on as the third talks and extends her hand to a girl with bare feet who appears to be a fishing rod. She has a large hat pushed away onto her back. He is charmed, and when Swan comes back, he only assumes he has been busy looking at something else. As far as Gus knows, Arnica is dry throughout the visit.

As far as Gus is concerned, Arnica sucks joyfully on soy milk in a bottle, and later an entire infant formula refill, not noticing that Swan dashes her off for three diaper changes in less than an hour.

A tactile infant, Arnica causes Swan to be spoken to twice by security people when he allows her to reach out and touch a seventeenth-century painting of a *Madonna with Child*. He is spoken to again in another room for letting her touch an eighteenth-century painting of a *Madonna with Child*, when he was, in fact, simply leaning forward to inspect. He begins to panic, afraid that they will be thrown out before they even enter the nineteenth century, and realizes Gus is a hundred years behind him, looking at a seventeenth-century French sculpture of *Leda and the Swan*.

In the subway, Arnica is extremely quiet and at ease with the crowd. Later, they find a man's wallet in her carrier. They argue over whether they should give it to a police officer or drop it in the mail to the last listed address. They decide to put it in a bubble-wrapped envelope. Swan uses a tissue to pick the wallet up and his shirt sleeve to purchase the stamps for fear of leaving fingerprints, as the wallet is so far only covered with baby fingerprints and those of the previous owner.

Because she is drooling anyway, Swan uses the baby as a handy source of saliva for wetting the stamps, while Gus pens in the address of the police station nearest to the subway stop where they found it.

All this takes the better part of an hour, and the two men are tired when they at last visit the area of town near where their friends are staying. They stop for a drink at a bar with a beautiful umbrella-filled terrace out front, and then stop to look at shoes. The shoe salesperson is extremely pleased to have a baby in the store and begins to play with her. Gus brings her out of the baby carrier and lets the shoe salesperson hold her.

"I am going to have a child," he tells the couple, and then rests his hand on Gus's tattooed arm. "When Wanda returns, she will marry me," he adds, and puts a package of shoelaces in the baby's fingers.

Arnica, who slips her pinky into the ring hanging from the shoe salesperson's nose, pulls down with all the strength of her new-found muscular abilities. The salesperson screams, and Gus disentangles them. "I think you would be a wonderful father," says Gus, and he lets the shoe salesperson jiggle the baby in his arms. "Wanda who?"

Swan seizes the moment to duck out the door and inspect the small street-level gallery that neighbours the World of Shoes. There seems to be no one in the gallery when he enters, only a wall painted a ragged pale lake blue, with a new peephole drilled in the centre. He looks for art on the walls, and then notices a number of photos of what seem to be a naked young woman posing next to stone carvings of herself. She poses in the same position as the sculptures but curves her body in a sensuous way around them. She barely looks sixteen, but there is something provocative about her face. The signatures under the photo collection say Skip Donkely, but Swan realizes with a gasp that the model is Vespa, or a very young look-alike, and surely underage. A man in a blue sweater emerges from behind the wall and greets Swan, rubbing his hands together and smiling.

"How much are these?"

"Those are not for sale," says the man, "but if you want something of this sort....."

"Do you have others with girls so young in them?" says Swan in a state of dismay.

"That depends on how much you are willing to pay," the man answers.

Swan feels the breath retreat from his throat. "You have other snapshots of underage girls?"

"I can possibly come by some for you," says the man, "and depending on your special area of interest, they are not all inexpensive."

"I am interested in this girl here," says Swan. "She looks so very much like a friend of mine, very much like her, a friend I met here."

"You are not from here?"

"Not really," says Swan.

"One is either born here or from some other place. No one is 'not really.'"

"I come from up North.."

"A Canadian?" says the man. There is a choked menace to his voice that Swan does not understand.

"I suppose so," says Swan. "I'm from the territory that straddles northern Ontario and the north of Québec, so I am First Nations, as well as what we call Québecois, which is derivative of..."

"A Canadian! Grave robber! What a monstrosity! The way they sell off their own Indigenous people! They wanted me to sell those bad things in here! I wouldn't do it! I told them no, no, no!"

"Look, I just told you I identify as Indigenous ... I think you are a bit confused."

Swan takes another look at the naked image of the girl that so resembles Vespa. He commits the signature to memory. "I wouldn't walk back into your shop if it was raining rocks," Swan tells him and turns on his heel.

The gallery owner returns to his chair behind the faux-finished wall. "Dammit," he mumbles to himself. "Lost another sale."

When Swan re-enters the World of Shoes, Gus has taken Arnica back into his arms and is telling the young man that he must be mistaken. "Please, the woman you are describing sounds like a very good friend of mine, one who would never engage in such adolescent-type antics! You have met my friend and you are fantasizing."

"You will see, when her belly swells out. Wanda is pregnant with my shoebox baby child...."

"A look-alike!" says Gus, and he storms out of the store.

"It's about Vespa?" Swan asks in the street. Arnica Montana begins to cry. Gus has put the snuggly on wrong. He hands her to Swan, who finds that she is wet.

"No, not Vespa, Wanda. I have never been so insulted in my life."

"Are you certain?" says Swan. "Are you sure an insult to someone else is more serious than one to yourself? Where do you find all the extra indignation?"

The two men cross the street and return to the bar, ordering a plate of curried rice while Swan changes Arnica and composes himself in the mirror. There is no time to wonder who he is, why he is Swan. Gus has been insulted. Gus and his world of untouchable European art. He does not know what Gus is going to say when he comes back out with the baby girl. She is laughing again and reaches out to pull the waitress by the hair.

"I must be suffering from some sort of an infatuation with Wanda. I defended her honour in a rage. Did you see it, Swan? That young man said he had had sex with her. And I was ready to fight him like a cock. I must be infatuated with her. I feel like I am," Gus tells him, adding, "because of how we met. And you know what I think about women."

Swan hands the infant to the waitress. "Do you mean you are in love with her?"

"I didn't say that. Did I say that? I am not in love with her. Like a painting, like a portrait, an infatuation, there is something, there is something I need to discover."

He takes Swan's hand before he can pull it away. "I am not in love with her. I am not interested in sleeping with her. I want to be with you for the rest of my life. I will never tire of desiring you."

"Even if I am a Canadian? Even if I am an American? Even if I refuse to be either one? Even if I have to walk through life with three feet?" asks Swan.

"Pardon me?" says Gus. He smiles for a moment, then takes the baby back from the waitress, who returns with two bowls of ice cream.

"Of course, Swan, I will always love you. But I am extremely distracted by a boyhood memory. It was my first real job. I rescued a girl with one hopelessly frozen hand, lying like marble in the snow. It must have been that museum. It's made me mad. They have a hundred statues of naked men and women with their noses chipped off their faces next to dinner plates with aroused men chasing each other around and around and around. Who am I in love with? Who was Leda in love with? A swan. You know I believe that we are destined, a closed logic system, and it makes you angry. But I am in love with you. Look how strong this girl is growing."

"Even if I have to think with three heads? You are so stupid. Leda was in love with a bird. What kind of a culture creates a story that would eroticize this? It's vulgarization of a beautiful myth, and you stared at that sculpture for half an hour."

"In a few years, she will walk into that shoe store and demand shoes for foot-long feet."

"Do you think she's going to be a ten?" asked Swan.

"An eleven, a thirteen ... the largest size for women."

"Those are men's sizes, Gus. You are all mixed up."

"I am mixed-up," Gus admits.

"I am mixed-blood," says Swan, "but don't bother asking how my day went. And I am a man, and I am not Leda's bird, and I am not your bird. I am a man of First Nations heritage, here in a maze of birds and imagery, and I intend to survive these insults and thrive in it."

"Don't you see," says Gus, "I defended her because I believe I knew her as a child. This missing hand. It must be her. But I, I am Leda."

"That's why you stared at that thing for an hour. In love with a Swan."

"Yes, if you are not in love with Celeste.... I am in love with you."

"Touching. I courted a few ladies, and many men, before I realized I myself was fond of you, as preoccupied and bad as you may be."

The baby cries. Swan takes her in his arms. "She's yay long, and yay tall, and all happiness and sunshine and dry pants and never mind Gus. He's silly, so *fait la bête*, and ignore his obsession with Wanda. Arnica will walk in bare feet like the girl in *Les Demoiselles de village*."

"Yes, darling, there is a child in a painting by a man named Gustave Courbet. I want her to be that free and happy."

"I wish the same thing," says Swan. There is a silence while he thinks.

"I just saw something I didn't like at all. More crass than the shoe salesperson. Photos of Vespa, I believe, posing with sculptures. As a mixed-medium. She has size seven feet, is about sixteen years old, and naked as the day she was born. On the wall across the street."

"You admire her."

"I am disturbed by this idea of her being exploited. And I want to talk to her very much."

A smile warms Gus's face. "Oh look, sweetheart. *Nudle s houbami.*"

29

ALASKA IS FURIOUS that such a large donation of money has been offered anonymously to spring Olesya out on bail. Olesya is free. It is more than enough, and once Olesya is spoken to during a rare, in fact, her only visit by Jackie, she decides it is tactically important to co-operate with the order that she stay away from the gallery next to World of Shoes and to report to a bail officer twice a week so that she is not able to leave the city.

The owner of the Gilera has located a new motorcycle of the same vintage model and in the same lousy condition in Belgium, and it has been purchased with Vespa's credit card. It cost over four thousand British pounds, and Vespa is wondering who deposited all of the money in her account. She looks at Jackie in an accusatory way, as if depositing money in someone's bank account behind their back is some sort of crime.

It was Ben who deduced his sister's charge card number from a pile of receipt, and quickly comes to Jackie's defense.

Vespa says she is tired of having her buttons pushed and then tells Ben not to jerk her chain. She is now certain that Jackie has been lying to her about not taking part in any more robberies.

Since Jackie has been spending countless hours in the shop compared to her brief, if passionate forays making love, she also feels that Jackie has threatened her sexual territory with yet more deceit.

Realizing she may have hurt her lover, expressively-challenged

Jackie leaves the equivalent of two thousand British pounds in Vespa's account as a gesture of goodwill. Ben coordinates the shipping of the Italian motorcycle and its various parts from Belgium to America by setting up a delivery account for his own motorcycle repair company.

He has decided to call it Didactic Motors and designates Alaska as the owner of the operation since he is not licensed to work in the U.S.

Alaska hires another lawyer to keep close tabs on the books, someone Ben reports to almost as often as Olesya reports to her bail officer. The company is quickly flooded with requests, and the money that he generates with his sister and Jackie, Alaska funnels back into legal expenses for Olesya.

Alaska thinks that for publicity reasons, it was wrong to spring Olesya, but now that Olesya is out, at least she is able to go to her gym again, spin on the stationary cycles, and tan herself an impossible umber. Alaska insists that Olesya has just been missing the sun. Jackie insists that Olesya is courting nose melanoma after seeing her bail officer and jogging around Central Park.

At her welcome-home party, Gus and Swan arrive with Arnica Montana and Wanda plays music by KISS and Queen and later, when the baby is tiring, Zappa and Patti Smith.

She tries to discuss the song, "Baby, Take Your Teeth Out," with Swan, but Swan does not want to discuss Zappa. He wants to talk discreetly with Vespa instead. Gus tries to cross the room so that he can talk to Wanda, who looks almost spectrally pale as she stands shunned in the centre of the room. The doorbell chimes. Gus notices the noise, turns away from Wanda, and drifts to the door with the baby in his arms. It is the woman from the gallery, the one who works for the man in the blue sweater.

"Don't open doors so casually in New York!" says Alaska. The young woman overwhelms her with an enormous bouquet of roses. "I quit," says the woman.

"You quit? Why? Because of the stolen Indigenous artifacts and the photos of exploited underage girls?"

"Partly."

Vespa, who has just been told by Swan that Donkely's photos are hanging in the gallery where this woman works, rushes to the door. She is offered a single rose.

Alaska goes to look for a vase big enough to contain twenty-three fresh-cut roses.

"What is your name?" asks Vespa.

"Washington," says the young woman shyly, "but some people call me Shinny."

"Your last name?" Vespa asks her.

The woman draws her breath. *This woman Vespa is more beautiful in life than the photos,* she thinks. She stares at her and can barely speak. "My last name is Madison," she tells her, and then feels as if her knees will sink under her and she will fall on her face in the hall.

"Well, so you quit?" says Vespa.

"Of course I quit. I had no idea what I was walking into, but I know what I want to walk away from now. He needs someone to help him when he sees spectres, but I didn't feel I could help. I told him to go blow his dog, and I will go back to flower sales."

"What was that?" Vespa asks her. She finds herself drawn to Washington Madison like a rose to pollination.

"Flower sales," says the young woman. "I'll need those back before I go, they're my livelihood now. That woman just took them from my arms."

"Oh shit." Vespa turns to call Alaska back to the door, but she has disappeared into the kitchen.

"It's okay, never mind that now. Vespa, I know that is you on the walls of the gallery. It was wrong the way you were exploited. I want to give you something."

The young woman peers at Vespa through her intelligent-looking, non-corrective lenses. She reaches behind herself and hands her a large cardboard-wrapped package that is leaning against the wall.

"Remember Skip Donkely? Here are all pictures of you. I thought you should have them back."

"Oh, holy fuck," says Vespa. She takes the young woman, whose friends called her Shinny, and leads her down to Olesya's storage lockers, where Vespa has a key.

"Let's lock these away safely in here for now," she tells her, and then, because she feels at a loss to thank her, she leans forward and kisses Washington (Shinny) Madison on the mouth. Shinny responds, kissing the new, strangely older and not-a-photograph Vespa on the neck continuously until the two of them fall backwards into the mess of upside-down furniture, and undress each other fully.

There in the gloom, they each make love as a pure act of surprise, enjoying each other until they are exhausted and salty with sweat.

30.

ON A DARK ARTERY entering Manhattan, a rider is approaching. It is Mimi. She is seated on her two-stroke twin, Velocette gearbox, 1969 Scott Flying Squirrel. The motorcycle sports the classic Flying Squirrel duplex frame and the front suspension system of telescopic forks that is now standard among motorcycles, of which the Scott Motocycle Company had the first.

She is coming to investigate the new motorcycle repair company. Glancing at her own reflection as she passes the window of a closed down automobile showroom, she smiles. Mimi's insistent electromagnetic force, which is more powerful than gravity, is empty and whole at the same time. She cannot help noticing that her 1969 Scott Flying Squirrel, looks very, very cool.

Upstairs in the apartment, the phone rings. It is Celeste, calling to see if Arnica Montana is doing okay. Baby Arnica is outside with Swan and Ben, who are talking about particle physics and Seurat. Swan is arguing that because Georges Seurat was a man who organized his paintings into planes of tiny dots, the dots demonstrated the subatomic structure of all things, including colour and sound.

Ben is interested in the idea that there are sounds emitted by Seurat's colours, at a frequency no one can hear. Swan hears the rattling sound of Celeste's telephone voice in Toronto talking to emptiness on the phone and reaches out to spare her the indignity of talking to no one. Arnica leans over the rail to look at the pretty shiny cars and begins to topple forward.

Ben, who once played football for Immaculate Conception High, throws himself through the air and catches Arnica as she begins to slide into nothingness and off the balcony. He is lying with his head underneath Olesya's barbeque with Arnica safely in his arms, awhile Swan lies in a prone position on top of him. Swan tells Celeste in Toronto that everything is going great. Celeste says she is coming on the next flight down and renting a minivan to bring back her baby.

Arnica lets out a gurgle of delight at the sound of her mother's voice and attempts to crawl away from Ben's grip to see if she can put the pretty cars in her mouth. She has already attempted to put one of the pretty charcoal briquettes in her mouth.

Mimi arrives at West 108th Street and parks her Flying Squirrel underneath the storage area where Vespa and Shinny Madison are making love.

Jackie takes Arnica from Ben's grip. The men continue to lie for one moment too long on top of each other in a mess of charcoal. Ben smiles, sits up, and, notices Wanda and Gus have retreated to the bedroom and closed the door. He lovingly paints pretty smudges like kohl around Swan's benevolent eyes.

31

ALASKA AND WANDA are feeling pretty good about the threat-to-disclose letter they have sent to Rudy. Alaska has photocopied every scrap and stolen memento in the large envelope and has even decided to withhold it from their lawyer.

She can no longer remember which one of her lawyers is in charge of the Condo Owners lawsuit anyway, and she is starting to feel aroused by her conspiracy with Wanda. There is an energy between the two of them, perhaps because they both have always been directing the irresponsible life of another person, and now they have found a source of fun in an irresponsible but powerful act all their own. In some ways, Wanda finds Alaska attractive.

As a straight Christian, Wanda feels confused by her own desire to nibble the soft downy hair on Alaska's tanned and lotion-scented face. Alaska has noticed this, and admits to herself that, like everyone who encounters Wanda, she also finds Wanda attractive, but she is too proud to tell a heterosexual woman how she feels.

Besides, she is involved with Olesya, a proud, out lesbian. And even if Wanda somehow looks more enticing and forbidding than her lover, she could never leave her side.

Olesya is her injured baby bird, and Alaska is happy in the position of nursing her sick little bird forever back to health. For both women, their desire takes the form of jealousy, and now, avarice in the form of blackmail. The letters offer them something they can get.

So, this is it. Wanda is caught in something wrong. But there are so many wrongs all around her that the only positive result has been a breakdown of her inhibition about wanting to ride a female, even if the female in question may be a high horse to hell.

They do not think about hurting Ben. Wanda even thinks Ben is now having a sexual liaison with Swan. It is ridiculous; last week she thought it was Jackie.

She wonders if she should go back to her therapist, Doctor Popair. Wanda wants to be a moral person and finds Dr. Popair's words difficult to forget. She likes him not because, unlike real therapists, he is an opinionated big mouth destined to found his own movement and make millions.

"Relax, baby Wanda, unsqueeze your mind. Tension is making you avoid getting to the milk," Dr. Popair is fond of saying.

She also found the physical touch of Gus at the party equally compelling—like a soul connection as opposed to the verboten feeling that Alaska creates in Wanda's panties. Her self-estrangement is like walking through a blizzard calling for help, and no one comes. It always seems no one comes until she falls and is waiting to die. She knows Ben was a very close boyhood friend of Rudy, and she thinks he is in possession of Rudy's strange papers because he is protecting him, and not because he wants them disclosed. Thinking this, she feels like a monster, but Alaska's enthusiasm is now unstoppable. She considers buying a gun and forcing Alaska to burn every copy on the spot. She had watched Ben sift through the papers at the diner, after she brought them out from under her shirt. Then, because she had not take a leak when she told Betty she was going to—instead, she had been caught in the middle of an adrenaline-charged act, had a pistol pointed to her head, and then had to sit politely afterwards drinking a pina colada—she ran to the diner washroom when she could. She was happy to see that Ben had recovered his photo of the CZ, but the rest was tucked away. When she returned, there had been only a few choice poems by juvenile Rudy on the table and a glass of water.

Yes, Alaska is butch. She even phoned Celeste and talked to her at length about proper care for baby Arnica, winning her the go-ahead from Celeste, who is preparing to drive down, to take the baby away from the boys. Once Alaska took charge, the collaborated threat-to-disclose letter was simple.

It contained the names of every company Rudy had removed documents from, including notes scribbled in his hand at the bottom of poems that he had written. Wanda said that their threat-to-disclose the poems might be enough to activate Turner's people right there. The two women had a good laugh. A sinister laugh, high-pitched but fun in that sophomoric, out of control way that Wanda has disapproved of in other women up until this point. But now, was caught up in herself, like a tight-fitting swimsuit that was too wet to pull back off. They realize that what they are doing is somehow very radical, or very criminal, or simply a departure from any sort of action that either one of them has taken before. Alaska pointed out that their loyalty to the hundreds of people housed in shoddy B.F. Turner buildings must take precedence. The email message to Rudy was simple:

"Your tenants have cracked the safe at Betty's. We have all of your mementoes. What a scrupulous thief you were, but your nostalgia is your downfall today. We know you are hiding out in the Adirondacks, and we can and we will track you down. We also know you are involved in business more unethical than any of your contemporaries. As the new head of B.F. Turner, you are now fully implicated in making it your business to construct towers that will self-destruct like time bombs. In response, we are preparing a legal case that will smash your position, smash your company, and grind your bones to dust. If you do not believe me, see below references to various businesses you broke into, and the innumerable records that you stole. Jeezaroo, are we going to open a Can of Whoop-Ass on you. Comply with our demands and have Camelia deposit four hundred thousand dollars into the following bank account number by Friday or we will begin to release this material not only to the press, but to your colleagues as we see fit."

Signed, "Society for Sellouts to get the Hell Out."

They considered using Vespa's bank account, since everybody knew her account number, and there wasn't a law against depositing money into someone's bank account behind their back. Then they worried that Rudy would have the account number traced, and think it was Vespa, since Vespa had a history with Rudy. They considered having the money into the Condo Owner's Fund, but then they realized that they were the only two signers. Finally, they resolved to have the money deposited into Didactic Motor Company because all monetary activities were first to be passed by Alaska's lawyers, and these were people that Rudy had never met.

The two women set up a public account, then send off the email to Rudy. They kiss each other formally on each cheek, making it official.

Wanda is wondering where Ben is, and Alaska is late for a workshop on Ethical Management and has to stop at Olesya's apartment first. Parting ways, one lady blackmailer trips off to a subway while the other lady blackmailer goes to the studio. Wanda wants to see if Ben is involved in another concept session with pencils and flow sheets and cigarettes and Jackie, the woman she cannot be. But there is no one at the studio and the door is locked.

Wanda presses her face against the cool surface to collect her thoughts. She has done something terrible. There is nothing to collect. Ben has not bothered to tell her where he is. This is because Ben is at the Carlton Arms, in a four-poster-bed next to a fresco of two women making love. He is lying there with Swan, a small fan stirring the curtains while Swan is lightly touching each one of Ben's scars with his tongue. Ben is discussing wave-particle duality, and how a photon representing the colour red, travelling at 5.25 times ten to the logarithmic power of fourteen nanometres per second, would create a frequency just like a particle hitting a membrane, or a stick striking a drum, and there would be a sound.

"A sound like this?" asks Swan. But Swan makes no sound. Instead, he does something unexpected to Ben, and Ben cries out. The sound Ben makes is the sound that the most primary of colours would cry out to the sun and stars if they were being prepared to be thrown onto a canvas by an artist of considerable talent.

Wanda does not hear the sound, or the other cries of pleasure that follow. Instead, she unlocks the studio door and takes the Triumph 750V Trident on a ride, swerving through SoHo and not wishing to see any of the galleries, blurring past art and someone else's passion, looking for her own.

32

A S WANDA IS TRAVELLING through the streets of Manhattan, trying to silence a devil on her shoulder that tells her she is, at this moment in the rotation or counter-rotation or rotations per second of time, the biggest loser to ever straddle a Triumph, she believes she sees Olesya. Olesya is headed in the direction of her bail officer, and it is the right day and time, but she is mounted on the back of a 1969 Scott Flying Squirrel with a man from her therapy group. Vim, that is his name; the one with the vivid childhood memories. But what are the chances, she is wondering, of that man being coincidentally on a motorbike with Olesya?

Wanda weaves through Little Italy, looking for a place to buy Indian curry, and is furious when nothing turns up. She admits she feels a little miffed because she heard Alaska talking in a long, romantic way to Celeste, and reminds herself that she is not the only one Alaska finds hot. She motors along West Broadway and is about to bully her way up crowded Broome Street, when she thinks she sees Gus, Swan's friend. She feels as if snow is blowing in her eyes. It must be a look-alike as she can no longer tell people apart. But now she has met the eyes of this man, and she realizes he has not stopped looking at her.

A pedestrian steps out in front of her, and she slams the Triumph to a stop. She finds, to her dismay, that the force has thrown her forward and off balance so much that she is forced to redirect the bike. She collides with a traffic pole, then falls and strikes a hydrant. Her head has taken a knock from the hydrant, and the pedestrian has hurried off, as if Wanda was deliberately trying to frighten him.

She lies for a moment, and now the blizzard of confusion and uncertainty is circling her much closer than before. Shocked, she pulls herself up. She checks that the fuel tank is not punctured or leaking and then waddles the bike to the nearest sidewalk ramp to catch her breath.

There, she buries the ignition key deep in her pocket, kickstands the Triumph, and runs her hands through her hair. Her eyes are spinning like epicyclical gears, and she feels as if her heart needs a timing check, as if it is speeding up and slowing down in a way that does not seem normal.

To her horror, she realizes that the blood has raced to her most vital organs, and that she is standing with snow flying all around her in the middle of July. She supposes it is ash, just like she thought an air-conditioner trickle above her the day before was rain. But there is too much of it, too much for her to even move her legs. Her face is white as plaster when Gus catches up to her, and he takes her face in his hands.

"I cannot move my hand," she tells him.

"That's all right, a spring or a mechanism inside it has been damaged by the force of the fall. But they're both all right," he tells her, and he takes her hands in her own.

"Who are you?" Wanda asks him, suddenly confused.

"I am the man who found you on the Schilthorn when you were just a little girl. After you ran away from your parents. Do you have to always run away?"

"I told them I was running. They wouldn't listen to me. They left my cat behind at the chalet that they rented, and then we were all going to the Schilthorn, but I wanted to find the cat. I still want to find that cat."

"You lost your first hand that day," says Gus.

"Yes, but I was given this hand. It's as heavy, as heavy as a club. How did you find me?"

"I don't know," says Gus. "Everyone was looking for you, and I was very good on skis. I think that I found you because I was as lost as you were, because I was not much more than a boy myself. I picked you up, and somehow, we made it back to a ski cabin. Slowly, you began to become warm in my arms. Doctors came, and after a while, I heard you were not dead."

"What did you do, to put the breath back into me? Because I feel snow all around me, and I am afraid of walking on."

"I did this," says Gus, and he put his lips against Wanda and breathes his minty breath into her mouth.

He places his lips a second time on hers and she feels the tenderness of the young boy who saved her in the snow. Around her, the blizzard is slowly beginning to subside.

"I am not going to freeze and die?" she asks him.

"Not today. Today I think you will live."

Gus takes her hand, and together they walk to a pharmacy for bandages. Wanda finds she is limping, and Gus buys her a cane. He dresses her wounds. They walk hand in hand through the park, talking like two children who, having met by coincidence, decide in opposition to the rules of the adult world to become faithful and lifelong friends.

The next morning, they will go to a clinic. Wanda has torn some ligaments. They will heal.

Olesya begins to houseclean, opening the patio doors now that there is no baby planning to crawl out. The baby is somewhere with Vespa, and because everyone trusts Vespa, because everyone even knows her credit card number and has access to her bank statements, no one is worried that the baby is not okay. The welfare of Arnica has not even occurred to protective Gus, who has rented a room a floor below the one where Ben and Swan are making love, so as to make illicit love with Wanda. It is painted by a local muralist, and has images of young, slender men with bodies like Swan and feet like Mercury chasing each other around the walls.

33.

OLESYA SIGNED THE FORMS, listened to a small speech, and then the patronizing bail officer told her to behave herself. Soon, she is in her apartment again, pouring a coffee for herself and looking around a space that no longer holds relevance for her.

Olesya wonders why she punctuates every new thought and topic with, "According to my therapist," instead of according to herself. No matter. She is free, despite her mild depression.

In comparison, Arnica Montana is happier than a neon pink rooster-poodle. The wind buffets against her, and she is blinking her eyes in a way that makes everything seem like a movie filmed through sun-dappled lids. She feels safe in the car seat of Vespa's new station wagon, and when Vespa pulls onto the I-87 and then the New York State Route 17, Arnica is delighted to be on a country trip.

Two days earlier, Jackie had not returned to their pop-out couch, which had caused Vespa to go looking for her at the studio, where they sometimes shared a mattress on the floor. She noticed new tire tracks on the floor, a visiting motorcycle that had come and gone, and a spark plug that had been replaced. The old one was lying in their garbage, and Vespa could not identify it, only that it had been changed at their shared garage. She drank some gin that her brother kept to splash on cuts and fell asleep on the mattress feeling wounded. She slept dreamlessly until dawn. She had not seen Jackie since, although she suspected she was with Mimi, who rode in on the night of Olesya's welcoming party and demanded to see Jackie's Flying Squirrel, but only if Jackie would come riding on her real Squirrel first. It made Vespa extremely jealous, but Vespa had not actually been there. Vespa had been making love in the storage room with Shinny.

She needs to talk to Jackie. She wishes Jackie would enter the modern world and carry a phone or a pager. Her eyes mist. She would not like a Jackie that carries a pager. She likes the Jackie that mends socks and cuts mittens out of her sweaters. So, if Jackie is so resourceful, if Jackie is such a called-upon and hotshot mechanic, why had twelve thousand dollars passed through Vespa's bank account. And what about the two thousand British pounds still sitting there? Why is Vespa using it to buy Shinny's roses when she doesn't even know where it came from in the first place? Who is the anonymous donor that had dropped the money into to Olesya's bail fund, just at the time when it would look best to the press? Why is Jackie always broke one day, and going to a pricey sushi restaurant the very next? And Ben too?

Both of them were now ordering parts and making unimaginable expenses that a few days before they had been complaining they could never afford.

Vespa is beginning to suspect Jackie has not only robbed something again but that she has involved Ben in the process. But why be so suspicious? Is she a suspicious woman by nature? Why doubt the ones she loves? Is she just losing her mind?

She parks the car in a small, pretty little town by the Hudson River intending to buy some strawberry formula for the baby and a carrot juice or perhaps even a caffeinated drink for herself. She realizes she has parked in front of a bank, and without covering her face, she walks in and demands a small envelope of ten thousand dollars in small unmarked bills from the teller.

Her adrenaline is raging, but the ease of it surprises her. The teller replies that this is ridiculous, and asks her why everything has to be small. Could she not make do with some larger notes? Vespa, a reasonable woman who has already been questioning the order of things, admits that she could probably break the larger notes at some other bank. The teller hands her an envelope as if she has already prepared it for such a robbery, which she probably has. As Vespa leaves, she remembers that she forgot to tell the teller she had a gun. It would have been a lie anyway, and it is wrong to tell a lie, even to a stranger. Telling the truth is a better, or the best policy, as her mother had always said. Then you can remember what you told people the second time they ask. As she is thinking these things, she is met by the familiar face of Mimi, waiting for her on the sidewalk outside the bank.

"Mimi!" says Vespa, remembering that she had not stopped to rob a bank, but to buy a soft drink and some formula for the baby in the car. Mimi says, "Now you are lucky we caught you when we did."

"I stopped here to buy a soda pop. I must have feathers in my head."

So, Mimi is not with Jackie; how wrong of her to be so suspicious.

"Hey, I'm not a mind reader," says Mimi, "but I saw everything, and there is no way you are going to walk out of this parking lot let alone drive out of town without our help."

"Are you certain?"

"I want half the cut," says Mimi, cutting to the quick, "on the condition that you get off Scott Squirrel free."

"Well, not if we stand here chatting about it on the sidewalk I won't," she comments.

"I can take care of it," says Mimi, and her eyes bore into Vespa's own.

It's best to be direct, or that's what my mother always said, Vespa thinks to herself. Shrugging, she digs into the envelope and hands Vim what seems to add up to a solid five thousand dollars.

"Good enough," says Mimi.

Her superior tone irks Vespa. She still thinks Mimi is having an affair with Jackie, but it isn't the time nor the place to talk. And no one can be two places at once.

"Help!" cries a young woman, and she runs out of the bank. It is the teller. Vespa, feeling intuitively friendly towards the woman, takes a step over to her to see what is wrong.

"Oh, it's you! You're still here."

"Don't worry, we're just leaving," says Vespa in a resigned way, remembering that it is because of her.

The teller runs back into the bank.

"I forgot to pick up an iced coffee," Vespa tells Arnica in her shoulder-check mirror as she heads back out to State 17, "and a strawberry formula for you," she shouts into the back of the car.

Arnica laughs and blinks her eyes.

The Scott Flying Squirrel speeds behind her with what Vespa at first perceives to be a troubled exhaust system and dirty fuel lines. She quickly realizes it is only a mist of evil and supernatural vapours. It blurs past her station wagon and disappears, leaving the held-up bank to find help on its own.

"Now, what were the chances of running into that woman in a sleepy little town?" Vespa asks the baby.

She drives through the rolling landscape with the money sliding back and forth on the seat at her side. Freed by the background gurgles of the baby, a buried memory surfaces, and she turns it over in her mind, checking for its veracity in the same way she stared at her balance slip after Jackie had deposited that extra two thousand pounds. It may be something to tell Ben. She glances back at Arnica and they exchange smiles.

Vespa feels herself at Arnica's age and remembers vividly riding like the wind with her mother on a large motorcycle, her little legs straddling the gas tank. She is held in front, inside her mother's jacket and between her mother's arms, while her mother's large gloved hands grip the steering. Together, with her mother, they were running away. From what? From whom? Where was Ben? When was her mother not running away? Would Ben even know? Was she even allowed to tell? The questions trouble her all the way back to Olesya's.

She parks the station wagon, takes the baby out of the car seat, and stops by a convenience store for iced coffee and strawberry formula. Moments later, she lets herself in through Olesya's door. Olesya is extended, naked, on the comfortable rug in front of the television. She fights a moment of shock, feeling her personal space invaded by a stranger with no clothes.

"Olesya, what are you doing here?"

"Come sit down," says Olesya, patting the couch.

Finally, Vespa smiles and the room becomes more relaxed. She is, in fact, a little ashamed of her original reaction; it is, after all, Olesya's place. Arnica begins to cry.

"Hush!" Vespa gives Arnica the new bottle full of formula.

"Look," says Olesya, "there's a robbery on the news! And look at her getup!"

A bank video plays and then replays on the screen. There is even an outdoor camera. The caught-in-the-act videos shows a woman in riding leathers and forties-style clothing pulling away on old Condor 500cc motorcycle with a baby between her thighs, auburn hair flowing out from an old-style leather biking helmet and aviator-type goggles.

"Wow! With two videos, they should have no trouble finding anyone who robbed that bank," says Olesya. "What was she thinking?"

"She looks exactly like my mother," says Vespa.

"Well, technically she looks a little young to be your mother, don't you think? But the bike and the leathers do look to be from another era!" says Olesya. She flips the channels, adding, "I hope she just vanishes, just like I'd like to do." To Olesya's dismay, the same woman is on three different news stations.

The next day, the fantastic goggles and flowing hair are featured in several newspapers. Swan brings them to Ben with his morning coffee. He clips the photos out and puts them in the pocket over his heart where they are safe. It is his mother, it is Vespa's mother, it is Mommy. No one else has a Condor 500; no one else has that auburn hair.

He and Swan have finished tumbling. There is nothing left but to go out into the world and discover new sensations, and then to unite again in secret. They have worn each other smooth, and for now, they are no longer touching each other's surfaces. Try as they may, they slip away from each other like two round stones. Ben presses his hand against Swan's, and Swan sets off in happy flight. Ben re-examines the newspaper clipping. There is a roar of an engine on the street. Wanda pulls up beside him on the Triumph. She is carrying a cane and has a bandage over her eye.

"What happened to you?"

"I fell down," says Wanda, and she drops her eyes. "It seems I fell down pretty hard."

34.

RUDY THOUGHT THE EMAIL was from Natalia. And he couldn't understand why she would have hurt him in this way. He knew that Camelia had visited New York, and that they had met, but he thought the two women had had a pleasant time. He had not considered that they were plotting to extort him.

Natalia had written a quick note he read as "Matriarchal deer slaps," causing him to wonder if his anagram coding method was the brightest way for the two of them to exchange ideas. He soon translated it to read, "Camelia parties hard," and he relaxed, dipping his hand-carved fishing lure in and out of a nearby stream. It was impossible to imagine that the two of them had somehow turned against him. He composed a letter and then sent it to Natalia, begging her to investigate the source of his threat-to-disclose email. Then he added in the most direct terms, with tears welling in his eyes, that Natalia must tell him if she no longer loved him and wished to break off their plans for a future.

"You must come back," Natalia responded from an Internet café. "How could I possibly love you if you are not here with me. I am not a detective, but I will investigate the threat you received, as you have requested me to do. This isn't my job, but you are busy eating pine nuts and berries, and psyching out the local wildlife with your endless poetry and staring.

"'I have lost friends,'" she concluded, "'some by death ...

others through sheer inability to cross the street.'"

Rudy did not recognize the quote was Woolf. He thought Natalia was more Dorothy Parker, and he was more Kerouac and Thoreau.

Later in the day, Camelia sends him a note, saying, "Rudy, come back to New York!" which Rudy encrypted before he had even opens it, thinking he was unencrypting a response from his beloved.

He reads, "Codebreak murky, town coy!" and presumes Camelia is having a good time. He now feels a little uncertain as to what a "coy town" has to do with him.

Is she just bragging? He wonders if Natalia's warnings were correct, and Camelia, who has just offered a multi-million dollar package to lawyers handling the Condo Owner's lawsuit, is partying to the point of being unfit for her position.

Is this happening while the lawyer is preparing documents for Alaska to consider, so that she can sign the right papers, the lawyer can be paid, and the Condo Owners can have more money dropped in their laps than they had ever dared imagine?

Preparing a small pack, Rudy hikes the treacherous trail he came in on back out of the heart of the Adirondacks to the place where he has parked his car. He drives it up the New York State route 8 to a nearby town and continues driving until he reaches a survivalist-oriented gun shop. Stopping, he buys a hundred dollars in blasting caps, a case of firecrackers, ten boxes of fire-starters, and three hundred energy bars in designer camo-colours. The cashier takes little notice of him. By sunset, he is back at a temporary camp inside the park boundaries, along a remote deer trail where he is certain to be undisturbed. He sleeps dreamlessly, and before the sky has time to gather clouds and strike him dead, Rudy pack camp and move on.

By sunset the next day, he is back in his treetop heaven and has set twenty-four traps around the only place where he has ever felt truly safe, all marked in ways only Rudy can identify. The traps are nothing like the little noose-snares he has set for squirrels in the past, or the elaborate commitments he has driven others to make in the boardroom. They are tin cans full of explosives that will be activated by a footfall. There is a message waiting for Rudy, but he already knows what it says.

The account has been traced. Natalia is no monkey, and she has not betrayed Rudy nor sat on her hands wondering what to do. The account belongs to one Didactic Motor Company, and it is under the trust of a series of lawyers and the minimum handful of shareholders required to give it the same corporate protectionism Turner enjoyed for decades. In other words, there is no one who is responsible or in charge.

Undeterred, Natalia went to Didactic Motor Company to see the individuals involved and met a hostile and grubby woman with tattoos on her arms who only said her name was Jackie before ducking back under a welder's helmet to patch a Norton Monocoque with the sudden flare of an arc. A friendly man about Rudy's age emerged from the back, and Natalia had noticed he had scar tissue that ran down his neck and disappeared into his jumpsuit. He told her that if she was certain the alternator on her Harley was broken, then he doubted she could have driven it right over to his shop. Before he had a chance to ask her what year and type of Harley, she ran back out into the street.

"His shop," was the key word Natalia was looking for. She quickly ran down the street and hopped into the first taxi she could wave. If it was of any assistance to Rudy, the man that she spoke with was called Ben.

35

RUDY NOW FEELS CERTAIN his blackmailer is the boy-friend who first taught him love and loyalty, Ben. He is in a fit again, a rage of heartbreak and fury. Natalia receives a notice from Rudy to take a poem by hand to Didactic Motor Company.

At the sixth-floor apartment, Olesya's phone is ringing off the hook from lawyers looking for Alaska. Camelia has been trying to get the deal through all day, and the other signer, Wanda, is the only other person in the Condo Owner's business record that the lawyers have on file. They have the names of almost everyone who lives in the building, including the man whose dog was struck in the ass by the carpenter's level that slid across his hall, but it is a group lawsuit, and Wanda and Alaska are the complainants at the helm.

Camelia is afraid to tell Rudy that this is the same Wanda who questioned her about her sexual orientation in the lounge of her hotel. Finally, she tells the lawyers to go ahead and find signer Wanda anyway, in order to at least get this thing on the board before formally approaching the residents with the offer. Camelia reapplies her lipstick and stares out at the Manhattan skyline from the B.F. Turner office tower, wondering if anything is ever okay.

Olesya steps out to a slide show on quilt-making at the library with Vim. She is convinced that a stay in a highway hotel would be more romantic than dealing with all the traffic running through her apartment. Vim has agreed with her.

Wanda presses a button and listens to the message on the answering machine from the lawyer for the Condo Owner's Association telling her to call at once, just as Ben is taking a shower and scrubbing the grease from his arms. Wanda and Ben had planned to go out that night to a dinner theatre that is presenting a psychological play by Pinter called *The Collection*. Ben is looking forward to the interpretation as the actors are trained to circulate through the restaurant performing their modified lines. Interactivity occurs as the actors taunt the audience about their homo or heterosexual inclinations with a personal and unrelenting series of suggestions. Since it is performed while the audience is eating as well as moving back and forth between a salad bar and their tables, there has been some actual physical combat between audience and actor. Wanda thinks it sounds exciting—the dawn of a new wave in theatre.

She is also hoping that a night out is a good time to tell Ben what she has done to Rudy. Ben must know that Wanda has been trying to confess something to him, and that there is something else she has been trying to say since she said that she had fallen very hard.

Perhaps he thinks she means Gus. Gus has told Swan everything, and Swan has told Ben everything, after Swan and Gus moved upstairs to the less lesbian-oriented, more masculine suite, and Wanda moved back to Ben.

Wanda hears Ben showering and singing in a carefree way and dials the number for the lawyer. The lawyer tells her that Turner Corporation wants Olesya's building inspected for any faults in its structure and that it wants to buy back each one of the units from the owners at between three-hundred and fifty and four-hundred and fifty thousand dollars, depending on whether they had one or two baths. Assuming the Owner's Association feels comfortable with this amount.

Since the tenants, in most cases, paid less than one-hundred thousand for their original units, which they are still paying off in the form of mortgages to the real estate firm that handles the property, the mortgages will be covered and the remainder will be forwarded to the original buyers. Turner lawyers are trying to attach a caveat that insists fifty thousand of each Condo Owners windfall be donated to a charity to help the homeless, and Turner lawyers, who are much more talented than Alaska and Wanda's real estate lawyer, are going to fight for it hard.

If the Condo Owner's Association does not agree, they are going to withdraw the offer and re-propose at fifty thousand less a piece, with the money going to charities not under the tax-deductible names of each Condo owner but as a project of Turner Corporation.

Wanda is stunned. They want her, as one of the first initiators behind the Condo Owner's protest, to sign papers to start the gears in motion. Wanda, and not Alaska, and not Olesya, who has run off to sleep by the highway. She allows Ben to listen to the machine.

"Not what we were expecting from Turner," says Ben, towelling. His face reads as stunned as Wanda's.

It is the first step in Turner's radically new path at sheltering every citizen who seeks shelter according and in compliance to their needs, by enriching and stabilizing their home environment. In other words, Rudy is the new CEO of Turner Industries. In this role, he has lost total interest in the needs of the affluent, and he is phasing them out politely, just as he did his more difficult colleagues and those loyal to the old-style B.F. Turner. To Rudy, the thug methods are no more. Nibbling on avocado energy bars in the treetops of the Adirondacks, the Upper West Side seemed to half-crazed Rudy like an interesting place to start.

In the hallway, Natalia runs into Ben and Wanda, dressed for an evening out on the town. Wanda leans lightly on a cane.

She is about to sweep past them, to dutifully cross the city and drop a note at Didactic Motor Company, when Ben snaps his fingers, points at her with a grin and says, "Harley owner, am I right?" He has such a peaceful, otherworldly look to him that Natalia is startled and then ashamed to think of how she hated him for doing what she believes he is doing to Rudy. She feels as if they should be friends, and wants to talk to him, because she knows he was the boyhood friend that supported Rudy through his father's death. Wanda's body language is possessive.

Natalia hesitates, then hates Rudy for putting her in this position, and hands the message to Ben. She hurries into the elevator and disappears.

"It's to me," says Ben, "I didn't know she even knew me. She came by Didactic Motors the other day...."

"Yes, I've seen her around. She's always avoided the Condo Owner's Association. I don't know if I trust her."

"How could you not trust her? She seems like a nice enough type." The loungy-orange elevator lights indicate it has reached the bottom floor.

"Why was she by Didactic Motors? What does she say?"

"It's not from her, it's from ... it's from Rudy!"

Wanda turns away, knowing what it might read.

"Way to go, Alaska! You really fucked things up now. Now we're really in it." She retrieves her cellphone to page the lawyer Alaska hired to handle the threat-to-disclose. Then she realizes Alaska didn't hire anyone. The money was to be directed through Didactic's legal group all right, but it was to be split fifty-fifty between Wanda and Alaska, without anyone working at Didactic knowing anything about the deal.

"Ben," she says, "I haven't fallen at all. I've only just crawled out of hell. Ben, I'm a visiting demon. Ben...."

He smiles. "It's okay, baby, just let me read the letter. Correction, a poem! The fuck-wad still writes poems."

In a singsong voice that grows more and more alarmed and miserable, Rudy's poem resonates though Ben's soul, through Wanda's bones and down the empty hall.

When power falls into your hands
A sleeping dreamer wakes and stands
He plans the vision dreaming gives
To build a house where freedom lives
Then looks about and finds the child
Of dreaming peaceful in the wild
Again withdraws blueprint and pen
Insistent life draws plans again
The beat of life and rushing crowd
Demand to live in shelters proud
You kissed me and you watched me act
Even my eye you did attract
And now betrayed with bloodless note
I promised Ben I'd cut your throat
My every move you put on freeze
And left me dying in the trees
The dream moves on, but without me
The sword swings now most grievously
Others move to seize my power
Built suffering from an ivory tower
As my single chance to change the pace
Of profit with a murderer's face
Is now destroyed and under feet
As friends I trusted on the street
Forget my name and lock me up
Nothing has changed since we grew up
You broke your oath and changed our rules
Then took away my only tools
I will love you as I always did
Until my death, the no-talk kid."

"Could he be referring to the lock-pick set we were looking for in the safe?" says Wanda.

"You blackmailed him," Ben answers.

"Ben, it's all okay now, everyone here is going to receive..."

"I know. I heard the answering machine. But not you ... not unless you used the receipts that Rudy and I collected over the years, covered with his handwriting, even scribbled on with poems. I should have burned them."

"I wanted to burn them when I realized what I had done."

"Then it is only you who knows, and he thinks it is me. And you have got his email address and can set the whole thing straight."

"Not quite, Ben. That's not how this situation exactly works. Not unless we find Alaska."

"Alaska?"

"And the baby."

"What does Alaska have to do with it?"

"She has the email, all the information. It was her idea. She set the whole thing up, beginning..."

"Beginning with a deposit to Didactic, which would be screened by her precious legal assistants."

"So that you would never know."

"So that Didactic would launder extorted money as the first year of taxable earnings. Alaska was never planning to let our company go, not with that tax burde....."

"A little blackmailing for a good cause isn't the end of the world, is it Ben? You can always get another motorcycle company."

"You, Wanda, can get some other company."

"I don't understand."

"I prefer not to be with you, beginning right now, tonight."

36

JACKIE HAS BOUGHT the pickup that she told Vespa she would get in order to salvage her reputation. She has polished the chrome to a shine, patched all the bodywork, replaced damaged engine parts, and slapped on new brake shoes. Vespa is nowhere in sight. Jackie has even taken Mimi for a ride in the Squirrel she and Ben built together. She flies effortlessly over a meadow in Orange County, setting her down by one of the oldest wineries in America.

She has enjoyed the feeling of Mimi's knees pressing tight against her hips. Although they decline a tour of the cellars, they buy themselves several glasses, smiling at one another on the terrace of a small restaurant. They are quipping, sipping, and eating a salad filled with walnuts, a gesture to the animal they have come to revere.

Mimi is extremely interested in the glider, wants to know how Jackie designed the complex series of cables that activate the three flaps on each side and change the rudder direction in the tail. Mimi looks into her eyes, and far from the caring, even doting affections of Vespa, Jackie sees the face of a woman who has been to hell many times, gotten to know the place her own way, and who even drops by now and again for a visit. Certainly Mimi is no angel, but to be fair, neither is Jackie, and Mimi's tough-bird attention is a breath of fresh air to Jackie, who seldom spends time outside, sipping wine on a terrace with a woman who has been inside, like her. If Jackie were to put a word to it, she would say that in the company of Mimi, she is bewitched.

She has a feeling that if she should leave their table even for a moment and call Vespa to say she is coming back, Mimi will pick up her charisma and be gone. So, she sits, and she sits, and she enjoys Mimi's informed questions, her devilish intelligence, and her speculation as to how much Jackie would accept in dollars in order to part with the Squirrel. She even forgets, as trees toss sunlight from their leaves and sparrows fill the air with chatter, that Ben, her dear friend, is half-owner.

Vespa is back from the hotel she slept in by the highway. Vespa sleeps until the proprietor taps on their window and tells her it is almost noon. "Since you are a girl," he said, "I won't charge you for the extra day."

Vespa leaves on the recovered Norton Monocoque and heads instead back into town, stopping in Central Park to have lunch. By that time, Jackie and Mimi are trucking back into Manhattan, and Vespa is already back at the shop, reading a note from her brother.

"I have gone to see Swan at his hotel. I am then going to look for Rudy. All of the papers I had saved have been put to evil use and he is being extorted. He believes that I am black-mailing him, but I have betrayed no one."

So *what,* thinks Vespa. A few years back, Rudy would have jumped at the chance to extort a millionaire developer. "Otherwise, I fear he has sent assassins already to kill me. Ben."

They are always afraid of assassins, she tells herself. She looks about her, and wonders how many people have access to the motorcycle repair shop. There are many gloomy places in this shop where a childhood fear could lurk. Then again, Turner is a multi-million dollar conglomerate with a track record that is less than squeaky clean.

Vespa rolls the Norton Monocoque out of the shop, powers into traffic, and misses Jackie in her pickup truck by half a minute.

She is going to see Gus and Swan at the hotel. When she arrives, Ben is in the room, and Swan is reclining on the bed.

"Where is Arnica?" asks Vespa.

"With Alaska," says Swan.

"I am being stalked by assassins," says Ben.

"I know, I read the note. You two always thought that."

"He might be right," says Swan.

"I thought that too," says Vespa, and she bows her head. "And where's Gus?"

"Pissing naked in a fountain for Wanda, who is going to make a thousand perfect prints of him on black-and-white film stock and sell them to the world of art," says Swan.

"He's not around," Ben clarifies, "because he's with Wanda."

"I don't understand, what is the great fault in what she did?" Vespa asks.

Swan responds, "Besides the fact that Ben appears to have betrayed his first boyhood love?"

"Maybe she was jealous. She didn't mean it to look like that. It's hardly too late to set things right again. And shit Ben, Rudy was really into it, you know, he was no longer the same boy, the same man that we loved. Or that you loved. He was messed up, and he was cruel, a psychologically cruel man who threw me out of his apartment on my ass."

Ben hands Vespa the phone, and dials in Olesya's message retrieval code. It is something they have all memorized, because they were using it to receive calls from other people.

"Man, I don't believe this," says Ben. "I loved him, and you fucked him. Who would figure that?"

"We were young then," explains Vespa, "and if he had cared about me I would have loved him as well." She listens to the urgent-sounding lawyer on the phone, explaining Turner's proposal to Wanda. "Okay, it sounds like Rudy's initiative had nothing to do with Wanda's games."

"Are you kidding? She went to every one of the residents in the building, talking up the idea of a lawsuit, and now it seems she's won."

"Well, what has she won? Perhaps the lawyer was going to arrange a generous cut for her if the class-action suit had gone through. It wasn't just from the kindness of her heart. But then a better thing came along, a sure ticket. Who could resist."

His sister can see that Ben is heartbroken over Wanda's bad behavior, she stumbles over what to say.

"All Wanda did was set up a little situation, without telling anyone else."

"Except Alaska."

"And that allowed her to receive a series of small gratuities for not revealing certain things that Rudy once wrote. It's like the opposite of publishing his writing and then getting paid. She offered to not publish his writing and get paid. What's wrong with that? She's been so lost this last little while. And it's not something Rudy would ever have hesitated to do himself."

"Unless he was breaking a blood vow."

"Well," says Swan, "we have to tell him it wasn't you, Ben. It wasn't you. That young woman, Natalia, she knows how to get hold of Rudy."

"Oh no, don't even think of it. I am not breaking into her apartment," says Ben a little too fast.

Swan smiles. "I never imagined you would even know how."

37

WANDA AND GUS BROWSE the showroom of Didactic Motor's crosstown competitor, and Gus decides to buy a Moto Guzzi, which Wanda insists was designed by a man called Gus. It is an 850 Le Mans 1, and despite himself, the styling and the masculine sound of the name delight him. Gus smiles at it, as if he has met a long-lost brother or a twin.

Wanda explains that it has twin carbs, a vertical twin engine, twin disc brakes, and a twin cradle frame. Gus, who spends more time statistically than the masculine median gazing in the mirror, sees himself in a streamlined windshield and allows his wallet to fall open in awe.

He feels that he is Narcissus, delightfully drowning in a pool, and Wanda has interrupted his reverie by pulling him by the roots of his hair from the water.

"It's too bad you can't drive this thing in the State of New York," she says, hopping onto the bike. Gus stares at the thing, then stares at the woman straddling the front. Wanda kick-starts it and Gus puts on the helmet that he has purchased to go along with the look. Now, it is Gus who is lost in a blizzard, only the snow is more like morphia, and the storm is Wanda's passion. Because of the volume of the motor, they both begin to shout.

"On the back roads!" Wanda laughs. "I'll show you, and then you can write your license and drive here!"

"I should have got a license in Ontario," says Gus. "Here I'm a motorcycling virgin. I Saint Joseph'd myself." How stupid to have one and not be able to drive.

"Pardon me?" says Wanda.

"It's an expression of Swan's. It means I have never had an experience, specifically sex."

"But you had sex with me this morning!" shouts Wanda. "And with yourself last night!"

The owner of the motorcycle store, who had, until this comment, been standing in the doorway proudly admiring their excitement, withdraws quickly into his shop.

"Hop on!" says Wanda, and they pull out onto the street. A few moments later, Natalia enters the shop and asks to buy a Harley. "I told someone I had one, and maybe I should. What do I do if I have no license?" she asks, looking disarmed.

"How much are you willing to pay?"

Natalia spends the rest of the afternoon training with the owner of the cycle shop in the parking lot of a gas station. When they are finished, they both open a can of Dos Equis, and the owner takes her into the back.

"I don't normally do this," he tells her, snapping a photo and laminating it with her vital information on an outdated licensing machine. It was his father who first showed him how to do it, but his father is now more interested in art and artifacts and runs the gallery next to the World of Shoes. He has never regretted the day that he bought the phoney-making machine. He charges Natalia four hundred dollars.

"Before the days of holograms and such," he tells her. "All you needed to carry was one of these."

Wanda and Gus are speeding along the highway at quite a quick clip, and Gus finds his mouth forced into a smile. With a top speed of over 200 klicks, the Guzzi cuts loose like only a real racing machine can do. *It was a wise decision*, he tells himself. He needs an indulgence. He feels like the men gambling together in Cézanne's painting series of the 'Card Players.' He loves risks and gambles. His memory examines the painting as he experienced it, and something tells him one of the players is someone he thinks he recognizes from a portrait, Cézanne's *Uncle Dominique*. How wonderful that he is an Uncle as well. And now he feels free as the girl Courbet painted with the naked feet.

In Jackie's pickup, Michelle Shocked's music is rattling from the dashboard radio. "Mimi, for goodness sake, wake up!" Jackie glances over to see that Mimi's eyes have rolled back in her head and her lids have fallen open. Jackie is glad she did not let her drive. Despite herself, Jackie has to admit that there are some aspects of Mimi she does not find perfectly attractive.

Mimi, spun out in a trance, has released her spell over Jackie, and is travelling from tree to tree, until she finds a man, sitting in a canopy perch among animals, with a small computer and piles of dew-damaged books. Her vision hovers, and she looks down over the man. He is in danger, but not in the way that he thinks. Instead, he is about to be consumed by his own childhood terrors. This is what attracts Mimi to him. A powerful soul that is dying of doubt has always been her special interest. There was a time when she would have reached out to help him. But since she has been sustaining Vim's love, a gear has slipped in Mimi's good character. In fact, she has become more and more interested in the bad. She hovers over the man and wonders how long it will take before he destroys himself in the dire search that has taken a wrong turn.

Rudy feels a chill and pulls his jacket closer, looking up to the sky for signs of change in weather. He sees only a squirrel as Mimi darts away, returning to her body and the pickup truck on the road.

"No," thinks Jackie, "*she has been asking too low a price. It is an insult. She should not have even been asking me if she could buy the Squirrel. It was crafted in silence; the precision parts were fitted and machined in an action of friendship and trust. Its construction represents the breaking of two solitudes.*

Mimi should understand, she has been in prison. The Squirrel is not for sale. "

When Swan sees Ben jiggling the tumbler lock of Natalia's apartment using a small wire pick and then flipping it open as if it were never there, he is struck by his grace, like a lion charging after and then striking down an animal running across the savannah.

"I didn't know you could get into everywhere so easily," says Swan. Vespa puts her fingers to her lips.

"Ben can, darling, but you cannot. It's something he learned. It's dangerous and you must not do it."

Swan sees in a flash the sinister game of trust and treachery that orbited Ben and Rudy's adolescence, and he looks away.

"Let's get on with it," he answers.

The inside of Natalia's unit is just like the inside of Olesya's, only it is has much more furniture. There is more art and electronic equipment than most people would cram into twice as many rooms. In the confusion of lamps, vases, flowers, drapery, and imported rugs, they locate Natalia's desk.

A computer sits on top of it, and Swan sits down in her chair. Activating it, they search for the folder that is the most important in Natalia's life, her exchange between Rudy and herself. Because they have not much time, they are only able to scan the notes.

"They are in love," declares Swan.

"Rudy's going mad!" declares Ben.

"Just find the button that sends him the email," Vespa cuts in, in a practical way. Swan races the little arrow cursor across the screen, as if it is a little Cupid's arrow that he commands to heal a man's heart. Swan, who has always been a lover, finds his way through the maze of Natalia's messages to a screen where Cupid can record his letter of love. He swaps seats with Ben, and Ben sits staring at the screen, unable to respond with love to a poetic threat to kill him.

"Oh, for pity's sake! Writer's block!" says his sister, and she reaches over his arms to hunt and peck out the letters.

"It wasn't Ben," she types, and then she snaps the arrow to "Send."

"Okay, good enough?"

"I guess," says Swan. "What else is there to say?"

"Here, this is where he is posting from! He's in the Adiron-dacks." Natalia has drawn an extremely rough map of Rudy's location based on information in his correspondence.

"We'll never find him like this," says Swan, while Ben scribbles down the notations Natalia has made.

"We are talking about a six- million-acre park," Swan adds.

"We'll find him." Ben finishes his scribbling and jams the scrap in his pocket.

"Do you think Natalia will miss her sticky note?"

"She'll recover," says Vespa, "Let's get out of here!"

38

"DO YOU ALWAYS roll your eyes back into your head and leave your lids open when you sleep?" Jackie asks Mimi.

Mimi smiles. Her indisputable charm back on the maximum available heat, sizzling enough to melt both Jackie's common sense and her ice cream if Jackie drops her guard.

"Because it looked kinda weird," said Jackie, focusing on the road so that she not be focused on the eye-rolling woman to her right.

"I was envisioning a man who is sitting in the forest. A powerful man who builds towers that rise into the sky. He built the building where you have been living, the same building that the cat fell from."

"I was just seeing a lady with her eyes rolled back in her head, who thinks she can charm me into selling her my glider for next to nothing."

"He is past the Blue Mountain, near the number twenty-eight. He is in love with the man who built the glider with you and with a woman at the same time. The woman you are in love with was once in love with him, but now she is going to see him. He is in danger, and so are all the animals that walk near him. He has made a terrible mistake, and many of your friends may die. You can change the future by selling me the glider that you built with the man he once loved, but you must sell the glider for twenty-eight bucks."

"You are so full of it. I can't believe I ever called you a friend."

"Animism. Giving a soul to inanimate things. Unexplainable by science. Unexplainable except perhaps in supernatural terms. You won't love the glider. You wouldn't even comb the tail."

Jackie narrows her eyes and accelerates the truck. Mimi continues. "You must take me to the mountain place where this man is hiding. He is near a place called North Creek. His car is parked on a utility road. There is a deer trail that leads into the woods, and it is marked by a book, an open book, lying on its face."

"I don't believe you. What is the book?"

"The book … the book is called, *The One Minute Manager*." She rolls her eyes back a second time with her lids open wide.

"The trail will fork eight times. Turn left, turn right, turn left, turn right, turn left, turn right, turn left, turn right, and there you are."

"What kind of a secret route is that? Quit that!" says Jackie.

"Oh cripes, that's so hard on my ocular muscle tissue," says Mimi. She returns to consciousness and smiles engagingly at Jackie.

"What do you mean, the woman I was in love with is also in love with him and is going to see him?"

"Yes, and she is in danger, as are all the animals that walk near him."

They sit in silence for a moment.

"Does that mean she is still in love with me?"

"Don't make me do that again. My oculars aren't as flexy as they used to be."

"It's okay," says Jackie. She is nearing Olesya's building. "Mimi, where is Vespa right now?"

"She's on the F 750 Norton, going to see … the man in the forest. Vespa is going to the forest, and she is … Vespa is in mortal danger."

"You're not kidding?"

Jackie slides the pickup truck up next to Olesya's building.

"Well then, you better get out of the truck. You may be able to see things beyond the range of normal people, but I have my powers as well. And I am about to break through bricks and rocks and concrete with my will."

39.

NATALIA, HAVING SPED up the I-87 without incident, stops her Panhead along the side of the New York State Route 8. She is wondering suddenly why it seemed as if someone had been meddling with her sticky notes. She wonders, and then she tells herself to stop dreaming things up. She wants to shake her hair out of her helmet. She wants to see Rudy. The Panhead is nice, and it can easily carry a second rider on the pillion back of the puckered leather seat. She powers it up again, and it hesitates for a moment before kicking in to the familiar, distinctive Harley growl. Natalia catches her breath, thinking she has been given a dud, but now the Panhead is purring as before.

She also recalls her pencil was set to the right. But she is left-handed. She must be less compulsive than she thought she was under stress. She relaxes and powers on.

Rudy has just finished distributing the last land mine around the area of his tree. They will not be detonated by the light step of an animal, and he is gambling that even a deer will leap away before it can be disabled by the charge. If it does not, he is primed and ready with his rifle to make a quick business of any suffering caused to the forest life around him. He feels himself a humane man, but he is fed up with being persecuted. The email from Ben's sister had been from Natalia's terminal. It was intended to read, "It wasn't Ben." Instead it Rudy reads, "It bent Swan." Rudy does not have the slightest idea who

Swan is, but if he is a lover of Natalia, he had better beware. *Beware assassins*, thinks Rudy. He is too confused to unbend the meaning that was intended to exonerate his childhood friend.

Mimi is riding to The Blue Mountain area of the Adirondacks when she is troubled by an image that blurs before her eyes. She is seeing a man pouring gunpowder into cans and wrapping the tops with flint and wire. She does not understand the energy that is around him— an electrical flow of confusion and heartbreak. She sees a guardian that cannot help, and a responsibility dismissed.

Mimi's eyes snap to awareness just as they are about to roll under her lids.

She regains her concentration on the road and repeats to herself the things that she knows about bikes. All the Triumph riders in England and even America used to wear jackets that said "Rockers" in the 1950s and 1960s. There were many bike gangs, but people who simply loved the motorcycle were no longer inclined to join obvious gangs.

Mimi knows a rhyme that she sings to herself as she speeds along. Every now and then, the bike begins to wander to one side, and she has a funny feeling that she is slipping in and out of her trance-state instead of focusing on steering the Squirrel.

She flies past hills and farmland and she chants in order to keep herself calm.

> *Too much whine is not so fine*
> *sounds like your rollers have lost their bearings.*
> *Hearing knocks on idle Rockers?*
> *cylinders and pistons wearing!*
> *If you hear singing, go see what's ringing.*
> *That's the timing, how are you doing?*
> *What's that pinging as you start speeding?*
> *What's the danger? Is trouble brewing?*
> *What can fix a bad fuel mix?*
> *If it gets louder with carbon powder*

it's burned-up combustion parts your sparing!
If there's a clatter, the valve's the matter!
A knock on start-up, bad shell bearings!
Extract sparkplug, press down finger
on start-up, seal compression's play.
If compression is flaring, you won't stand staring.
The pressure will push your pinky away!
If then no broken rings you're wearing,
the beast's alive and off your tearing!
No piston holes just one highway,
the Rocker's free to chase the day.

The vehicle Mimi is driving is not a Triumph, but Mimi is fairly certain that the rhyme she has memorized will help if her Squirrel starts to choke.

She spots Natalia up ahead, stopped by the side of the road, and pulls over behind her.

"Hey!" says Mimi, pouring on the charm. Natalia feels as if this woman can see right through her, and she feels comforted by her and full of desire to burst into tears in her arms at the same time. The Panhead has made some terrible noises, and Natalia has stopped, not being sure what they mean.

Mimi is overcome with empathetic loneliness for companionship, expressed by Natalia's face and her desire to be with Rudy. The two of them stand there, love-lost, trying to hide it from each other.

"Engine trouble?" asks Mimi. Natalia neatly folds her hands together in front of herself as if she is about to begin a dance recital and nods.

"It won't turn over at all," she tells them, and she smiles, her hair pressed into an interesting wave by the helmet.

"Could be your battery," says Mimi. She looks at the Harley.

"Yep, probably the electrical system, maybe just the ignition circuit.... Do you have water with you?"

"Yes, I have a small jug of spring water," says Natalia.

"Is it spring water, or is it glacial runoff that can never be renewed?"

"I don't know," say Natalia hesitantly. "They're both bad. I should stop buying bottled water entirely."

"True, true. Could you go get my tools from under the seat?" asks Mimi.

When she comes back, Mimi is fooling with Natalia's ignition and trying to reach back to the battery behind her engine to check water levels. Shinny sets down the tool kit and looks Natalia up and down. She smiles at her and Natalia grins. Mimi scratches the back of her head, and then opens the gas cap on Natalia's tank.

"You're out of gasoline."

The two women begin to laugh. "I won't pull your whole electrical system apart quite yet," says Mimi, "because you just ran out of gas."

Natalia turns to Mimi who is now standing. "Could you siphon off a little gas from your tank, and I'll pay you for a fill-up at the next station? It can't be that far from here! We'll ride like a convoy...."

Mimi begins to say that it would be no problem at all and her lips extend in a smile as she sees the energy force of the man who is hiding in the forest, circling Natalia. Mimi begins to shake, and her eyes roll back into her head, so that she can get a better look. Because this is the way she can contact psychic channels, overpowering curiosity has often been her social downfall. Natalia takes a step back in surprise.

"*Hum, hum-hum...*" says Mimi. She thinks she sees that Natalia is in love with the man in the forest. Yet there is another force. A man in a pleated white shirt and teal-blue leotards. It is her dance instructor. He has been using a pheromone-based cologne. It is attracting Natalia, but Natalia fears the dance instructor only wants to stick her hard with his leotard-laden *lingham*. Natalia is angry with the man in the trees. So far, she has remained faithful. But the cologne and those tights are driving her to her limit. If Rudy does not shape up, she may have an affair.

And Rudy is paying for the dance lessons! Mimi sees that this has created a conflict. She sees Camelia, Rudy's secretary, first dropping a spoon and touching Natalia's leg. She sees Camelia boogie-woogie down a New York discothèque in an attempt to seduce her while drunk.

Suddenly, she realizes she is standing at the side of the Interstate, shaking and rolling her eyes. As usual, she has left her lids open. She rolls her eyeballs back into focus, and notes she is being stared at.

"Are you alright?" asks Natalia, holding up a half litre of siphoned gasoline.

"Fine," says Mimi, straightening up in a winning way with a smile.

Natalia takes the siphoned gasoline and pours it from her half-litre soy-milk box into the Panhead's tank. She throws her drinking straw at Mimi's feet.

"You were shaking, your eyes...."

"It's nothing. Just energy. It sent me into a sort of a trance. It's stupid really. I can control it if I want."

Natalia smiles in a worried way.

"I don't believe you were in a trance, I think you would have looked more entrancing. I think you were having some sort of seizure, and I'm not at all sure you should be on the road in your condition."

"Nonsense. Of course I was in a trance. And I was just going to suggest that you and I go to the nearest service station...."

"I'm not going anywhere with you. And I no longer think, my bug-eyed friend, that you should be getting back on your bike."

"Well, I don't think you should be fantasizing about your dance instructor. Forget his pretty white blouse, his teal tights and his nappy nylon nightstick. He's wearing a pheromone cologne, and his interest is purely...."

"Back off!" screams Natalia. "Stop reading my mind! You're sick! It's not a blouse!"

"I'd hate to be stranded by the road."

"Thank you for the gasoline. I hope that you fare well."

"Well yeah, now that half the motor fuel's gone...." Mimi begins. The two women glare at each other. It is a dangerous looking eye-lock. Mimi clears her throat. "Um, I'm going up to the Adirondacks. Whereabouts you headed?"

"I'm going crazy," says Natalia. The engine turns over perfectly, a friendly sounding growl.

"Fine," says Mimi. "Go crazy, but don't drag all my friends into your romance with a madman." Mimi mounts her bike and starts her engine. Her movements are fluid, and for a moment, dancer Natalia widens her eyes.

Mimi pulls into the traffic, causing a car to swerve. It blows its horn and Mimi waves her leather fist.

40.

JACKIE IS NOT HAVING the greatest time with the Chevy pickup. It is moving with a misaligned drive shaft that coasts slightly into oncoming traffic, and her steering has to be corrected every few moments. It wasn't something it was doing before Mimi got out, but she dismisses the idea that Mimi has powers to fudge with mechanical things. Otherwise she is moving swiftly along New York State Route 28, to an area called North Creek.

It is because she knows Vespa is headed there, not because she gives a damn about Rudy. Jackie senses Vespa is approaching danger, and approaching it with a forgiving, kind-hearted attitude that is about to blow her to bits. Jackie curses the pickup, then apologizes to it. She believes in an unwavering, agnostic way that machines can feel her vibes.

"I'm sorry," says Jackie aloud.

The pickup truck corrects and suddenly Jackie is driving in a straight line again, without having to adjust the misalignment. A shudder of truck-woman kinship moves up and down her spine. In the back of the truck, the Squirrel glider is held down by bungees and a tarp. In the rear-view, she can see the furred rudder moving happily back and forth with the wind.

Arriving outside of North Creek, she parks the Chevy at a lookout point to assemble the motorless aircraft. A strong wind is tugging at her. She grits her teeth and pops together the component parts. Roping it to a tree, she runs over their craftwork with the tips of her fingers until she is satisfied that every part is joined tightly and in place. The cliff she chooses is four hundred feet above the mixed-tree forest. Throwing a pack on her back, she launches the glider, the wind speed-reading at thirty knots an hour. To any observer, it would appear that Jackie was committing suicide. To Jackie, it is merely a challenging fly.

In Manhattan, Olesya's bail officer laughs and settles back in his chair. A sense of hilarity has swept in through the windows and into his bones, and he has started to giggle. The judge has rendered the evidence against Olesya as inadmissible on the grounds that the videotape is black and white and the jacket is tangerine. Eyewitnesses aside, even the city workers tearing up the block in front of West 109th Street are wearing tangerine. Even the PR men and some of the cops brought in to control the Internet site picket chaos were wearing tangerine. The judge himself has a tangerine Speedo. The papers are flaring in tangerine ink: "Olesya case acquitted, Judge rules lack of evidence."

Several miles of hardtop behind Mimi is Ben and Gus's lover Swan on the back of his Trident 750V. They are following a map taken from Natalia's apartment. Ahead of them is Ben's sister. Vespa has been thinking about him on idle, not crazy about him, just a regular guy now, when the idea suddenly strikes her that Ben has been a real worm.

First, he broke into that woman's apartment, then abandoned Wanda for doing nothing more than conning a few filthy thousand out of dirty Rudy. Rudy—the man who had Vespa thrown from his building. The man who had laboured in the corporate boardroom of a company that had killed, defrauded, and caused death and injury to hundreds, possibly thousands of people. And he had mistrusted Jackie, when all Jackie had ever done was to saw open a few bank machines, breaking into a few places that would not miss the cash. It was something Ben had done himself.

The price tag in damage and death behind corporate crime was apparently in the millions, and B.F. Turner had not paid a cent. At least Rudy seems informed. Now, he is somewhere up in the trees. And she is supposed to love him and forgive him? She is supposed to convince him it had not been Ben who sent the threats? Why? So that Wanda could be targeted? So that Ben could have Swan to himself?

Vespa allows her bike to slow and then dodges and trails behind Ben. As ever, even with the sides of his face smushed like a Shar-Pei inside his helmet, his smile is magnetizing. When Ben and Swan have rumbled ahead of her a decent distance, she turns onto a sideroad, and then another, and another. Ben finally slows to have a poutine and a fried fish burger with Swan, and realizes his sister is not behind him. "Oh no! She doesn't understand!"

For a moment, he is flooded with fear that she has been swiped off the road and killed. He feels as if he has been torn apart, as if a tornado has ripped off the roof of their home and dropped a raging river between himself and Vespa that is too wild for him to cross. He argues with Swan that they should turn back and look for her, but Swan is insistent that they should push on. Ben is not used to not getting his way. He steels himself. He cannot let concern for Wanda surface. After all, Wanda is shagging Swan's beau. He has an absurd feeling of rootlessness, something like what Olesya must have felt when she first came home from the prison psychiatric infirmary to find her home was packed with the busy lives of many other people.

Swan laughs and shovels a French fry into Ben's mouth, and Ben accepts it, like a baby bird, like a cygnet. If it had been Wanda, he would have pushed her hand away. He might have said something angry. He is beginning to think about how he treats Wanda. Perhaps he has not been playful enough. With Swan he accepts, even peeps like a baby bird. Swan laughs and feeds him another. The sun beats hot, and they are enjoying each other's inner child. Swan tells him not to worry about his sister, she is probably having fun. For a moment, Ben thinks he meant Wanda, having fun in the arms of Gus. He drops his eyes before they can discuss it. Instead, they look at the map they have gleaned from information in Natalia's house. It is confusing; it is chicken scratch, Ben has become separated from Vespa, and they are lost.

41.

ARNICA HEARS THE RUMBLE of Gus and Wanda's Moto Guzzi coming towards her at their picnic spot by the Hudson River. Celeste has only been in new York a few days, and is overcome by Alaska's caring attention to her child. As well, Alaska seems to appreciate Celeste for what she is, a hot artiste. They sit closely together, the door of the minivan left open, a radio warbling from within. Arnica however is tired of staring at her mother's friend's French easel, being bounced on Alaska's knee and listening to them discuss forgiving and nonforgiving watercolour paper. She misses Gus and Swan.

Celeste looks furtively around her. The sound of the motor-cycle engine has disrupted her meditative state. She looks up guiltily, as if caught *en flagrant délit* stoned on absinthe *avec la bébé* on the banks of the Seine. But Gus is far from a judge-mental mood. For one thing, thanks to him, Arnica's father is with Ben and he is with Wanda, having the time of his life.

"Hello, my dear friends," says Gus, and he hits the kill switch on the Guzzi. Wanda hops off and saunters over to the group. As ever, Wanda is intimidating, something she has never noticed, preferring to hide behind men who frighten her more. She is only now beginning to realize and think about the effect this may have on other people.

"Hello," says Wanda. Only the baby looks impressed.

The grown-ups look like they are about to burst into tears. "It's okay," Wanda tells them.

"What do you mean?" asks Celeste.

Wanda drops a newspaper on Alaska's lap and saunters over to look at the painting of *Trees By The Hudson* that Celeste has painted.

"This is stunning! You're really good. It's captured every flash of light in the tree! Everything is in that painting! Gus, come look!!"

"Holy Smokin' Foot-longs!" says Alaska, reading the bright tangerine print. Ignoring her, Gus steps lightly over to look at the painting.

Alaska falls back in her Cape Cod recliner, and Gus takes Arnica in his arms.

"Mary, Joseph, Java, and Tee Tee. Holy Dog Nuts and Hashish Hannah!" Alaska holds up the newspaper.

"I know, it's good," says Gus, unsure if he should be referring to the newspaper report of Olesya's acquittal or to Celeste's work. "You didn't know?" he adds politely.

"It's first-rate!" says Wanda. She moves closer in her leather and traces the motion of the brushwork in the air with her prosthetic.

"I always wanted talent like this," she murmurs gently.

"Gorgeous!" says Gus. His hair is sweaty and sticking every which way. Arnica laughs and presses her fist into his mouth.

"We really, really love your work," says Wanda.

"You do?" asks Celeste insecurely, and she stares at Wanda, the expression of a brilliant and tormented artist that will become her everyday resting face is just beginning to accent her features. She falls into Wanda's embrace, and fits Wanda's body in a way that makes Wanda feel good and warm and gentle.

Gus sits the baby on the newspaper. The river light Celeste had caught in her painting plays in Gus's dark hair.

"We really do," says Alaska. "We love you."

"Yes," says Gus, "and we love sweet baby Arnica too."

42.

ALONE, MIMI DOES NOT find it difficult to visit Rudy in his trees. She has parked her Scott Flying Squirrel in the bush, and then followed the open book that has been left as a marker into the woods. She finds a deer trail, and begins to follow it, turning as her instincts tell her to do. Finally, she feels a sense of arrival. She is not entirely wrong, as she is standing in the centre of his mines.

"Hello!" she calls out, not sure why she is here alone, only that this is the place where she has been led.

"Dear God! Look out woman!" calls a voice from above her, and then, "It's all my fault!"

She begins to take a step toward the voice, then steps back.

She realizes that many small animals around her are watching her, and that the place has become a sort of temple to the forest, with pines as spires. Rudy, in the trees above, is its silent worshipper, who, only just now, has become terribly troubled.

She begins to walk to him and stops a second time. Something is telling her not to approach him, but a powerful compassion pulls her forward.

"What's the matter with you?" she shouts at him. "What the hell is your problem?"

"The whole place, this whole place, is surrounded by mines. Do you hear what I am saying? I would come down and help you to safety, but I am crazy with sorrow. I don't even remember where I placed them. Each one is more damning of me than the one I buried previously. And they are all around, surrounding me where I hide. I cannot come down to help you, and you cannot come here to help me down."

Mimi looks around for a moment. She realizes that any perceptions that may have brought her here cannot help her at this juncture in her life. She also realizes that she has arrived here alone because she has always been interested by excesses of evil. She had always thought it was something she could touch without being harmed. She thought that her ability to go into a trance and see things as they really are would protect her, but she cannot see the land mines buried in the ground. They are rooted in paranoia and misunderstanding, and she cannot see where they are placed. "I can't see them and I don't know why."

"Because curiosity has brought you here," says Rudy, "and curiosity is pure." It is a riddle he should not have constructed. To be in the same place as Rudy because of her purity, and now find that she has been rendered powerless by fear and evil, is an answer she does not accept. Mimi resolves that even if kills her, she will take all risks to remove the danger—and not so as to rescue another person or to learn what turned him into who he is, but to clarify who she is to herself.

"How many?" she asks him.

"Twenty-four."

Mimi looks at the various ways the treetop could be approached. She looks at the sky, then she looks around for a rock, a stick, an object with some weight.

"I know you are not here to assassinate me," Rudy tells her.

"Not for that," Mimi answers him.

She takes off her boot and turns her back away from the direction in which she is walking. She is glad she is wearing leathers. She puts on her helmet and braces herself. Then she throws the boot into the air onto the path where she was about to step. When the boot falls, there is an explosion. The explosion sends gravel and dirt high into the air. The fireworks and gunpowder make a spectacular flash in the sky, catching the attention of Jackie, jumping with mastery in her lightweight craft from tree to tree to tree.

The force of it knocks Mimi onto her stomach.

It leaves a crater in the ground. She gets up slowly and looks about her. Her boot has landed next to her, as if it was frightened and had returned to the protection of its mate.

"Twenty-three!" says Mimi.

She steps into the crater with her boot in her hand. It is a well-made boot and is barely damaged by the force of the blast. She slips it back on. Then she tosses a dislodged rock onto the path, creating a second explosion. Mimi tosses more rocks, triggers a third. The force of the third explosion strikes her in the solar plexus, causing her to fall.

Another boot fall strikes its mark, and Mimi is showered with rocks and debris. A sting strikes her foot, and she sees that she is cut. Anger starts to rage inside her.

"What the fuck were you trying to prove? Are you completely out of your mind? What the fuck kind of hotshot dipshit do you think you are? Rudy, I am going to kill you when I get my hands on you, you candy-arse prick."

"I have a gun," he tells her. "And you are creating me a path to freedom. You will not kill me. You are serving me. I will shoot you first. It is the law of the forest."

"Okay, okay, I won't kill you," says Mimi. She smiles and sees his face peering out at her from between the branches. She stares back and locks onto him with her eyes. She is determined not to die at the hands of this twerp. His anger softens, while hers grows hard. "I'm just coming to help you down because something told me you were in some kind of trouble."

She picks up a largish rock fallen at her feet after the last explosion. "What are we at, honey?"

"Twenty," he says. He is the saddest-sounding man she has ever heard. A shadow passes over him. It is Jackie, flapping her glider wings in the trees and landing on the trees next to him with her glider. Both Mimi and the man in the tree can only see the silhouette.

"Sweet mercy!" cries Rudy. "What am I seeing?"

He fires his rifle up at the glider, and a bullet tears through the wing.

There is a crashing sound as Jackie drops down onto the trees.

He fires a second shot and misses his target. Landing on his platform, Jackie grabs him by the collar and sinks her fist into his stomach. She takes the gun from him and throws it from the tree. A kick leaves him begging for mercy.

43.

"YOU'RE RIGHT. Alaska was right. Celeste really is talented!" Wanda is gushing. They have enjoyed a pleasant visit with the painter, the woman-who-knows-a-whole-ton-about-art and the baby. They have left them with their minivan and they are nearing the end of their long road trip with the Moto Guzzi near a shady place called North Creek.

"Listen Gus! Explosions!"

"Yes," says Gus in an informed-sounding voice, "they may be doing some type of mineral extraction in these hills. The Adirondacks are old."

"I thought it was parkland," shouts Wanda underneath the helmet on his head.

"Oh, yes, this part may be, but I'm not sure," says Gus. It does not cross his mind to feel afraid. He is unsure how to act. The quiver in his gut is something he feels more closely to be a cousin of social danger. He is right. He is worrying about seeing Swan and Ben on the Triumph when he should be worrying about losing his life. Because he is with Wanda, the woman whose life he has saved, whose girlhood was swept away from the grip of snowy death in his arms, he is unable to see through his own blizzard of confusion over his own mortality or the fact that they are doing this for Ben. They have arrived at the end of the utility road on the map.

Wanda is feeling the letdown feeling that something between

herself and Alaska has been lost. Gus turns off the engine. The two of them sit there, smoke a joint, and ponder how to proceed. They stare at the beautiful mountains and smile blithely as a red Corvette pulls up next to them. It is Natalia and Camelia, Camelia at the wheel, looking like FBI agents in matching Raybans. Natalia, who panicked and abandoned her Panhead, contacted Camelia by phone for a ride. Since Camelia was already driving out from the New York offices, and already tracking Rudy, it didn't take long for the red Corvette to find Rudy's mistress on the highway. Camelia jumps out, and her boardroom power voice makes itself known as she takes command of the little group. "Whatshisname has really gone over the deep end, kids. This is no small matter. I have a cellphone and I'm going to use it."

"What for?" cries Gus.

Vespa arrives on her Honda. Gus and Wanda smile in surprise at the solo rider because they were afraid she was Ben and Swan.

"Because he's planted land mines around the perimeter," says Camelia. "I'm calling the police."

Another explosion sounds from down the path where the book marker lies face down. Camelia picks up the book. *The One Minute Manager*. This is the spot alright. He marked it." She sighs mightily, the sigh drawing Wanda's eyes to her bosom.

"He's in there!" cries Natalia. Breaking away, she begins to run to the path. "My boyfriend! He's in danger!"

Vespa and Gus grab Natalia, who has been working out several hours a day with a personal trainer, and wrestle her to the ground. "Let me go, you fucked-up dyke!" she screams at Gus.

"Free me, faggot!" she snarls at Vespa.

"Never," says Vespa.

"We don't want you hurt!" Gus says, and looks at Vespa in confusion.

"Hello, police, there is a man...." barks Camelia into the phone.

"How did you find out?" Vespa asks Camelia from her position on the pavement. She has captured Natalia in an especially painful armlock. "Just calm down, straight lady," she whispers to her. "Calm down or I'll snap your arms like a stick."

Natalia throws back her head and screams an operatic falsetto.

"Goddamn it, the police hung up. Would you tell her to be quiet? The goddamn police thought it was teenagers. Natalia calm down. I'll redial...."

"But how did you know?"

"I was driving down here anyway. I knew something was wrong. I kept emailing Rudy, trying to find out what was going on. He only told me a few moments ago, on the email."

"On the Internet?"

"Sort of," says Camelia. "This isn't an ordinary Corvette."

"He's got email in there," says Gus. "He must have a satellite dish in the car."

"Well, it wasn't actually Rudy who sent off the message," says Camelia. "It was someone named Jackie, and my -mail makes a *dong*, a *donging* sound, whenever...."

"What?" Vespa is off the ground and out of there like a shot.

"Stop!" shouts Gus.

Natalia makes an effort to kick him in the testicles. "You pitiful hormone-crazed hetero! I could out-tango your overly compact ass on any dance floor on the planet!"

There is another explosion. Gus jumps away from Natalia, who is hissing and gnashing her teeth. She grabs the phone from Camelia and throws it with a clatter to the ground. "Nooo way! My good thing's in there! My multi-million dollar daddy, and I'm not going to let cops or anyone else take him away from me now. We are driving away to Manhattan to be married and enjoy our money and our love. The rest of you can butt out!"

Natalia dashes into the forest after Vespa, who is in pursuit of Jackie. Gus looks about him and realizes that injured Wanda, heavily favouring one leg with her cane, has rambled down the path ahead of the rest. Gus opens his mouth in a cry of horror when he spots scavenger birds wheeling in the sky.

"Uh-oh," says Ben and then Swan almost at the same time. Lost, they are still enjoying each other's company and trying to make light of the fact that they cannot actually find the highway they think they should be on. They do know that they are surrounded by beautiful mountains, snaking rivers, and that the Triumph is a hot sexy rumble between their thighs.

Wanda has made it a very good distance up the path and past several land mines, tapping them lightly with her cane and then stepping another way. She is trying to catch Vespa, who has passed her now and is further ahead. "Vespa, come back! I can feel the ground. Trust me with this cane! You'll get hurt without me, Vespa!"

Vespa, who is no idiot, has made a rush through the trees, avoiding the path, and splashing through a brook that follows it.

She does not hear Wanda. Wanda hears a crashing sound behind her as Natalia leaps past with the grace of a white-tailed doe.

"Be careful, young woman!" she calls to her, even though Wanda is the same approximate age as the dancer. She calls again, then continues to pick her own way along the path. Behind them, Gus is feeling a sense that, twenty-five years later, the terrible avalanche has now swallowed the girl.

"How many more?" Jackie calls to Mimi.

"Seventeen!" says Mimi.

Rudy begins to stir. "Oh holy masters of forest and leafage, oh cherished and whiskered animals, oh six-legged friends that munch upon the foliage and bounty, oh mice and rat and birds and bat...."

"He's talking to himself!" says Jackie.

"Smack him! Wake him up!" directs Mimi from the centre of a crater. Jackie does both.

"Oh winged beasts that ... oh ... Mama, someone slugged me."

He reaches out his arms to Jackie like a little child and begins to cry. Jackie sits down beside him and unwraps a mocha and vanilla energy bar. She strokes his hair—something she is not used to doing to a male.

"So, little sweetheart, it looks like you planted a whole mess of little bombs around your fort."

"I didn't mean to, Doctor Pop-Tart."

"He just called me Doctor Pop-Tart," calls Jackie.

Mimi is pitching stones. Another bomb goes off and when the rubble is finished raining around her, she says, "That's a good sign. Dr. Popair. I went to that psychotherapist too. He's a group regression therapist."

"What the hell is a psychotherapist?" starts Jackie, and then realizes it must be of no importance. She begins to take her own munch of the candy bar before she realizes it is infested with weevils. Furious, she pitches it over the side of the platform. Another mine is detonated at the foot of the tree.

"Jesus, Mary, Jo Jo, and Donkey! Would you be more careful?"

"Sorry," Jackie apologizes.

"Sixteen," says Mimi. "Good shot."

"Honestly, there's way more than twenty-four, Doctor Popcans. I know where each of them are. I can take them all out again, and make this place sacred again for the birds, the eight-legged, eight-eyed companions of man, the...." Rudy says.

"He just said there are more than twenty-four. And he says he remembers where they all are and wants to help take them out."

Mimi gives out a cry of despair. Real tears are now mixing with the sweat that is running down the inside of her helmet. "Well, untie him then. Let him come on down here."

"If he's coming down, I am too," says Jackie. She unties his hands, and Rudy scrambles away down the swinging rope ladder.

"Fuck!" Jackie remembers she has thrown the rifle at the foot of the tree. She shakes the rope ladder violently, causing Rudy to fall the last few feet onto his ass.

"There's one right around here!" says Rudy, and he picks up a rock that had held down a tarp. He tosses it. Unlike Mimi, he is not wearing riding leathers and a protective helmet. He throws up his arms to protect himself from the blast but is knocked off his feet. He staggers upright, bleeding from the gravel and nails that he had packed inside and have now struck him.

"Oh lovely, terrific," says Jackie, swinging from the ladder. She watches Rudy staggering over to Mimi like a real-day zombie and wonders what to do. Gingerly, she picks up the rifle.

Vespa bursts from the woods. Rudy focuses his eyes on her and says her name, first in a whisper, then in a shout. "Vespa, it's Vespa! She finally made it past my security people!"

"Jackie!" Vespa cries. "You're okay!" Her face drops as she surveys the scene. "You're with Mimi again!"

"This is not a sex thing, believe me," says Mimi.

"Vespa," says Jackie, "do not move one more inch forward or I will have to shoot you."

"Shoot?"

"There are land mines everywhere and I will have to shoot you for your own protection."

"That doesn't make any sense."

"I don't care. Put your hands on your head."

"Jackie, can't we save this for the bedroom? I really wanted to see you, but this is a little extreme, don't you...." She makes a move toward Jackie and then stops.

"I don't love you, Vespa!" says Rudy. "But there is a land mine one boot-width from your running shoe. And I don't want to see you lose your legs. Your pretty, honey-coloured, silky smooth..."

"Shut up, guy!" says Mimi.

"Yeah, shut up!" says Jackie.

"She has a chisel injury above the left knee and a sweet little old mole on her right thigh..." Rudy continues.

"Rudy!" screams Natalia, emerging from the bushes. "I thought you really loved me. I thought you were going to marry me in Manhattan. She's a lesbian, you screwball fuck. Half the men and women around here are lesbians. Even Camelia is a lesbian. I'm all you've got, honey, I'm all that's left. Don't you tell me about her cute little chisel scars. I'm here to get you away from these people. They were threatening to disclose your past and blow everything out of the water. If Vespa's here, don't you think that Ben is lurking somewhere around here as well?"

"Ben," says Rudy. "I did love Ben like a brother. I wanted to make love to Ben. And he betrayed me."

"That's why we came here," says Jackie. "To tell you the threat-to-disclose letter was not actually sent from Ben. Ben loves you, and better yet, he is on his way here now to tell you that in person," says Jackie.

"No clue why, but that much is true," says Vespa.

"Don't you remember the email? I sent it. It was supposed to read, 'It wasn't Ben.'"

"No! All I got was the one that came from Natalia's apartment. It said, 'It bent Swan.'"

"No, Swan is Gus's boyfriend. That makes no sense."

"Sent from my apartment. These fucking scumbags broke into my..."

"Oh, I used to do that kind of shit all of the time," says Rudy.

"Don't you see," says Natalia, "the letter was encrypted, and you didn't apply your usual fastidiousness to unravel the code. You're losing your mind, Rudy. 'It bent Swan' has the same letters, but it was sent by people who broke in."

Natalia moves closer to Vespa, across an area that Mimi had been convinced was peppered with mines. "Nobody move!" shouts Jackie, but the tree she is standing next to has started to fall.

The few mines detonated by Mimi and Rudy have dislodged the old tree and blasted the stump, and it is beginning to topple. "Everybody, look out!" shouts Jackie. "This whole tree, it's coming over!"

The group freezes and looks at Jackie. "Where are we to go?"

Mimi stares at Jackie. The toppling tree is headed straight in her direction, and directly beyond her, Vespa, and the dancer, frozen in a quarrel. "Well, kid, guess this is it," says Mimi.

"Move!" shouts Jackie.

"Which way?"

Jackie turns and begins to scramble up the tree even as it is beginning to fall. "What the hell are you doing?"

"I'm getting the Flying Squirrel! What the hell are you doing?"

"I'm running for my life!" Mimi starts to run forward, jumps into the protection of another crater, overcome by the enormity of the tree about to crash down on their group. Other mines will be detonated, and the forest around them is already starting to burn.

"At the beginning, I was attracted to the mystery of evil. But later on, I just felt like they needed my help," says Mimi weakly. She feels overcome by emotions. She is alone and concussed in a crater.

44.

JACKIE FINDS THE GLIDER difficult to control. It is snagged on the branches of the tree next to the one that she first scrambled up, and she jumps to it, then pulls herself with the strength of her upper body into the machine she built with Ben.

The glider wing that has been shot has grown into a tear. A few moments later, she lets herself drop and swings past Vespa, grabbing on to her with her legs. The heat of the burning forest ignites another mine and the force of it throws them together up into the air and across the convection of heat over the small clearing Rudy has called home. Vespa is not holding on to Jackie, who grips her tightly between her own thighs.

Jackie sweeps above the trees, and sees Wanda and Gus stumbling back down the path, away from the fire. Neither sees the other one and both are calling each other's name. Swan and Ben have arrived in the parking area and are no longer wondering what is going on. Ben sees the fire and rushes to it, running straight through the woods. He meets Natalia who is carrying Rudy in her arms. They are both covered with blood.

"I'm so glad to see you," says Natalia. "You really loved him, as much as I do."

"I did once. I don't know if I do now. But I would never betray him. I can carry him out if you like, if he's not too heavy."

"I guess love is love," says Natalia. She shakes her head. "I can carry him out. I work out four hours solid twice a day with a personal...."

The smoke has grown so heavy that they can no longer speak. Ben is glad that Natalia sounds like a bit of a dull blade. Swan finds Gus along the path and leads him out along the footsteps they can see through the thickening smoke, while Wanda continues wandering the path calling his name. When Ben stumbles out to the parking area, he finds Gus is passed out on the pavement and Wanda nowhere to be found. Natalia loads Rudy into the back of the Corvette with Camelia. Ben begins to panic and starts up the path. It is thick with smoke.

He hears an explosion behind him.

"Oh God, I've killed her," he says, not sure why it would be his fault. He runs in the direction of the detonated mine, certain he will find Wanda in bits.

"Take your helmet!" shouts Swan, who is giving CPR to Gus. Gus sits up and tells Swan to take a mint. When Ben reaches the site of the mine crater, he looks around in terror. Lying by the side of the path, mangled and burned even more seriously than Ben was the night of his collision, is Wanda's prosthetic hand. It seems to be reaching for him, reaching as it always did, but it is still too hot for him to touch. Then he hears her voice, the voice of his love.

"Gus!"

She is standing in the little brook of running water that follows the path. Ben runs down the slope. "My name is not Gus," he tells her.

"Well then, treat me right," says Wanda.

"Could you find your way out of here without me?" asks Ben.

"I think I detonated that mine fairly well with what was at hand so to speak. And I felt my way along the rest of the distance with my cane."

Another blast issues behind them, the fire igniting the powder.

"This is awful. To think I ever loved him, let's get out of

here before we are killed!" Ben yells. He reaches for her hand and it is not there.

That particular hand will never be there again. She has given it away to Gus.

They wade through the creek and emerge at last a short distance from the group by the car. The group is shaking with shock.

Jackie is leaning over Vespa, across the lot from the others. The broken glider is smouldering in pieces at their side.

Ben runs to his sister. Wanda follows him more slowly, as if there are still mines on the surface of the pavement.

"She's not ... she's not responding. She's like you were, when you went over the cliff. She's hardly breathing...."

Vespa does not react to touch. Her limbs are cold, her breath is shallow, her face is expressionless of life.

"No," says Ben. "I think she might be even worse off than I was that night, even worse."

Wanda sets down her cane and rests her head lightly on Vespa's breast, an intimacy Jackie has never seen before. Wanda takes Vespa's hand. "Her heartbeat is irregular. Don't die, kid," she tells her.

Ben's eyes fall on the mangled glider, then onto Jackie's face.

"How are we to get her out of here? She won't make it. She needs emergency medical help. Even if we all packed in to the Corvette, we might not make it...."

"A Corvette can move pretty fast with the right woman at the wheel," says Wanda.

Ben turns his head back to look at the others, and then stands and breaks into a run. He stops at the Corvette and leans into the window. "Rudy, please wait, Vespa is ... she's..."

"I saw," says Natalia. "She's dying. Now back off so I can get him out of here."

"Please wait. Can you take her to a hospital? Rudy, it's Vespa, can you, can you...."

A voice rattles out from the back seat. "Natalia, you will

wait for Vespa to be carried to the car. Otherwise I will die, and I will leave you with nothing."

Natalia bites her lip. "But she's slipping away, even if we got her medical help...."

Jackie looks up at the sky, and sees a small furry animal jumping through the air. The clouds are beautiful; the mountains are too pretty to be missed.

"Vespa, Vespa, look up at the clouds," she says. She is greeted by silence. She brushes a strand of hair clotted with blood away from Vespa's face. A shadow falls over them, and for a moment, Jackie bows her head. Then she touches her lips to Vespa's lips and again runs her hands through her hair. "Don't die, baby. Please, sugar, don't die."

Mimi, shambling out of the woods, unscathed but for a small trickle of blood at her temple, has a more squirrel-like countenance than Jackie has ever noticed before.

"Sorry to arrive so late. I had a small concussion. Thanks for looking for me."

"Mimi!" says Jackie. "it's Vespa."

"Rough shape, huh?" says Mimi. Jackie nods. It has always offended Vespa to speak the obvious.

"What kind is she?" asks Mimi.

"What do you mean, 'what kind?' The fighting kind. What kind of shape?"

"I suppose." Mimi bends to listen to the younger woman's heart, laying her hand on her breast. "Four valves, and four cylinder, if you count both arms and legs," she remarks.

"What're you doing to me?" asks Jackie. "She's dying."

"No, she's resting. She's still alive."

"Is she paralyzed?"

"Not at all. She's trancing. She's talking to someone. She's angry with the man in the back of the Corvette. She's talking to his spirit."

"Will she come out of it? When will she be able to talk to me?"

"Rudy says all the mines have been detonated now by the

heat of the fire," Vespa murmurs, and she opens her eyes slightly.

"Tell him thanks for giving me credit," says Mimi.

"He says he's going to tell the police straight up what happened, and he's not going to implicate us or get us involved," Vespa adds.

"Tell him you have over forty shrapnel-type wounds on your body and the rest of us aren't looking all that hot either. So, we're already involved. But thanks for being so considerate."

With a comforting rumble, The Eleanor Roosevelt Memorial Fire Watch Service, in a vintage 1928 biplane, flies over the fire. The plane dumps a load of Perrier on the simmering wooded area and circles back into town.

"He says he's a millionaire, so he'll get in a lot of trouble, but he'll find a way to cover it up. He says he thanks you for your understanding."

A second Cessna passes by with volunteers of the Culinary Institute of America and drops a large *mousse à la vanille* onto the centre of the blaze, all but extinguishing the fire without polluting the forest with artificial creams.

Vespa's eyes flutter. "He shot him," says Vespa. "He shot the guy, Turner. He murdered him in cold blood. I'm not getting in the Corvette with him. He shot him." She falls back into Jackie's arms.

Ben returns to her side. "Well there's a seat waiting for you in the Corvette. I think you better go to the hospital."

She takes Jackie's hands.

"What am I thinking? There's no need for Vespa to ride in the Corvette. I brought the pickup! I must be a little dizzy in the head myself!" says Jackie. She slaps herself in the forehead as a gesture of forgetfulness and sees she is bleeding as she draws it away.

"Oh, crap."

"I'll drive the pickup," says Mimi. "We'll get her there that way."

"Let's get a move on then," says Vespa." Rudy says the Blue Mountain Volunteer Police Department will be here in a couple of minutes."

"Okay, Mimi, you grab the pickup. Even though you probably don't even have a license to drive a pickup. I don't even know how you pulled through all this..."

"Sometimes rules get broken," says Mimi.

Jackie fishes her truck keys from her pocket.

"I'll come and see you as soon as all of this is over," Mimi tells Vim. She runs to the truck.

She is glad to know that confronting her fears has given her the power to breathe life back into the dying. Vespa was a goner. She looks back and sees Jackie crumpled pitifully on the pavement next to her true love and she quickens her step.

Rudy had certainly played all the wrong cards—a hopeless case of a different sort. He has taught her everything he will never understand himself on the subject of evil—a mastery she will handle with care. Mimi is grateful that he took her there, and she knows how deep his terror is that he should be taken back. She understands the depths of the emotional suffering he has endured, the heat of the flames, and the sting of the weapons he constructed to keep away his fears.

There is still a part of Rudy that would like to lay the blame on shaggy Gus, soft-hearted Swan, on anyone else but himself. She realizes Rudy will have to own what he has done from the beginning. Mimi drops by the Corvette as she runs to the truck and leans into the back seat. "Don't you hurt them, Rudy. Time to be honest. Because I'm on to you now, baby," she tells him. "Don't forget that I'm the one who can take you down. I can take you there anytime."

"What a slut!" says Natalia. "Pay no attention to her."

"That's not what she meant," says Rudy. "She means that she has the power. The power to fly me straight to hell."

ACKNOWLEDGEMENTS

The author wishes to thank Connie Frey, Susan Mayse, Ursula Pflug, Heather Spears, and the Kootenay School of the Arts and the Victoria School of Writing for their editorial assistance and ongoing support.

Thanks also to Editor-in-Chief of Inanna Publications, Luciana Ricciutelli, to Inanna Publicist and Marketing Manager, Renée Knapp, and to cover designer, Val Fullard.

The author would like to acknowledge the following sources:

Baudelaire, Charles. *Les Fleurs du Mal*. Alençon: Auguste Poulet-Malassis, 1857.

Bergman, Ingmar. *Autumn Sonata*. Oslo, 1978.

Shelley, Percy Bysshe. *Oedipus Tyrannus*. London, 1820.

Descartes, René. *Discourse on the Method*. Leiden, 1637.

Diderot, Denis. *Philosophical Thought*. Paris, 1746.

Kerouac, Jack. *On the Road*. New York: Viking Press, 1957.

Lessing, Doris. *Briefing for a Descent into Hell*. London: London: Jonathan Cape, 1971.

Shakespeare, William. *Macbeth*. London, 1623.

Thoreau, Henry D. *Walden, Or, Life in the Woods*. London : Chapman and Hall, 1927.

Tsu, Lao. *Tao Te Ching*. 4th Century. Mawangdul.

Whitman, Walt. *Leaves of Grass*. Brooklyn, NY, 1855.

SK Dyment is a writer and visual artist with a love of political cartooning. SK likes take to the stage at open mic events to perform
poetry, short prose, and stand-up work, and they have written several plays which were produced at Buddies In Bad Times Theatre.
Their illustrations were most recently published in Ursula Pflug's
flash fiction novel, *Motion Sickness,* which was longlisted for the
ReLit Award. Their humour and cartooning work has appeared in
a number of magazines including, *Peace Magazine, This Magazine,
Open Road Magazine, Healthsharing, Herizons, Kinesis, The Activist
Magazine, Kick It Over Magazine,* and *Fireweed. Steel Animals* is
their debut novel.